ALSO BY
DARCY COATES

*The Haunting of
Ashburn House*

*The Haunting of
Blackwood House*

The House Next Door

Craven Manor

*The Haunting of
Rookward House*

The Carrow Haunt

Hunted

The Folcroft Ghosts

*The Haunting of
Gillespie House*

Dead Lake

Parasite

Quarter to Midnight

Small Horrors

The Haunting of Leigh Harker

From Below

Gallows Hill

House of Shadows

House of Shadows

House of Secrets

Black Winter

Voices in the Snow

Secrets in the Dark

Whispers in the Mist

Silence in the Shadows

Gravekeeper

The Whispering Dead

The Ravenous Dead

THE TWISTED DEAD

DARCY COATES

Poisoned Pen
PRESS

Published by Poisoned Pen Press, an imprint of Sourcebooks
P.O. Box 4410, Naperville, Illinois 60567-4410
(630) 961-3900
sourcebooks.com

Library of Congress Cataloging-in-Publication Data

Names: Coates, Darcy, author.
Title: The twisted dead / Darcy Coates.
Description: Naperville, Illinois : Poisoned Pen Press, [2023] | Series:
   Gravekeeper ; book 3
Identifiers: LCCN 2022029865 | (trade paperback)
Subjects: LCGFT: Ghost stories. | Horror fiction. | Novels.
Classification: LCC PR9619.4.C628 T87 2023 | DDC 823/.92--dc23/eng/20220624
LC record available at https://lccn.loc.gov/2022029865

Printed and bound in Canada.
MBP 10 9 8 7 6 5 4 3 2

CHAPTER 1

"THIS *PROBABLY* ISN'T GOOD."

Keira, standing outside her burnt cottage, stared at the small, neatly addressed letter she held in both hands. The note had been left for her on her front step, resting against the lightly charred wood of the door, its envelope blank.

She turned to look at the scene around her. A low stone fence formed the boundary of the cottage's front garden. Beyond that, mist flooded the earth. Gravestones rose out of the ground, crooked and cracked and discolored from age, but they became scarcely more than vague, gray forms as the fog wrapped around them.

Keira felt for the muscle inside her head, just behind her eyes, that controlled her second sight. It ached faintly when she pulled on it, but additional shapes came into focus, like she'd lifted a veil.

Figures appeared through the fog. They were white and ethereal—not quite real and not quite solid—as though they had been made out of the condensation itself. The only part of them that had any color were their eyes. Those were pitch-black.

Some of the shapes were so clear that Keira could see the creases around their mouths and the dirt under their fingernails. Others were so faint they were barely more than a shimmer. There were dozens of them. They were Blighty Cemetery's ghosts.

That was her gift—if *gift* was even the right word—to see the dead.

She didn't know where the gift had come from or much else about who she'd been before she arrived in Blighty. She remembered waking in the forest outside of town and being hunted by unknown men, but nothing before. Figuring out who she'd been—and why and how she could see the dead—was turning out to be more complicated than she'd expected.

Keira lifted the note for the specters. "Did anyone see who left this?" she asked, a joking smile twitching over numb lips. As expected, there was no answer. Her ghosts weren't especially chatty. A few heads turned at her voice, but others strode away, vanishing entirely. "Right. Didn't think so."

A haze of blue canvas was visible near the forest's edge. That was her temporary home. Technically Mason owned the tent, but he'd lent it to her while she made her actual home habitable again. She'd woken just at dawn, which meant the note must have been delivered during the night. And they'd been discreet about it. Keira had gotten good at detecting when strangers were entering her domain, even when she was asleep.

She looked back down at the message, frowning, then pushed the cottage door open.

Her home—the groundskeeper's cottage lent to her by the town's kindly pastor—had suffered an arson attempt from a doctor with a grudge. The damage could have been a lot worse, all considered. One of the windows was broken, but Keira had already taped cardboard over it. A healthy layer of soot hung across all surfaces. Some of the floorboards and fixtures were damaged, but the cottage's walls were made of stone, and they could be restored with some aggressive scrubbing. She'd already made a start on one.

A small dark shape flitted past her ankles. Keira glimpsed the swish of a tail and called, "Hey, Daze."

The small black cat sent her a frenzied, wide-eyed glance. She held a dead leaf in her jaws: the mighty hunter returned victorious. Keira barely had time to chuckle before Daisy slipped beneath the bed and vanished into the shadows.

Keira opened a can of cat food and served it up for when Daisy grew hungry, then grabbed a handful of biscuits for herself. She chewed her way through them as she stared at the message in her hand.

So what am I going to do about this?

She needed a second opinion. Keira unplugged her cell phone from the kitchen counter. It was an outdated flip model with an abysmal battery and only a few numbers programmed into it, but it worked fine as a lifeline to the outside world. She selected Zoe's name and pressed to dial.

The call was answered on the first ring. "Keira, bestie, light of my life, it is a joy to hear from you this morning."

"Same to you," Keira said. She was more grateful than she'd expected to be to hear her friend's voice. "Sorry, I know it's early."

"Oh, don't worry about that. I have a new bonsai tree on a strict watering schedule and I had to get up for that. But what's got you in a chatty mood at such an unmerciful hour?"

"Ah." Keira glanced down at the note. "Someone left a message outside my door this morning. I wanted to get your thoughts on it."

"That sounds like something we should meet over. I'll see you in a second."

The phone beeped as the call was disconnected. Keira barely had time to frown at the display before the cottage's door slammed open. She flinched.

"He-e-e-y," Zoe crowed, leaning through the doorway. Early-morning light glanced over her cropped black hair and emphasized the mischief in her eyes as she grinned.

"Okay." Keira let herself slump with relief. "You meant *literally* in a second."

"It was too good of an opportunity to pass up." Zoe stepped inside and a taller figure followed: Mason, doctor-in-training, his dark brown hair brushed back from his face. "We were on our way here when you called."

Mason raised a hand in greeting. "Sorry. We weren't sure if you'd be awake yet."

"Yeah, but we figured this was worth disturbing you over." Zoe held up a sheet of paper, and Mason mimicked the motion, showing a note of his own. "You weren't the only one to get a message."

Keira felt a sinking in her stomach. She laid her own note out on the table, and the others gathered around as they did the same. The contents, handwritten in formal cursive, were identical save for the name at the top. Keira's said:

Ms. Keira,

You are cordially invited to dinner at the Crispin Estate this evening, Wednesday, at 6:00 p.m.
Please attend Farrier Street, Blighty. The gates will be left open.

Sincerely,
Dane Crispin

"So," Zoe said, folding her arms as she looked down at the three notes. "It's pretty safe to say we're going to get murdered if we go, right?"

"Oh, yeah," Keira said. "Definitely."

Mason made a faintly unhappy noise but didn't argue.

Keira had met Dane Crispin once before. Descended from the wealthy family that had founded the town and then fallen from grace during a scandal, Dane was now the sole heir still living in

Blighty. He occupied a crumbling mansion outside of town and was notoriously unwelcoming to visitors.

A woman had been murdered on the estate, and her ghost had appealed to Keira for help. While trying to untangle the woman's history, Keira had trespassed onto the Crispin grounds in the dead of night, along with Mason and Zoe. They'd been seen. And then shot at. Keira had been followed through the forest and only managed to keep her life by hiding in the abandoned mill.

Apparently guessing her thoughts, Mason said, "It might be unrelated to that night. It was dark. Dane shouldn't have been able to see our faces."

Keira chewed on the corner of her thumbnail. "It seems too much of a coincidence, though, doesn't it? The three of us went onto the estate. The three of us now have these notes. Even if he couldn't see us, he must have figured out who we were."

"How did he even know you were in town?" Zoe asked. She pulled a chair out, sitting on it sideways, apparently unconcerned about getting soot on her sweater and sleek jeans. "He's not exactly a regular visitor at the pub. Or anywhere, for that matter. Sometimes people go up to the gates to try to catch a glimpse of him wandering around his gardens, but they only really do that to make sure he's still alive."

Mason tilted his head. "When you say *people*, you're mostly talking about yourself, right?"

She grinned up at him. "Yep."

"He really must be isolated." Keira traced a finger over the message. The paper was old, yellowing around the edges, and the words' ragged lines and tiny splatters told her it had likely been written with a fountain pen and an inkwell. "This could have been teleported out of the eighteenth century."

"Everything about this note is amazing," Zoe said, ticking off on her fingers. "The formality. The way he gives you his address as though it's possible to miss the biggest house in town. The absolute class he displays by keeping his threats of violence veiled."

"We don't know that he *actually* wants to harm us," Mason said, arms folded. He made a faint, disgruntled noise. "It's just… an uncomfortably high probability."

"And it leaves us with an important question." Zoe took a deep breath. "With the full knowledge that we're most likely never leaving the Crispin estate alive, do we attend?"

"I feel like the answer to that should be obvious." Mason looked from Zoe to Keira. "Please tell me it's obvious."

Keira rubbed the back of her neck. "I think I should go."

"Yes. *Hell* yes." Zoe pumped a fist, a victorious smile lighting her face. "No one has seen inside that house in decades. What's he hiding? How many skeletons are in there? Death is a fair price to pay for a glimpse behind its doors."

Mason only sighed.

"From my perspective, if he wants to meet me, I can't reasonably avoid him." Keira shrugged. "He left the note outside my cottage. That means he knows where I live. And, well, I'd rather face him directly than have him sneak up on me in the middle of the night or something." She glanced at Mason. "That's my choice, though. I wouldn't blame you if you wanted to stay home."

He grimaced. "If you and Zo are going, I'll come too. It seems less awful than the thought of trying to form a vengeful mob when you inevitably fail to return home by morning."

"Friends that stick together…" Keira gestured vaguely. "Die together, I guess?"

"I believe that's how the saying goes." Daisy had appeared and wove between Mason's legs, purring. He bent to pick her up and cradled her gently as he scratched her head. "It sounds like it will be a proper dinner party. I hope Dane Crispin is a good cook."

Zoe inhaled sharply as her face lit up. "I'm going to wear my fancy black dress. I'll look *so cool* when I'm being stabbed to death."

"I will also be wearing my best clothes," Keira said. "You remember the sweater with the bug-eyed cat face on it?"

"Ooh, good choice. He'll love it."

"He'd better. I'm overdue for laundry and it's all I've got."

Zoe chuckled, leaning back in the chair, one arm thrown over its back. "D'you want to borrow an outfit? I'm sure I'd have something I could alter to fit you—"

Keira waved a hand. "Don't worry. The cat sweater's part of my identity by now. If Dane Crispin wants to chop me up with an ax, I'm at least going to be comfortable while it's happening."

"You're both way too calm about this," Mason muttered.

"Eh." Keira shrugged. "I've cheated death plenty in the last couple of weeks. Might as well go for one more round."

"Let's meet up at the fountain," Zoe said. "Say, five forty or thereabouts. We can walk up to the house together."

Mason clicked his tongue. "Zoe, that reminds me. You said you wanted to meet up today regardless of the invitation, right?"

Zoe's eyes lit up. "Oh, yes. And you're going to love the reason for it. Keira, I think I have a lead on the people who've been hunting you."

CHAPTER 2

"SO YOU REMEMBER HOW I offered to ask around with some of my contacts in case they had any clues about the logo you saw on that van?" Zoe asked. "But then you decided that we should put that on pause because it was vitally important that we hike through a mercy-forsaken forest in search of clues to help us kill a serial killer who was already dead?"

"Gerald Barge, yes." Keira folded up Dane's letters and pulled out a seat so that she could face Zoe. Mason carefully lowered himself into a chair of his own, with Daisy purring furiously in his arms.

"Well, I finally got back to the main project and made some progress. There's a guy I know from an obscure forum who's super into corporate conspiracies. He's hard to reach, though. He has, like, five phone numbers and if you call the wrong one, he'll basically go into hiding for most of a week. And the *correct* number changes any time an unfamiliar car parks on his street. So. You could say he's a little paranoid."

"Maybe a little," Keira conceded.

"Anyway, I got lucky and managed to get through to him." Zoe reached into her pocket and wrestled out several tightly folded sheets of paper. She spread them out on the table. "Check this out."

The first page was a photocopy of the drawing Keira had made. She'd created it after visiting a hospital with Adage, the pastor, and finding the mark on a van parked outside. None of her memories from her time before arriving in Blighty had survived...but she'd recognized that symbol. It had filled her with dread and deep, deep loathing.

The mark was comprised of a hexagon made of thin, curling leaves. There had been no company name attached. Keira had drawn the mark as accurately as she could from memory, but neither Mason nor Zoe had been able to recognize it.

"So he thinks he's found a match." Zoe unfolded another sheet of paper and laid it out beside the first.

"That's it," Keira said, sick horror rising through her like a nest of cold snakes writhing toward her throat.

The image on the second sheet of paper was made of low-resolution black lines on a white background. The edges were pixelated, suggesting it had been enlarged. It was an almost perfect match for the logo she'd drawn.

As she stared at the new image, she could feel cold, dead memories stirring in the back of her mind. She knew the logo.

Almost too well. She hated it. She feared it. But as she reached for the memories, they blinked out again, vanishing back into her subconscious.

She tore her eyes away from the papers as she turned to her friend. "What is it? Who are they?"

Zoe's smile was thin lipped and sad. "The group goes under the name of Artec. That's all I know about it so far."

"Artec…?" There was something there. Just like the image, the name sparked a distant familiarity that Keira couldn't quite catch. "Do they have a website? Are they a business or government or…?"

"They're a publicly traded company." Zoe tapped the paper. "That's where Mr. Toast recognized the icon from: the stock market."

"Sorry." Mason flicked a hand up. "I know this is too important to interrupt, but…*Mr. Toast?*"

"I met him on an anonymous forum, okay?" Zoe shrugged. "He's way too nervy to tell me any personal info. Apparently he secretly had a legal name change a few years back and now not even his parents know his real name. Everyone online just calls him Mr. Toast."

"Right, sure." Mason returned to stroking Daisy, who was halfway to melting off his lap. "That's not weird at all."

"*Anyway.*" Zoe glared at Mason before continuing. "Mr. Toast doesn't trade, but he likes to watch the stock market. Especially smaller companies. And he came across Artec a while back, and his curiosity got sparked by how little information they have online. They've been active for four years but have no website. No social media presence. Even their company description is a string of nothingness."

Zoe unfolded the third and final sheet. It was a printout of Artec's registration. Under *description* it simply read *A midsized, publicly traded company in the renewable energy sector.*

"That's as far as I've gotten," Zoe said. "Mr. Toast is trying to dig up some more info on his side, but last time I spoke to him, he said he saw a plane flying at the wrong altitude so I wouldn't be surprised if we didn't hear from him for a while."

"Okay," Keira managed.

"Every trail I've tried to follow so far has led me to a dead end. Their registered address doesn't exist. Their CEO is listed as—get this—John Doe. No phone number. Reverse image searches for the logo don't bring up any results. I can't even find any employees, past or present."

"Well, at least we know we've found the right company," Mason said. "There's no way they would be so secretive if there wasn't something they wanted to hide."

"Exactly my thoughts." Zoe took the papers back and folded them up. "The bit in their bio about them being a part of the renewable energy industry might be another false lead, but it's what I'm going to focus on next—see if I can find anyone in the industry who's heard of them before. I'll keep you posted."

"Thanks," Keira said. "It's kind of hard to protect yourself from an unknown threat when you're not even sure where they're coming from."

"Or what they want," Mason said. "I'm having trouble seeing how your ability to speak with the dead would be a threat to a renewable energy company."

"Maybe I was super into fossil fuels in my life before Blighty?" Keira shrugged. "Nuke the whales, burn down the forests, convert the marshlands to shopping malls. And etcetera."

Zoe laughed as she stood. "Bestie, you've got *way* too much internalized anxiety for that kind of life. No, I have a theory of my own. This Artec company is doing something they desperately need to hide. Something so big they're willing to *kill* to keep it buried. And maybe that's the key. Maybe they *have* already killed over it."

The implications clicked into place, and Keira frowned. "Killing someone with unfinished business would leave a spirit."

"A spirit who knows too much," Zoe said, approaching the kitchenette window and gazing through the fogged glass. "And the secrets would have died with them *unless* they found a way to reach you. You're the dead's only link to the living world."

Keira chewed the idea over. It was the most plausible theory they'd come up with yet. It still didn't help her much, though. If a ghost had really tried to pass on secret knowledge to her, it had been lost along with all of her other memories.

She was fairly sure, if she could just get closer to the company behind the twisting-leaf logo and the skull-mask men she'd seen, she could pull the lost memories back. But that was easier said than done. Especially when every shred of prudence left in her said she needed to stay as far away from them as possible.

"I'm going to kick this toxic can a bit farther down the road," Keira said, rising. "In the meantime, who wants breakfast?"

The three of them jostled around the kitchenette, frying eggs and slotting bread into the soot-tinged toaster. Then they brought their plates outside, shivering slightly against the cold. They ate while sitting on the edge of the low stone fence and watching early-morning light cut through the bare tree branches and slice into the lingering fog.

"Are they any ghosts hanging about?" Zoe asked through a mouthful of heavily buttered toast, her heels tapping against the stone.

Keira opened her second sight. The hazy shapes bled into view. None had come close to her cottage, but they weren't trying to hide either. "Yep."

"Nice." Zoe's grin was ferocious. "Breakfast in a haunted graveyard has to be the most metal thing I've done in my life, and that's pretty high praise considering I went through a punk phase."

Keira laughed. "I still can't believe you're both so willing to take my word on it."

Mason had his head tilted back, apparently enjoying the thin sun on his skin. "We *all* felt something when we had that brush with the shade in the forest. And even if we hadn't...well..."

"You're a shocking liar," Zoe supplied. She tilted her slice of toast in Keira's direction. "You think you're good at hiding stuff, but it shows *all* over your face."

"Oh no," Keira groaned, hunching forward.

"*Don't worry, the ghosts can't hurt me,*" Zoe mimicked. "And then six hours later we watched you face-plant straight into the ground when a cranky spirit got hold of you. You're just lucky we like you so much; otherwise we wouldn't put up with half your nonsense."

Mason had started laughing and didn't seem able to stop. "Sorry," he managed between gasping breaths. "But it's the truth."

The laughter was infectious, and Keira couldn't help herself from joining in. Daisy, attracted by the noise, appeared through the fog. She approached them at a calm trot, gazed up at Zoe with huge amber eyes, then darted forward and snatched the last of the buttered toast from her hand before turning and fleeing.

"No!" Zoe called, arms outstretched theatrically. "Bring my toast back, hellion!"

But Daisy had already disappeared back into the fog, a flick of her tail the last sign of her.

They cleaned up from breakfast. Zoe had a shift at the grocery store that morning and left reluctantly. Mason stayed a little longer, though, helping wash out some of the cupboards where soot had managed to creep inside. By the time they walked back outdoors, the mist had thinned as the sun warmed the ground.

"You're really not scared about tonight, are you?" Mason asked.

"About Dane?" His features flashed behind Keira's eyes. Dane—gaunt, ferocious, his hair greasy and long, the rifle held in the crook of one arm. She blinked, then shook her head. "I really don't know what to think. If he wanted to hurt us, why go to the effort of the invitations? If he never leaves his estate, how did he know where I live? And if he *didn't* see our faces on the night we trespassed, why is he contacting us?" She raised her hands in a broad shrug. "At this point, the curiosity's outweighing the nerves."

"Ha. Fair enough."

Mason was smiling, hands thrust into his long coat's pockets as he examined the field of sickly shrubs and leaning grave markers around them, but a tinge of unease lingered behind his eyes.

"I meant what I said earlier," Keira added. "You shouldn't feel pressured to come just because Zo and I are."

His smile seemed slightly more genuine. "I appreciate that. I'll still be there, though. We'll all be safer if the three of us stay together. And, I have to admit, I'm curious. Why does he want to talk to us, and why can't it be conveyed in a letter?"

"That's what I want to know too. I've been joking about certain death, but Dane must want *something*, and it has to be important if we're going to be allowed into a house that never has visitors." Keira paused, then nudged Mason. "Thanks for staying with me, by the way. It'll be nice to have your company."

"I wouldn't have it any other way."

For a moment they stood, their shoulders nearly touching, as they watched Daisy stalk insects through the long grass. Then Mason drew a deep breath, filling his lungs, and let it out in a sigh.

"Considering this might be your last day on earth, do you have any plans?" he asked.

"Mm." Keira gazed across the ocean of gravestones. "Well,

technically, I'm still on duty as the graveyard's groundskeeper. Otherwise, it'll be cleaning, mostly. If I can keep up my pace, I should be able to make the place habitable enough to give you your tent back by tomorrow."

Mason glanced toward the one-room cottage. "You're welcome to it for as long as you like, though I'm sure you want your home back too. We should replace the mattress. I don't think you're supposed to keep them once they've been fire damaged."

Keira wrinkled her nose. "It's really not that bad."

"It is, and we both know it." Mason's smile was warm. "My parents have a guest room in our house, but they're away so often that it never gets used. You can have the mattress from there. It's virtually brand-new, which is more than can be said for the current one."

The thought was desperately tempting. She'd examined her mattress the previous day, and the smell alone made her think she'd prefer to sleep on the floor. But Keira was already hyperaware of how much she'd imposed on her friends and their generosity. "Mattresses are expensive, though—"

"Good thing this one doesn't have a price tag." Mason stepped past her, grinning. "Did you want it today or tomorrow?"

"It's way too much—"

"And it's gathering dust where it is. Seriously. It'd be a waste not to use it."

She smiled. "Okay. Thank you, Mason. Sincerely. Let's move it tomorrow; that will give me a chance to clean the house so I don't get it sooty the moment it comes through the door."

"Sounds like a plan." Mason moved through the opening in the stone fence. "I guess I'll see you tonight, then, at the fountain."

"It'll be a proper date with death," Keira said. "And I think I'm actually looking forward to it."

CHAPTER 3

SHORTLY AFTER FIVE, KEIRA left her cottage, closing the door securely behind her. She wore the demented cat sweater, as promised, with a beanie that didn't match in the slightest. That was one benefit of having a wardrobe made entirely from church donations: she had a good excuse to wear bad fashion.

The sky was a steely kind of overcast that threatened rain later. Keira pulled a jacket over the sweater and hiked its collar up to protect her throat, then set out into the graveyard.

Blighty Cemetery was old. While modern graves dotted the space—most of them closer to the small stone church near the road—the bleak ground held graves dating back hundreds of years. The stones were cracked and worn, many of them listing, some so faded that the names were no longer distinguishable.

They didn't end at the clearing either, but spilled into the trees surrounding them. Keira still hadn't found where the markers ended, only that they spread farther than she was comfortable thinking about.

Her own cottage was tucked between the graveyard and the trees. She liked it there; it was sheltered from sight, and very few visitors came that far. Neglect was apparent in the areas around it, though. Adage, the pastor who had offered Keira the cottage, tried to keep the graveyard maintained, but it was more than he could keep up with.

It was technically Keira's job now. Adage knew about her ability to see the dead. He'd offered her the cottage and a small allowance to speak to the spirits there and move them onto the next life if and when she could. As far as the town was aware, though, she was a groundskeeper. She supposed she'd better start keeping some grounds to make the story convincing.

That will have to be a tomorrow job. Assuming I'm getting a tomorrow. The light was beginning to fade. She moved through the cemetery, carefully weaving around the plots so she wouldn't step on any graves. She pulled on the muscle that opened her second sight and smiled as the vague forms appeared around her.

The spirits were still standoffish…but less than they had been. Trust wasn't something that could be earned overnight.

She was doing her best to learn the spirits' names, but it was painstakingly slow work when they weren't always visible and didn't always stand near their grave markers. She knew a few, though.

"Marianne!" she called, raising a hand in greeting toward a small, sickly looking spirit whose wispy hair was tied down with a shawl. Marianne stared back at her, the blank, dead eyes unreadable. Keira kept moving.

An enormous statue of an angel blocked her path. Decades of rain had left tracks running from its folded wings and over its face. They bled from its closed eyes, looking uncomfortably like tears. Keira skirted around it and pulled up short. A man stood in her way. Rags were tied around his hands and across his eyes. Based on his clothes, she thought he might have been from the early nineteen hundreds. He'd died blind, but his head turned to track Keira's motion as she approached.

"Hey," Keira said. "I haven't met you before. Which grave's yours?"

He faced her, seeming to stare at her despite the weaving strips of cloth circling his face, then he faded, vanishing into the mist.

"Cool. We'll catch up again later." Keira thrust her hands into her pockets.

The spirits couldn't always control how long they were visible. Some were strong and could stay present almost constantly, but others were weaker and faded within minutes. They'd be back—sometimes hours or days later—but they seemed to need to gather energy before they could manifest again.

The mist seemed to make it easier for the ghosts to appear. Possibly because their forms were made out of something vapor-like. Foggy mornings and rainy days saw her graveyard light up with spirits.

Two small spirits ran from between listing monuments—children. They darted as they played some kind of unfathomable game, mouths open in laughter that Keira couldn't hear. They passed behind another gravestone but didn't come out the other side.

One other familiar spirit was near Keira's path. The steely Victorian-era ghost stood facing the trees, her chin lifted high, her wrinkled hands folded on top of the ornate cane she carried with her. She was one of the brightest spirits in the graveyard. Her high-collared dress flowed in a breeze Keira couldn't feel. Gray hair was tied up at the back of her head. She showed no acknowledgment as Keira drew near, not even a twitch of her tightly pressed, creased lips.

"How're you doing today?" Keira asked, hopping from foot to foot to keep her legs warm against the growing chill. "Anything interesting happening?"

She knew she wouldn't get an answer. She never did. But despite the Victorian woman's apparent indifference, she'd helped Keira once before. And Keira would never not be grateful for that.

"I'm heading into town," Keira continued. "I guess I'll see you later tonight, or maybe tomorrow. Your gravestone's overdue for a clean, yeah? Don't let me forget."

The spirit blinked once, very slowly, still without looking at Keira.

"Great. Good talk." Keira hitched her jacket slightly higher and stepped around the woman's massive, ornate monument. Ahead, the rectory appeared through the mist, its shingles catching flecks of gold in the fading light. Adage already had his lights on, and distant tunes floated from a scratchy record player. As she rounded the building, she found the pastor pulling weeds from the ground surrounding his front step.

"Hi!" she called.

"Keira!" Adage straightened, dusting his hands on his knees, a smile lighting his gentle face. He wore one of his trademark cardigans, the sleeves rolled up. "How are you this early evening?"

"Oh my gosh," she said. "I'm mostly just grateful that at least *one* person around here answers me when I say hello."

"The dead aren't great conversationalists, I take it." Adage nudged his spectacles slightly higher on his nose as he joined her at the edge of the driveway.

She gestured vaguely at the cemetery behind them. "They're not exactly clamoring for attention. I guess I should be grateful for that, anyway. I don't know what I'd do if I had, like, fifty sets of unfinished business to figure out all at once."

"Ask them to form a queue," Adage suggested. He stretched his back, sighing. "You're heading out for the evening, my dear?"

"Yeah. I got invited out to a dinner party somehow." Keira considered telling him who the invite had come from, but Adage had a tendency to worry, and this was one thing he couldn't help her with. "I should be back later tonight. Fingers crossed."

"Well, that sounds ominous, but I can cross as many fingers as you'd like me to."

"Not to make a habit out of being ominous or anything, but..." Keira gave him an apologetic shrug. "If I for some reason never come back, would you look after Daisy?"

"Of course I will." Adage squinted at her through his glasses. "But, child, you're not in any kind of danger, are you?"

She grinned. "No more than I can handle."

"Well, I can add you to my prayers, if you like. I did my rounds this morning and I have a whole list of them. Mrs. Mullion's in the hospital. Edith wants me to pray that her roses will beat Mildred's in the regional fair. Mildred wants me to pray that a pox will strike Edith—I don't think I can in good conscience do that one—and Greg wants me to pray that his neighbor's lawn mower will explode the next time he tries to use it at six in the morning."

"People hold grudges in this town, huh?"

"That's what happens when a population stays stagnant for so long," Adage said mildly. "There are feuds going back generations. In some cases, families hate each other but can't even remember why. I find it keeps things from getting boring."

Keira said goodbye and continued along the driveway. It wasn't quite dark, but the overcast day dampened the world. Ahead, she could see parts of the town where lights were already blinking to life inside homes.

The driveway wended, flanked by spreading trees, and crossed over a creek before it let onto the main road. Keira turned left, following the familiar path to town.

Blighty felt like it existed as part of an older world. Most of the buildings were made of stone and had shingle roofs. The stores that formed the town's center had hand-painted signs hung above their doors. She rarely saw cars on the streets. She supposed there wasn't much need for them when the town was small enough that everything important was within walking distance.

The town was shutting down for the night, with bells above the doors ringing as owners left their businesses. Keira glimpsed Polly Kennard inside the florist's and waved. Polly's face lit up as she waved back.

Keira followed the path to the crossroads at the town's center. An elaborate fountain created a roundabout at the juncture. Keira was early, but Mason had still beaten her there. He sat on the fountain's edge, gazing toward the sky.

"Hey," Keira said, dropping down to sit next to him. "Have you been here long?"

"Only a minute." He stretched his long legs ahead of himself. "I dropped in on Zoe on my way here. She looked like she was dealing with some stuff, but she said she wouldn't be long."

Keira looked toward the corner grocery store where Zoe worked. The lights were still on. She could make out faint shapes moving inside. "I hope she's okay. She's had a long shift."

"They overschedule her pretty horribly. Can you believe she's their most reliable employee?" Mason lifted his shoulders into a shrug. "Lots of people underestimate Zo, but she's actually really good at the things she cares about. She just…works in unorthodox ways."

As if on cue, the general store door banged open. A middle-aged woman appeared in the opening, staggering as Zoe physically shoved her out of the store. Keira couldn't hear their words, but their mouths were moving at a blinding speed as they engaged in some kind of argument. Zoe gave the woman a final shove to get her off the sidewalk and onto the road, then yanked her apron off over her head and vanished back inside the shop. The woman stood there for a beat, scowling, then stalked off in the opposite direction.

The lights inside the store turned off in quick succession, then Zoe appeared again, slamming the door and locking it behind herself before jogging across the road to reach them. She was decked out in a huge black ball gown and Keira realized, with a mix of incredulity and awe, that Zoe must have worn it through her shift.

"Sorry, sorry, I know I'm late." Zoe grimaced as she reached them. "Mrs. Keene wanted cat milk. So I showed her the kitten formula in the pet aisle. But, no, she didn't want milk *for* a cat. She wanted milk that came *from* a cat. Kept saying things like, 'Why do they make milk if we're not allowed to drink it?' and 'You have almond milk. How hard can it be to get cat milk?' Told me to special order it in. Refused to take no for an answer. Then she asked me if I owned any cats and if I'd ever tried milking them myself."

"Ew" was the only thing Keira could manage to say.

"I swear I have to get out of retail or I'm gonna die." Zoe dropped her head against Keira's shoulder and released a low, slow moan muffled by her jacket. "No," she said after a moment. "I lie. My love of gossip and complaining means I can never truly leave retail without starving myself of material."

Keira patted the top of her head. "That's a heavy burden, but thank you for carrying it. Speaking of starving, are you ready for dinner?"

"Oh *heck* yes." Zoe lifted her head, and she almost looked like a different person. The exhaustion had evaporated into bright-eyed eagerness once again. "The thought of Ol' Crispy's mansion is the only thing that got me through today. Let's go."

CHAPTER 4

AS THE THREE OF them turned down the road leading to Crispin Manor, Mason cleared his throat. "You're not planning to call him that to his face, right?"

"Ol' Crispy wanted the pleasure of my company this evening." Zoe flicked a hand carelessly. "He'll take what he's given."

Mason's smile came out closer to a grimace. "I know we were joking about dying in Crispin Manor earlier—"

"*You* can joke; *I* make plans."

"—but at least let us live long enough to get to dessert. Please."

Zoe sighed heavily. "Well, obviously. We're not missing dessert. I'll do my best to behave until then, promise."

Mason sighed. "Thanks, Zo."

"Anyway, I don't think I should be taking lessons on politeness from you, considering the way you chose to dress yourself."

Keira took another look at Mason. He was wearing a relatively low-key charcoal suit and scarf. They looked good on him, accenting his broad shoulders and clean jawline. Zoe, meanwhile, had worn a jet-black ball gown, resplendent with bustle and black lace and elbow-high gloves. While Keira was opting for casual, and Zoe had leaned hard into the elaborate, Mason had chosen something in-between.

"Huh." She tilted her head. "We've an eclectic group tonight."

"Yeah, and it's kind of a problem." Zoe pointed to herself. "Hot stuff." She pointed to Keira and the bug-eyed cat sweater. "*Mega* hot stuff." Then she pointed at Mason. "Dumpster fire on wheels. You're letting the team down, buddy."

Mason smiled good-naturedly. "I made the mistake of spending all of my money on textbooks instead of medieval goth cosplay."

"Excuse you, *Victorian* goth cosplay." Zoe began digging into the folds of her dress. "And it was hardly wasted money. This thing has *pockets*. Check it out." She pulled out three chocolate bars. "In case dinner is inedible." From another fold in the dress she retrieved a small glass bottle with clear liquid inside. "Holy water. Well, holy-ish. I asked Adage to bless it but he said he can't because he's a pastor not a priest, so I just told him to shake it up real good. I've been holding on to it for years, and I might finally get a chance to use it."

"Wow," Keira managed.

"That's not all." She took out a tightly folded piece of paper and flattened it out for them to see. It read *I WAS MURDERED BY DANE CRISPIN AND ALL I GOT WAS THIS LOUSY NOTE*.

"If things look like they're going bad, I'm going to eat this really quick so they find it in my stomach during my autopsy."

"You truly have covered every eventuality," Mason said dryly.

"Not quite. I couldn't find a way to hide a sword in my dress. But I did bring these." She drew out three cloves of garlic and passed one each to Keira and Mason. "In case he really is a secret vampire."

"Is that a high possibility?" Keira asked.

"The facts don't lie. He's almost never seen during the day. He never leaves that creepy old house. He just plain *looks* weird. And sure, vampires are allegedly mythical creatures. But I could have said the same about ghosts until you showed up. Vampire isn't the worst conclusion to draw."

"Holy water. Garlic." Keira frowned down at her clove. "This is starting to feel a lot like we're bullying a lonely man with a bad sleep schedule."

"Dane gave me an entire day to prepare for this dinner party, so that's what I did. I'm only mildly surprised that neither of you did the same."

"Well…" Keira glanced behind herself, afraid there might be someone within hearing distance. The roads were bare; they'd left the town, and the houses were thinning into empty fields. She cleared her throat. "I brought a gun."

"You *what*?" Zoe stumbled before catching herself. "You have a gun? Since when?"

Keira lifted the corner of her sweater. The grip of a small silver pistol peeked out from her jeans pocket. "You remember how my house caught on fire? That was Dr. Kelsey. He was trying to chase me off. And, well, it didn't work, and he dropped his gun on the way out and never came back for it, so I guess it's mine now."

"This isn't fair." Zoe stuffed her garlic clove back into her pocket. "It's impossible to be cool in this group when you're around. You just bring out surprises like *bam*, I can fight; *bam*, I have a gun; *bam*, I talk to ghosts."

"If it's any consolation, they were all surprises to me too." Keira grimaced as she dropped the sweater back over the pistol. "To be clear, I have exactly zero plans to use this. I'm not even sure if I know how. But it might buy us a few seconds if we need to run, understood?"

Mason thrust his hands into his pockets. A furrow had developed between his eyebrows. "Why was Dr. Kelsey trying to chase you off?"

Keira ran her tongue across her teeth. She'd already shared more than she felt was safe. Shortly after arriving in Blighty, she'd had a run-in with the resident doctor's son, Gavin. The boy's steel-cold eyes and the cruel twist to his pale lips had chilled Keira, but that was nothing compared to what she'd experienced when she'd touched him. She'd seen a vision: Gavin Kelsey approaching an older man on the town's bridge during winter. A terse conversation. Then Gavin pushing the man and watching as he plunged through the ice and failed to resurface.

Apparently, she could know when someone had killed just by touching them. Another side effect of her gift.

She wasn't sure she was ready to share all of that with her

friends. It was already weighing on her heavily. She knew Gavin had murdered someone, but she had no way of convincing anyone else. There wasn't a single piece of evidence she could bring to the police. She couldn't even lie and say she'd been an eye witness, as the event had happened months before she arrived at town. Gavin walked free and there was nothing she could do about it. She didn't think it was fair to pass that same burden to anyone else. Not yet.

On the other hand, she'd spent too much of her time in Blighty lying to her friends. Both Zoe and Mason were watching her, and their expressions were slowly turning from curiosity to concern. She opted for an abridgment. "Long story. But Gavin Kelsey hates me, and now his father does too."

"Gavin Kelsey hates everyone," Zoe muttered. "The little weasel."

"A gun, though…" The worry refused to fade from Mason's face. "If he was willing to pull that on you, what else will he be prepared to do?"

"I don't think he's coming back." Keira remembered the way his eyes had flashed with pure terror as he'd watched a storm materialize above them and felt the icy touch of specters pressing in. She doubted Dr. Kelsey had an open mind toward the supernatural, but she still thought it would be enough to keep him at bay. For a while. "I can keep myself safe."

Slowly, the crease faded from between Mason's eyes, and he gave her a soft, private smile. "Sorry. I worry. But I should trust you more, shouldn't I?"

"A little bit." She grinned back at him.

"I suspect we're *all* going to have to trust each other a whole bunch over the next couple of hours." Their walk had slowed, and Zoe turned to face two massive wrought-iron gates ahead of them. "We're here."

The gates were almost invisible under their blanket of ivy. A high stone fence ran along the property's exterior, along the edge of the road, but it was so overgrown with vines and craggy plants that it was hard to see as well.

Keira leaned close to the gate and used one hand to lift a mat of ivy away. Through narrow gaps, she caught glimpses of the distant mansion. It was derelict. Dark. The massive building appeared to sag, as though the weight of its history were grinding it into the earth.

Zoe tilted her head to look at them, her owlish eyes bright. "We're a couple minutes early. If anyone has any deathbed confessions, now's the time to share them. Keira, you got any more cool surprises you're hiding from us?"

"Uhhh…" She frowned. "I saw a deer outside my tent yesterday."

"That's…it?"

"It was a cool surprise for me."

Zoe sighed. "Okay. Mason. Are you in the mood to unburden your soul? Want to tell us why you dropped out of med school?"

Something flashed through his eyes, but it was gone before Keira could fully catch it. "Nope."

"Really?" Zoe folded her gloved arms as she glared up at him.

"Top of your class. Beloved by teachers. Blighty's one glimmer of hope for our generation. And yet you quit less than a year from graduation. And no one knows why."

"Firstly, I wasn't top of my class." His smile was unshakable. "I was fourth. And secondly, no, I'm not talking about it. Not right now."

Keira couldn't stop herself from watching him. His familiar smile was firmly in place: calm and steady, the way she'd always known him. But unspoken emotion flickered deep in his eyes. Whatever it was, it looked like it hurt him.

She'd asked Mason about it once before, but his answer then had been just as noncommittal. Whatever had caused him to drop out, it was something he kept close to his chest. She wanted to believe it was burnout. But she already knew the truth wouldn't be that simple.

"Okay, great talk," Zoe said, deadpan. "Glad we're now emotionally ready to march into certain doom."

"We're probably going to be fine," Mason said, and only the uncomfortable tilt to his brows told Keira he didn't fully believe his own words.

"Time?" Keira asked, and Zoe pulled an antique fob watch from her pocket, flicked the lid open, and held it up for Keira to read. The hands were stuck at half past twelve. Keira squinted. "Actual time?"

Zoe brought out her phone. Its display showed two minutes to six.

"Right," Keira said, and reached toward the metal gate. The

wrought iron was so stiff and heavily draped with plants that at first it seemed like Dane had left them locked out in spite of his promise. But then the metal began to shift inward. Rusted hinges screamed as they turned. The bars shuddered under Keira's fingers, and small leaves and bits of debris fell as the vines were separated. Mason and Zoe joined her, shoving on the metal until it had drawn open far enough for them to move through.

Keira glanced at both of her friends. They each gave her a firm nod. She took a deep breath, then moved forward, stepping into the ancient Crispin estate.

CHAPTER 5

THE SUN WAS FADING. Shadows, long and blurred, stretched across the mansion.

Both the house and the grounds had been left to neglect. Paths wove through overlong grass, carved out by restless feet over the course of years. They formed unsteady patterns, crisscrossing in strange places and looping around trees that were beginning to collapse under their own age.

At the end of a weed-riddled driveway, the three-story mansion waited. The roof over one of its wings had collapsed. There were no visible lights inside the building.

"We got the date right, didn't we?" Zoe whispered.

As if on cue, golden candlelight flickered to life in what had to be the foyer. The light shimmered through windows set into the front door. A dark silhouette moved beyond.

Keira flexed her hands. They were damp with sweat. For all

the fun she'd had joking about inevitable death, now that she was so close to actually meeting the reclusive Crispin heir, tension thrummed through her veins. The gun felt heavy on her hip and less comforting than she'd thought it might be.

You can't back out now. Just don't let him see that you're scared.

She didn't think she was alone. Zoe had gone uncharacteristically quiet. Mason held his head high, but a pulse jumped in his throat. The three of them stayed even with each other as they approached the doors, relying on the security they provided each other.

Four weathered stone steps led to the alcove around the front entrance. Dead leaves lay scattered over them, appearing to not have been swept in years. Dry, prickly weeds poked through cracks in the pillars and in the alcove's corners where dirt had accumulated.

Keira strained to see through the windows. The space beyond was nothing but a blur of light and shadows. She'd seen Dane Crispin's silhouette just a moment before, but now she couldn't place him.

Do it. Quickly. Before you lose all of your courage.

She lifted her hand to knock. A sonorous boom echoed as her knuckles hit the wood, but she didn't have a chance to repeat the sound. The door rushed open, swirling dead leaves around her ankles and sending the lights inside the house guttering.

Before them stood Dane Crispin.

He was tall, something that a heavily stooped bearing couldn't hide. Rough stubble grew across sunken cheeks. The spaces around his eyes were hollowed out, the skin there paper thin, and the eyes themselves were both cold and almost feverishly bright.

A long, straight nose and sharp jaw left him looking angular in a way that set Keira's own bones on edge. His clothes were old and faded and mended many times over. The knuckles holding the door seemed to swell uncomfortably, as though he didn't belong in his own skin. He couldn't have been older than forty. He looked twice that age.

The chilled eyes flicked from Keira, to Zoe, then to Mason, and finally back to Keira. Dane took a step back, releasing his hold on the door, to leave a gap for them to enter. He didn't smile.

Mason's fingertips found the cuff of Keira's sweater and gave a slight tug. It was a discreet question: *Are you sure you want to do this?*

Keira glanced up at him. His warm brown eyes were waiting for her signal. She understood what he was offering: if she was in past her comfort zone, he would help her get out. If she was committed, he would be as well.

She gave a very small nod, then looked at Zoe. Her face was alight with curiosity, but the set to her jaw suggested her own misgivings were coming thick and fast. She saw Keira's look and raised an eyebrow.

Dane Crispin still waited inside his home. The lights were at his back, and they forced dense shadows across his sunken skin.

Hungry was the first thought that flickered through Keira's mind. He looked ravenous. Like a man who had been starved for years. Something like morbid pity ran through her, and she stepped over the threshold.

"This way." Dane turned and led them across the foyer. His voice sounded dry and raspy. If the rumors were right, he rarely had the chance to use it.

His gait was loping and uneven and surprisingly fast. Keira struggled to see the foyer. It was immense and its ceiling so high above her that the intricate designs around the cobwebbed lights were barely visible.

Portraits hung across the walls. Dozens of them, spreading up vertically until almost every inch of surface was covered. Ornate gilt frames surrounded inscrutable, pale faces. Keira had the uncomfortable sensation that the eyes were watching her.

There was precious little other furniture in the space, except for small side tables with vases of faded silk flowers. Dust had been allowed to collect in the hall's corners and across the paintings. The house smelled of mildew and age. Distantly, Keira thought she heard the chatter of bats.

The house was far too large for one man to manage. And so, from what Keira could tell, Dane hadn't even tried.

Prickles spread across her skin. Keira flexed her hands, her breathing shallow. She knew this sensation. The room was tainted with emotional imprints.

She'd felt the sensation before: at the abandoned mill and at the hospital. It was the feeling she got when death and suffering had tainted a space. It set her stomach cold and churning, and the hairs rising across the backs of her arms.

Mason had noticed. He dipped his head so she could hear his whisper. "Are you okay?"

She didn't trust herself to speak but nodded.

Dane had reached the opposite side of the foyer. A lantern rested on a small, round table there, and he took it up.

Zoe's bright eyes had been darting across the room, absorbing every detail she could. No one had seen inside the house in years, she'd said. Keira imagined that, to her, this must be like an archaeologist discovering one of the world's lost treasures. As Dane raised the lantern, though, Zoe's focus switched back to him. "Looking to boost the atmosphere, huh?"

He sent her a very brief, cold glance. "Not all of the house has lights."

"Cool," she managed.

They entered into a long hall. More portraits lined the space, making it feel desperately claustrophobic. The flickering lantern's light washed over pinched, severe faces. The portraits must have been created over hundreds of years, based on their clothes. The subjects all appeared wealthy, possibly even noble. There was a trace of something familiar about their eyes. Keira recognized the hollowness from Dane's own gaze.

Her attention switched back to the stooped man and his threadbare coat. The last of the Crispins was a stark contrast to his ancestors.

Their pathway twisted through the mansion. It was hard to keep track of where they were, and Keira wasn't sure she could retrace the path if she needed to. That idea left her abruptly cold, and it was followed by a far more unnerving thought.

What if Dane had made their path disorienting on purpose?

They passed through another door. This led into the formal dining room. A long, elegant table filled the space's center. Windows along one wall might have looked out over the gardens, but the curtains had been drawn, leaving the space stifling and dark.

Candles had been lit to provide light: three candelabras spaced along the table's length and clusters of candles stood on side tables and in sconces in the walls. They created the effect of bobbing pools of light among an ocean of gloom.

The table had been set for four people: a seat at each end and one on each side. It left an uncomfortable amount of space between them all. Each setting had a bowl of soup and an empty plate. Platters of bread, poultry meat, and fruit had been left between the candelabras. There was enough to feed them all, but it still seemed paltry compared to the table's size.

"Sit," Dane said, and his voice sounded like a broken sigh. His eyes moved across them, lingering a second too long at each interval, before he took a step back from the table. "I will return."

He left, closing the door behind himself. There were a few precious seconds of silence, then Keira heard the faint click of a small digital camera as Zoe took a photo.

"This might be the strangest night of my life," Mason whispered. "And I *am* including the murder cabin camping trip in that equation."

"Meanwhile, I've never felt more alive," Zoe retorted, taking another photo of the room. "I wouldn't recommend eating the soup, by the way. It's pre-portioned, which means it's the easiest to poison. The shared platters should be safe. Well, safe-ish. Can't discount a murder-suicide scheme."

Keira slowly paced around the room as she took in the details. The table's plates were ornately painted, though they were so old that cracks spread through the glazing. It didn't feel like the kind of surface you were supposed to eat off. They were flanked with heavy silver cutlery, covered in baroque flourishes and heavily tarnished.

"You're sure you're okay?" Mason asked her. "You look pale."

She hunched her shoulders. "This place doesn't feel right."

"Preach it, sister," Zoe muttered as she carefully dropped her garlic clove into Dane's bowl of soup. "Vampire den. I'm calling it now."

"No. It's…" Shivers rolled along her spine. "It's the energy. It's so bad here. Like this place is full of horrible things."

The deeper she'd been led into the estate, the worse the sensation had grown. It seeped out of the walls. Through the floorboards. It hung in the air like a poison she couldn't see but was slowly succumbing to.

"We should have a signal," Mason said. "In case any of us want to call an end to this discreetly."

"A bird call," Zoe suggested, and followed it with an echoing "Ka-*kaw!*"

Mason made a face. "I was thinking more like a word or a phrase we can slip into conversation. Like *crimson* or something."

"Oh, yeah, that's a word I use in everyday conversation, sure."

"I'm open to alternatives."

"Ka-*kaw*!"

Keira held up a hand to silence them. Footsteps were growing nearer. "He's coming," she hissed, and the three of them rushed to the nearest chairs. Keira, who'd been pacing around the room's edge, found herself at the table's head, opposite Dane's seat. Zoe and Mason took their places on the table's longest sides, and Zoe took one last wildly aimed photo before stuffing her camera back into the folds of her dress.

The door groaned as it opened, and Dane stepped through. He carried some kind of fabric bundled in one hand. He lingered in the doorway for a beat, cold eyes flicking across them, and Keira felt a sudden fear that he'd heard their conversation. But he only said one word. "Eat."

Keira stared down at the bowl of soup ahead of her. It looked like some sort of vegetable broth, but she couldn't identify everything floating in the cloudy liquid.

Zoe caught her eye and gave her head a tiny shake. Keira reached forward and picked up one of the bread rolls instead.

"We were surprised to get your invitations," Mason said, smiling as he took up a bread roll of his own. "I don't think we've ever spoken before, though I was always happy to see you at the town hall meetings."

Thank you, Mason. He was good with people. He had a way of making them like him. Keira was grateful he'd taken the initiative to break the awful silence.

"I try to attend the meetings." Dane's fingers twitched across the fabric. He still hadn't sat. "This is still my family's town after all."

Keira couldn't take her eyes off the material. It was a deep, rich blue and seemed out of place in the crumbling mansion. Everything else in the building was old, faded. This material looked almost uncomfortably bright by comparison.

Dane saw her looking. There was something tight about his expression, as though he was trying to preserve a mask of civility over something colder hidden underneath. He stepped forward, pacing around the table with slow, deliberate steps.

"Well…it's certainly nice to meet you properly after all this time." Mason's smile hadn't budged, but an edge of quiet anxiety had entered his voice.

Dane didn't answer but kept steadily walking toward Keira. His eyes didn't leave her. They were chilling. Predatory. He hadn't blinked since he'd entered the room.

Keira didn't know where to look. She tore a corner off the bread roll just to occupy her hands, but her mouth was too dry to eat it, so she dropped it back onto the plate instead.

"I'd love to hear about your home," Mason said, turning desperate. "Or…your gardens. Did you plant them yourself?"

"I did plant one tree," Dane said, and Keira's blood ran cold.

Dane's grandfather had been responsible for the murder of a local girl who had fallen in love with his son. He'd killed her in the garden behind the home but had been caught before he could finish burying her. And Dane had planted a tree directly over the place where the murder had occurred. Keira had used it to piece together clues about the woman's death on the night Dane had caught them trespassing on his property.

He stopped directly beside Keira. She tore another chunk off her roll.

Back then, when Keira was just learning about the Crispin family, Zoe had commented that the tree was morbid. Keira hadn't considered its significance beyond that. Now, she didn't know what to think. Was it a monument to a woman taken before her time? Or a monument to a grandfather who had killed for supposed family honor? What had been running through Dane's head when he planted it there?

Slowly, Dane extended his hand. He released the balled-up fabric and let it fall onto the table beside Keira. Up close, she could see it was a knitted material. One that was all too familiar.

"I believe this belongs to you," Dane whispered, and Keira's heart turned to ice.

CHAPTER 6

KEIRA COULDN'T BREATHE. SHE was frozen, staring down at the scarf Dane had placed beside her. She recognized it. It had been in the bundle of donated clothes Adage had given to her. She'd worn it on the night she'd ventured onto the Crispin property. The night when Dane had fired his shotgun at her. She'd fled into the forest, but the scarf had threatened to snag on branches and choke her, so she'd discarded it. And apparently, Dane had found it.

Slowly, she lifted her gaze. Dane Crispin's icy, gray eyes bored into hers. The mask of civility was slipping.

"Crimson," Keira said. "Uh, ka-kaw?"

A crease formed between Dane's brows. He leaned forward, and that small motion was enough to snap something in Keira. She darted up, twisting her chair to put it between herself and Dane, blocking his path. He reached toward her. She bolted.

Zoe and Mason were already on their feet. The three of them ran toward the exit, Zoe stuffing the slip of paper that incriminated Dane into her mouth without missing a step.

"Stop," Dane barked, and his voice reverberated through the room. He was coming around the other side of the table, trying to reach the door before them.

Keira didn't let herself slow. Fear set a tinny whistling in her ears. She hadn't seen Dane's shotgun, but she didn't doubt he'd kept it close.

They darted through the still-open door. Keira had just enough time to slam it closed behind them and felt the heavy wood reverberate as Dane hit its other side.

It wouldn't buy them much time. A couple of seconds, if that. But seconds counted if they wanted to get out of the estate.

The windowless hallway was nearly pitch-black without the lantern. Her friends had hesitated, waiting on her. "Go," Keira hissed, and they set off again, racing along the passageway half-blind.

Keira was faintly conscious of the eyes following her every movement. Even without any lights, she could feel the walls of portraits hanging over her, staring down at her.

The door behind them banged open, and Keira flinched. Zoe was panting. Someone misjudged the hallway's width and hit one of the massive portraits, sending it clattering against the wall.

"We should be back in the foyer by now," Zoe said between heavy breaths. "Did we miss a turn?"

"We must have," Mason said. His steps slowed, and Keira

bumped into him, then shoved a hand into the small of his back to push him forward.

"Keep moving," she said. Dane's long, loping steps echoed in the hall behind them. He was gaining. "We can't go back. We'll find another way out."

Zoe grunted as she collided with a side table. The hallway turned to the right. Even Keira, who could see better than most in the dark, was struggling to navigate the tight passage. They were at a disadvantage; Dane knew the house better than any of them. If they tried to run, he would be faster. If they tried to hide, he would find them. Their only chance relied on finding an exit—and fast.

"Look for a door," Keira hissed, hoping that Dane wouldn't be able to hear her under their pounding footsteps. They might be able to lose him for a moment. Or, she hoped, it might lead them to a back exit or a room with a large enough window to fit through.

"Here." A doorknob rattled as Mason opened it. Keira squeezed close behind Zoe as the three of them slipped through, then shut the door behind them again.

They slowed, their breathing ragged, as they tried to dampen the sounds they made. Keira could no longer hear Dane behind them. She didn't know if he'd guessed they'd left the main path, but she prayed he would continue along the passageway, at least for a little longer.

There was a glowing light up ahead. Keira pushed forward, squinting as she tried to guess what part of the building they might be in. The wallpaper was dark and peeling, its ornate pattern lost under the weathering effects of time. Furniture cluttered the space: tables, display cabinets, and shelving full of trinkets Keira couldn't name.

Then the passage opened into a room, and Keira blinked against the light. It was a sitting area. Bookcases filled the wall to their left. Two wingback chairs were positioned ahead of a fireplace. The fire supplied the only light in the room, and it had been allowed to burn down to embers. A leatherbound book and a glass of wine, nearly empty, had been left on a table beside one of the chairs.

Dane had been here not long ago, Keira realized. He'd probably sat in front of the fire as he wiled away the time waiting for Keira and her friends to arrive.

A large window took up the wall to their right, but metal bars latticed the glass. Mason crossed to it and felt around the frame. The window rattled as he pulled, but refused to open.

Keira turned in a slow circle, her shoes sinking into an old, thick rug in the room's center. There were no other exits. "We'll have to go back," she whispered. "Find a different door—"

A floorboard creaked. Keira swung toward the passage they'd entered through. A tall, dark figure approached, cloaked in shadows. The head lifted, and the firelight set shimmering sparks across Dane's eyes.

Keira put her arms out, pushing Mason and Zoe behind her as they backed up. The fire's waning glow heated her back. There was nowhere to run to. Nowhere to hide. As Dane entered the sitting room, Keira felt for the pistol hidden under her sweater.

Dane's face was a mask of simmering fury. The earlier civility had vanished. He didn't try to speak.

Keira pulled the pistol free. Her chest was tight, making every breath ache. She didn't think she could take a life. Even if it was in self-defense. Death already stalked her every footfall; she felt the stains it left on places and on people. What would it mean to be stained herself? Would it follow her for the rest of her life, turning her dreams to nightmares and leaving her clammy and sick through the days?

But Dane was advancing on them. Not just her, but on Mason and Zoe as well. And she needed to keep them safe. No matter the cost. She raised the pistol, aiming it at Dane's chest.

"You're going to shoot me?" he snarled.

Keira's hands shook. She tried to fit her finger around the trigger. It felt desperately unnatural. *Pull it*, her mind whispered, but her hand refused to respond.

Dane came to a halt just four paces from her. He glared down at her, towering above her despite his stoop. Then the snarling grimace began to fade.

"I suppose I did the same to you that night," he said. There was something in his voice—sadness, Keira thought. "That's why we're here. Why...I opened my house to you. I am trying to apologize. As poorly as I'm able to achieve it. Shoot me if you like. It will put an end to things one way or another."

Zoe's and Mason's hushed, rapid breathing echoed behind Keira. She couldn't stop her hands from shaking. *This has to be a ploy. He wants me to drop my guard and lower the pistol.*

But Dane was no longer looking at her. He'd turned his head to stare through the window, where dark leaves scratched across the glass. "I am so very tired. I would not be sad if this was the end."

Slowly, almost against her better judgment, Keira let herself lower the gun. If Dane was trying to feign sadness, he was doing a very convincing job of it. "You invited us to dinner… to apologize?"

"Yes." Dane's eyes flicked to her, then turned away again. "And to ask a favor. Though I suspect the window for that is long gone."

From over Keira's shoulder, Zoe made a faintly incredulous noise. "You think maybe chasing us through your house wasn't the best way to apologize?"

"You were the ones who started running," he snapped. Then he grimaced. "I don't want to be angry. It just…happens. Like on the night you first came here. I heard something in my garden and I thought it was children from the town again, come to throw eggs at the house or pull up my plants. I just wanted to be left alone."

Keira kept her voice low and level as she tried to fight the frustration creeping into it. "You fired a gun at me."

"I shot over your heads." His shoulders shifted in something like a shrug. "And then I ran after you. I wanted to teach you a lesson. Make sure you never came back. I wish to heaven I'd kept my head, but it's what happened."

Keira glanced back at Mason. He placed a hand on her shoulder, warm and steady, and it gave her the courage to finally tuck the pistol back under her sweater.

Dane saw. He drew a deep breath, then let it out in a sigh. "I've made a mess of this as well. You can leave if you choose. I'll show you how to find the door."

Keira chewed on her lip. She glanced to Zoe, who looked heavily skeptical, then at Mason, who was slightly paler than he'd been earlier that night. He lightly pressed her shoulder, and she knew he was telling her that the choice was hers.

"I can stay a bit longer," Keira said.

"If this is an apology, I'm gonna get my money's worth," Zoe added. "And that means eating a whole bunch of your bread."

Dane's face, heavily dampened by the room's thickening shadows, was unreadable. He stood quietly for a moment, then gestured to the hall they'd entered through. "The dining room is this way."

An uncomfortable silence fell over them as they followed Dane single file. Keira's skin felt itchy as the lingering adrenaline faded. She still wasn't sure she was doing the right thing by staying. Only, the way Dane looked bothered her. He appeared exhausted…and deeply, bone-achingly sad.

Dane's loping gait rang on old floorboards as he led them back along the near-black hall. Keira couldn't stop imagining him roving the house alone, late at night, with only his own shadow and the beat of his footsteps to keep him company.

Pools of wax had started to form around the candles in the dining room. Dane indicated to the table, then took his own seat. After a second's hesitation, Keira circled the space to reach her place. The scarf still waited on the polished tabletop. She felt faintly ashamed. When Dane had first presented it to her, she'd taken it as a threat: *I know what you did.* Now, it seemed like more of a peace offering. He'd held on to it, waiting to return it to her. She already wore a sweater, but the room was chilled enough that she lifted it and layered it on top.

Dane dipped his spoon into the soup. He drank it quickly, and the thought again returned to Keira: *He's ravenous.* She slipped her own spoon into her bowl and gave it an experimental swirl.

"So," Zoe said, cautiously tearing a corner off her bread roll. "Presumably you've chased people off your property before. How come we get an apology, and they don't?"

After a beat, Dane answered. "Something recently came to my attention that made me believe you were not here to vandalize or to mock."

Keira ran her thumb across the cold metal spoon's handle. She wasn't sure how much was safe to tell him and opted to keep it simple. "No."

"That is all people seem to do anymore," Dane said. "The house is already in a poor state. It can't take vandalism. *I* can't take it."

Keira lifted her eyes to the ceiling. Cracks ran through the plaster. The manor was so old and so badly damaged that she wasn't sure it would be possible to save it. "Why do you still live here?"

"Where else am I to go?" He lifted his spoon from the bowl again. Inside was the clove of garlic. Dane stared at it, his eyes narrowing in bewilderment, before slowly lowering his spoon back into the bowl. Then he reached across the table to scoop pieces of poultry onto his plate instead. "Excuse me. I am hungry. I haven't eaten yet today."

"Oh," Mason murmured, and Keira felt him switching into doctor mode. "That's not good."

"I wake late." Dane's shoulders hunched into something like a shrug. "It's easier to feel like myself at night."

Keira ate carefully. A distant clock ticked, chronicling each second, though it seemed to run slow. Each minute she spent in the mansion made her feel more and more uneasy. Not just because of Dane, either—but because of the way the walls felt tainted. Even when she blocked her mind to the sensations as thoroughly as she could, it still leaked in, leaving her clammy and unsteady.

What happened here to poison the air so badly?

She knew of one murder: Emma Carthage, the woman Dane's grandfather had killed behind the house. But one death wouldn't be enough to leave such a strong imprint.

The house has stood since the town was founded hundreds of years ago. Generations could have lived and died here. But I've been in other old, historic buildings without feeling like this.

She lifted her head from her soup and saw Dane was watching her. The candles between them flickered, casting strange lights across his eyes. Keira put her spoon down. "Earlier, you said you wanted to ask me for a favor."

"Yes." His voice was dry, raspy. He hunched back in his chair. "My friend visited yesterday. He talked about you."

"Since when do you have a *friend*?" Zoe blurted. Keira was pretty sure Mason was trying to kick her under the table but couldn't quite reach.

Dane's expression darkened, but his voice stayed dispassionate. "You would know him. Harry, the florist's son."

"You're friends with *Harry*?" Zoe lifted her head to look at the grand, dilapidated room again. "Okay, yeah, that tracks."

Keira's path kept crossing with the sullen, dispassionate youth who lived with his mother above the florist. Ashen, pale skin and smooth black hair that swept over half his face were accented by dark eyeliner and a thorough disdain for life and everything it offered.

He'd helped them, though. He'd allowed them to take a skull he owned. Keira had believed it belonged to a spirit in the forest that was slowly consuming the graveyard.

Keira took a sharp breath. The skull relocation had come at the end of a two-day hike through the forest where Keira had barely slept. She'd been stressed, exhausted, and frankly fed up with the ghosts, and most of her memories from that evening felt like a fever dream. Harry had told her where he'd originally obtained the old bones, though. "I remember now. You gave him the skull, didn't you?"

"He saw it in a display cabinet." Dane's bony shoulders once again shifted in a shrug. "I had no use for it, so I said he could have it."

"How did you guys even meet?" Zoe asked.

"I find it hard to sleep at night. Sometimes I walk through the streets to calm my mind. I kept encountering Harry. Eventually he invited himself back to my home. We understand each other better than most, I suppose."

"Yeah, you guys have a *lot* in common. That's not a compliment by the way," Zoe said. Once again Mason desperately tried, and failed, to kick her under the table.

Dane ignored her but turned back to Keira. "Yesterday, my friend told me something interesting. He said you might have some gift with the occult. With spirits. Specifically, *removing* spirits."

Her mind raced. Harry had been present when Keira destroyed the shade that had been consuming her graveyard. He'd even placed his hand on her shoulder, allowing her to draw some of his energy.

He wouldn't have been able to see the shade. But he'd likely felt the air prickle with electricity. A normal person would have discounted the experience as something they didn't understand. But Harry, already open to the macabre, might have very easily accepted that he was a part of something supernatural.

She tried to avoid revealing her gift to too many people. Every time she opened up felt like a gamble: Would they believe her? Would they think she was delusional or lying? Would they betray her trust and tell others who would be less accepting?

But there was something in Dane's expression that arrested Keira. He wasn't asking out of morbid curiosity.

"Yeah," she said. "I can see them. Sometimes I can influence them too."

"Please…" He caught himself, then leaned forward, one hand resting on the table. An animalistic desperation filled his face, pinching around his eyes and his mouth. "I need to know. Are there restless spirits in my home?"

Keira clenched her hands in her lap. She didn't want to open herself up to the dangerously bad energy in the place any more than she already was.

But she was the only person she knew who could answer Dane's question. He seemed desperate; he'd prepared this dinner for her and returned her scarf, all as tokens of apology to ask for this favor. Not that he'd needed to. This was supposed to be her job, after all.

She took a quick breath to steady herself, then pulled on the muscles to open her second sight.

CHAPTER 7

"OH," KEIRA WHISPERED.

Dane had half risen from his chair. He was trembling. He held one hand braced on the table as his flickering eyes fixed on her, and inside she saw an emotion she hadn't seen in him before: hope. "Please," he said. "Can you see them? Are there spirits of the dead here?"

"Yes," Keira managed. She swallowed thickly. "Yeah, you have a ghost problem."

Ethereal shapes clustered around Dane. The figures overlapped, making it difficult to tell exactly how many there were, but Keira saw washes of flowing hair and loose billows of clothing, drifting as though underwater. She didn't take her eyes off the clustered figures as she stood and slowly rounded the table.

A head lifted. The spirit was entirely white except for its eyes, which were pits of transparent black. It was a woman in her fifties. A long nightgown floated about her, drifting in a wind Keira couldn't feel. Her face was pinched but had a square jaw. Her eyes locked onto Keira, and she smiled. Keira flinched.

The spirit's mouth was a dark hole framing its teeth. And the teeth themselves...

It took all of Keira's self-control not to step back. The teeth had been sharpened into points. Like a shark's, but narrower and longer, with needle-delicate tips.

She thought the spirit might be laughing at her reaction, but it was hard to tell when she couldn't hear it. The woman turned back toward Dane. Her head nuzzled into the crook of his neck, where it joined his shoulder. The delicate, sharpened teeth plunged through his top and into his flesh. Dane's arm twitched a fraction, though he didn't seem to be fully aware of what was happening.

The woman wasn't the only spirit attached to him, though. Four others clung to him, their arms wrapping around his torso, their heads buried into his flesh.

"Stop," Keira said, horrified, but the ghosts didn't react. "No. *Stop!* Why are you doing this to him?"

She had no response, except a man adjusted his grip on Dane, burrowing his teeth deeper into his shoulder.

Realization hit her like a slap. They were feeding on him. Spirits were made of energy, which they normally accumulated slowly from the atmosphere. A ghost could gain energy from other sources, though. Keira had watched the shade tear apart other spirits in the graveyard to fuel itself. It had even sapped energy from her when she got close enough for it to touch her.

And she was fairly certain that was what was happening now. These things—these *parasites*—had latched on to Dane as their source of sustenance.

It was no wonder he looked so old. So tired. So hungry.

And it was no wonder the house's energy felt so achingly poisonous.

"What can you see?" Dane asked. He watched her keenly, and the hope was now so visible that Keira felt she would be cruel to crush it. She couldn't lie to him, though—not about something like this.

"They're…" She wet her lips. "They're feeding off of you. Like leeches."

"There is more than one?" He seemed surprised at that.

"Yes. Five." The ghastly shapes hung about Dane like a cloak, their arms wrapped around him. Their backs flexed as they sucked. Keira wanted to relax her second sight, to let the shapes fade from view again, but forced herself to hold it. "How long…"

She'd wanted to ask him how long it had been like this, but the words died on her tongue. She already knew the answer: the specters had been feeding from him his whole life.

Dane's tongue darted out to wet his lips. "I don't know if you've heard this, but a very long time ago a woman was killed outside this house. By my grandfather, in fact. I suspect her spirit might have stayed and is trying to seek revenge. I've tried everything I can think of to appease her. I planted a memorial tree. I have tried speaking to her. But what can I do to right a wrong that was committed before I was even born?"

"I know who you're talking about," Keira said. "But Emma Carthage's ghost stayed in the graveyard. She's passed on to the next life now."

"Oh." Dane seemed faintly stunned. He blinked rapidly, not able to meet Keira's eyes. She could imagine how hard this news might be to take. He'd spent his whole life believing he knew the source of his suffering, only to discover all of his efforts had been directed to the wrong place. He cleared his throat, his fingers twitching. "If not her, then…who?"

Keira had been asking the same question. She took a step closer and pulled on the muscle to bring the spirits into brighter relief. She focused on the closest specter, the one that had bared its teeth at her. "See if you can recognize any of this. A woman in her fifties. She's short, about five foot two, with thin hair past her shoulders. She has a very square jaw. And the space between her nose and her lips is larger than normal."

Dane didn't answer but abruptly turned and strode toward the door. Keira sent a confused glance back at her companions. Mason gave her an equally confused shrug in return, but Zoe was already scrambling out of her seat. "Come on," she hissed. "We have to follow him."

The three of them did, breaking into a jog to catch up to Dane's loping pace. He'd picked up the lantern from beside the door and used it to light his path through the dark halls. The spirits flowed with him, like seaweed clinging to an anchor, and Keira wondered if Dane might feel their weight in every step he took.

As Keira watched, a sixth ghost shimmered through the wallpaper and closed in on Dane. Its arms threaded around him as it burrowed its teeth into his back. Revulsion sent shudders through Keira.

Dane turned back into the foyer. He approached the opposite wall and stopped there, staring upward.

The wall was covered in portraits of men, women, and children. One subject per painting, all posed at a three-quarter angle, all staring toward the viewer. Each gilt frame had a different design, but all of them were competitively ornate. The paintings stretched up the wall's height, carefully arranged to create a mosaic of faces staring down at the house's guests.

Dane wordlessly pointed to a portrait just above head height.

"Yes," Keira managed. Her throat was tight. "That's her."

The woman in the portrait had a fuller face. She seemed younger and had an air of quiet dignity about her, and, although her mouth was closed in a tight-lipped smile, Keira didn't doubt her teeth were normal. Most of the spirits Keira encountered were mirrors of who they had been in life, but the woman clinging to Dane's shoulder seemed to have changed. She'd grown shriveled and more angular, even spindly.

It's because she's feeding from a living human, Keira's subconscious whispered. *That will twist a spirit. Not quickly, though. She's likely been doing this for longer than Dane has been alive.*

"That is my great-grandmother," Dane said, and there was a dull resignation in his voice. "She was considered a great lady in life."

"Well, she sucks now," Keira said, and immediately regretted her word choice.

Dane's jaw quivered a fraction. "You said there were more."

"Yeah." Keira took a step back, glancing from the spirits attached to Dane to the wall of portraits. "Uh…a man. In his eighties. He has sideburns. And he's missing his pinkie finger."

"My great-uncle." Dane pointed to another spot on the wall without even looking. He had the portraits memorized, Keira realized. Living alone in the house, he'd probably found himself wandering past them often. Staring up at them. Maybe even talking to them when the loneliness became too much.

She wondered how long it would take her to do the same if she found herself cut off from the outside world.

It was hard to see the spirits around Dane when they overlapped, but she struggled to identify more features among the cloud of white. "A man in his sixties. Large stomach. Heavy-lidded eyes. He's wearing some kind of medallion on his shirt."

"That would be my father's cousin." Dane flicked his wrist to indicate farther down the wall. A sense of defeat was spreading through his expression. "The spirits that linger here are all my family, aren't they?"

"I…" Keira swallowed, stepping back from the wall. There had to be more than a hundred portraits there. "I think so."

Motion caught her attention, and she turned. Faint, wispy shapes roved through the hall—men and women, wearing jackets and nightdresses and gowns, moved through the house.

Do they all eat from him?

She swallowed as a larger, more daunting thought occurred. *How many are there?*

"Something has been wrong for my whole life." Dane's eyes were bright with desperation. "The house feels sickly. Despite trying in every way to control myself, my temper burns like a flare. I am either exhausted or bitter all of the time. Every attempt at change feels as though I am pushing against a stone wall. Others can alter themselves so easily; I am trapped in this circle of weariness and resentment, and I cannot find my way out."

The man attached to his shoulder lifted his head, his lips peeled back to reveal the tiny, sharpened teeth protruding from his gums. Keira couldn't tear her eyes away.

"Can you help?" Dane's voice dropped to a whisper. "Can you…make the dead leave me alone?"

Keira swallowed. Two more spirits had moved into the room, drawn by the commotion. The same question swirled around her like a fly. *How many are there? How many? How many?*

Dane saw her hesitation. He reached for her, his bony hand grasping her wrist. His fingers were clammy and trembling, despite his heavy jacket. "I will pay you. Everything I have."

Keira managed a thin chuckle. "I can promise you I'm not in this for the money. I…don't know how much I'll be able to do. But I'll try."

His head dropped, and a shivering sigh escaped him. "Thank you. Thank you."

"Okay." Keira prayed she wasn't promising the impossible. "Let me see what I can do."

CHAPTER 8

KEIRA TENTATIVELY PATTED DANE'S hand, then extracted herself. "Give me a minute."

She turned to examine the room. The overhead lights, encased in layers of cobwebs, left a pale golden glow across the immense walls. Mason and Zoe stood not far away. Mason had tucked his hands into his jacket pockets. Even though he pretended to study the nearest portraits, he couldn't completely keep the concern out of his expression. Zoe, meanwhile, watched Keira with unabashed rapture.

"Go on," Zoe hissed. "Pretend we're not here."

Keira took a deep breath. A woman, her long hair cascading behind her, had drawn near. Her expression was cold as she gazed at Keira with black, empty eyes. It was still better than the pure indifference the others had been showing her, though, so she took her chance.

"Hey," Keira said, wrapping her arms around her chest as she stepped up to the woman. "Can we talk?"

Chilled air radiated from the spirit. She tilted her head slightly, eyebrows lifted. There was disdain in her face. Keira tried to ignore it as she forged on. "You understand that you're dead, don't you? You've been dead for a long time. Something's holding you here, though. Some kind of unfinished business."

The woman showed no reaction. Keira hunched her shoulders slightly higher to protect against the chill. "I want to help you move over. Please, show me that you understand. A nod. Anything."

She waited. So did the woman. Keira was about to give up when a flash of light made her flinch. She turned to see Zoe holding up her camera.

"Sorry," Zoe whispered. "Ignore me."

Keira sighed and saw a plume of condensation leave her lips. The spirit ahead of her seemed to be growing bored. Its attention was drifting toward Dane, who stood under the medley of portraits, his head down.

"Don't you want to move on to the next life?" Keira pressed. "I can help. Just show me what's holding you here."

Finally, the woman's expression changed. A wicked smile grew, showing dark gums and two rows of narrow, pointed teeth. She drifted past Keira, eyes alight as she approached Dane.

Frustration boiled in Keira's stomach. The woman's answer had been more than clear. If she'd had unfinished business at one point, it was no longer any kind of priority. She didn't want to move on. She only wanted to feed.

"Does *anyone* here want to be untethered from their resting place?" Keira raised her voice, desperate. "I can help you. But you have to *want* help."

More ghosts had appeared while she was speaking to the woman. Grim, gaunt faces stared at her from every corner of the room. Keira turned, meeting each gaze in turn. Everywhere she looked, she met the same expressions: disdainful, derisive. Cold, thin smiles sent her heart racing. They were laughing at her.

"Fine," Keira muttered. She rolled up the sleeves on her bug-eyed cat sweater. "Fine, we'll do this the hard way."

In her brief stint as Blighty Graveyard's groundskeeper, Keira had found three ways to get rid of trapped ghosts. The first, resolving their unfinished business, was the most complicated but also the kindest to the spirits.

Almost universally, Keira found herself pitying the dead. Many of them had spent decades or even centuries shackled to their resting places, bound there by some heartsick wish or twist of fate they could no longer resolve. When possible, Keira tried to give them closure. They had waited so long for it, it felt cruel to deny them their final wishes.

She felt no such pity for the spirits of Crispin Manor. They didn't care about being trapped. Their sole purpose was to cause suffering, and as she stared at the figures around her, she realized not a single one of them showed any hint of remorse or shame.

And Keira, in turn, was certain she wouldn't feel even a shred of remorse if she forcefully eradicated them.

Dane took a half step back as Keira approached him. "Hold

still," she said, and he obediently froze. She picked her target: the woman who had disregarded Keira's offer of help. She had bitten Dane's upper arm and hung to him as she fed.

Keira focused on the center of the woman's chest. The ghosts were made up of something not unlike fog. When Keira strained, she could see a point inside the spirit's chest, close to her heart, where the brightness seemed more condensed.

She knew what she would find there. A delicate, tangled thread. Every spirit had one; it was their life essence, the thing that tethered them to earth. And Keira's gifting allowed her to untangle it...if she could just get ahold of one of its loose ends.

Reaching into the spirit's body felt like plunging her hand into freezing water. Keira grit her teeth. Her questing fingers felt electricity course along their tips. The woman's energy was stronger than any of the normal spirits Keira had encountered in her graveyard, most likely because she'd been feeding from a human.

Keira could visualize the threads. They tangled into a ball only slightly larger than a marble. Her fingers found a loose end, but holding it felt like trying to pinch a fragment of shattered glass. Sharp. Aching.

The woman finally reacted, lifting her head from Dane's arm. Her lips pulled back into a snarl, exposing a seemingly endless black pit ringed by the awful sharpened teeth.

The chill was spreading up Keira's arm. Her fingers burned from touching the hissing electricity that coursed through the threads.

She tightened her hold, then pulled.

Sparks of pain ran along Keira's arm, like she was touching a high-voltage fence. The woman convulsed. She clamped both hands over her chest—over the ball of thread—trying to shield it.

Keira pulled harder. The thread refused to untangle. An uncomfortable numbness spread along her arm, and she realized the ghost was sapping *her* energy.

Sweat beaded across her skin. Each breath came thin and stuttering. Distantly, she thought she heard Mason say something, but the words came through muddy and vague.

"Let...*go*..." she hissed.

The woman's mouth stretched wide. She was howling, even though the noise was inaudible to Keira. She convulsed backward, trying to escape Keira's grip. The thread slid a fraction before the specter redoubled her grip over it. She was fighting to prevent it from unraveling.

"Keira." Mason's voice came through again, sharp with alarm. It broke her concentration. She let go of the thread and staggered back. Mason caught her before she could collapse to the floor, his arms wrapping under hers and folding around her. "Easy," he said. "Just breathe."

She felt achingly, uncomfortably weak. Her legs didn't want to carry her weight, so she leaned back against Mason, grateful at how warm and solid he was.

"Here," Mason said, adjusting his grip on her to press one hand to the back of her neck. "You can take energy from me, right? Borrow some now. I don't mind."

Keira wasn't sure she even had the strength to answer, but she opened herself to his touch. A soft, steady flow of energy came through where their skin connected. She felt it spreading through her limbs and took a deep, stuttering breath. "Thanks."

"You want some of mine too?" Zoe asked. She fired off another photo before waving a hand in Keira's direction. "I have plenty to spare."

"I think I'm good for now." Keira pushed away from Mason and was relieved that her legs seemed prepared to carry her again. "Sorry. I shouldn't have pushed it so far. I picked a stubborn ghost."

"Did it work?" Zoe asked. "Is the spirit gone?"

Keira pulled her second sight open again. The woman stood barely four paces away from her. The earlier dignity had vanished; she now stood with her legs wide, her hands flexed into clawlike shapes at her side. Her face had contorted, lines forming around her mouth and eyes and nose as she snarled.

"No," Keira said, and felt frustration bite into her. "She's still here."

Dane stayed with his back to the wall of portraits, hunched with his arms folded across his chest. Figures continued to move about him, ghosts releasing their hold on him and drifting away, and others moving in to take their place. Worry flickered in his eyes. "I am sorry," he said. "I did not realize it was so taxing for you."

"That's the thing: it normally isn't." Keira swiped the back of her hand across her forehead to clear off the cold sweat that had built there. Even after drawing from Mason's energy, she still felt breathless. "When they're ready to go, it's as easy as opening a door. These ones don't *want* it to be easy, though."

The woman slowly drew back into herself, the ferocity in her expression fading into cold resentment. She kept her eyes focused on Keira as she began to move back toward Dane.

Anger burned in the pit of Keira's stomach. Even after coming so close to being untethered, the woman still only cared about feeding. She felt no qualms about it, even though Dane was the last of her family line. She was willing to drain him until there was nothing left.

Keira knew of one final way to get rid of ghosts. She'd only done it once before: with the dark specter in the graveyard.

She could push her energy into the ghost, feeding it faster than it was prepared for. If she could push enough energy into it, she could overload it. It would swell and swell and swell until it couldn't contain any more and burst.

The idea of doing that to the ghosts around Dane was incredibly appealing. If they wanted to feed, well, let them have more than they could contain.

Keira flexed her hands at her sides. As badly as she wanted to see the spirits burst at their seams, she knew she wasn't able to make it happen. She'd lost almost all of her energy doing it to the shade in the graveyard. That had only been a few days before, and she was still building her way back to feeling normal. She wasn't strong enough to eradicate even one of the spirits around her. Especially now.

One of the spirits—an older, stooped man—left his hold on

Dane. He drifted away, and Keira half expected him to fade back into the ether, only he didn't. He turned toward Mason.

"No." Keira took a sharp breath as she watched the ghost's bone-thin arms thread around Mason. "*Don't.*"

Mason's eyebrows rose. He glanced at where Keira stared, even though he wasn't able to see the spirit. "Should I be worried?"

"I said *stop.*" Keira moved forward. She smacked her hands through the ghost's form, trying to buffet him away. All she felt was the ache of frost across her palms. The spirit showed no reaction.

"Do you want me to…do something?" Mason, nervous, glanced between Keira and what must have looked like empty air to him.

A sly smile appeared in the ghost's eyes as his mouth opened to reveal rows of teeth.

"No!" Keira forced some energy into her hands as she shoved at the spirit. It worked. There was a burst of light as the figure tumbled backward, shock and anger twisting its face.

Keira, panting, stared down at it. She stretched her hands wide, a threat: *I'll do it again.*

The ghost's lips curled. It turned away from Mason, instead drifting back to Dane.

Keira staggered back and leaned against the wall, ignoring the way the gilt frames pressed into her shoulder blades. She felt shaky and slightly queasy. She closed her eyes, unable to watch as the specter joined his companions in their feast.

"I'm sorry, Dane," she said. "I can't stop them."

"Ah." She didn't like the way he sounded. As though he were resigned. As though this was the outcome he had expected all along. "It was always a long shot. Thank you for trying, regardless. Will you be all right to see yourselves out?"

He was already turning away, moving toward the doors leading him deeper into the crumbling maze of a building. The shimmering specters turned with him, closing in around him. The helpless frustration redoubled.

"No. Wait." Keira pressed her palms into her closed eyes, rubbing at the ache forming behind them. She'd overtaxed her second sight as well. The muscles there were growing stronger, but she still wasn't used to pulling on them for so long. "I'm not done. I just need more time. And…I'll need to ask a favor."

"Anything."

Keira let her hands drop as she stared at the scene ahead of her. More than a dozen spirits had gathered in the foyer, their forms strange and eerie in the sickly light. Their faces were cold and unwelcoming, surreal echoes of the artwork above them as they stood surrounded by the portraits they had commissioned during life.

"I need to know your family tree," Keira said. "I need to understand the people these spirits once were."

"Research," Zoe said, lowering her camera. Her expression held unbridled delight. "I know this whole situation is straight-up horrendous for everyone else here, but if it's any consolation, I'm having the time of my life."

"Great," Keira managed. She turned to Dane. "Do you have your family tree recorded somewhere by any chance?"

A small, bitter smile pulled at the corners of his lips. "I am a part of the great Crispin family. They would have rather drowned themselves in the river than forgotten their ancestry. Follow me."

CHAPTER 9

DUST SCATTERED ABOUT THEM as Dane unfurled a roll of parchment. It was huge, taking up most of the dark wood table in the room's center.

Keira, Mason, and Zoe all approached from different sides, craning to read the aged ink markings. The parchment held names, all interconnected by lines drawing out a complicated family tree. Dane placed smaller sheets of paper, a nibbed pen, and an inkwell beside it.

Zoe reached for the note-taking material. "I was going to be a pain and ask if you have any pens from the current century, but it's hard to say no to such a slavish devotion to aesthetic. What's the plan here, Keira?"

"We're going to log some ghosts." Keira folded her arms as she turned away from the table. The room was small and felt cramped with an accruement of odd trinkets. Animal skulls stared out at her from glass boxes. Silver platters, vases, and ornaments, all tarnished, shimmered inside a cabinet. An assortment of elaborately framed mirrors filled the gaps in the walls, and it left Keira with the uneasy sensation that she was being watched from every direction.

That wasn't too far from the truth. Dane had brought a cluster of feasting ghosts into the room with him. Still more arrived, shifting through the patterned wallpaper. Cold, glittering eyes fixed Keira with hostile glares.

She took a slow breath to steady herself. "Dane, you and I are going to ID as many of these as we can. Zoe, copy down that family tree. Mark which ghosts are present. I want to know how many I'm dealing with and who they are."

"Got it." Zoe was using the inkwell as though it was second nature, her hand flying across the parchment as she re-created the Crispin history. "Wow, you guys liked weird names, huh? There's actually a Marmaduke in here."

Keira turned back to Dane. His eyes seemed to sag at the corners, weighted down by age or tiredness, but his nod was resolute as he gave Keira the go-ahead.

She described the spirits to Dane. When he'd heard enough to identify them, he cut in with a name and a place in the family tree, and Zoe marked it down with a large asterisk.

It wasn't fast work. Ghosts drifted in and out. Sometimes their forms overlapped as they ate from Dane, and Keira's eyes ached as she fought to tease out details. Sometimes there weren't enough distinguishable features to make a positive identification, and

Dane would suggest two or three potential names. Zoe marked them down with a question mark.

As night grew deeper, Mason left the room, then returned a few minutes later with glasses of water and plates of food from the dining table. Otherwise, he was quiet, standing in the back of the room as he let Keira work.

"A woman in her fifties or sixties." Keira tracked a new spirit who had entered through the closed door. "Her hair is cut with a fringe that covers her eyebrows. Long fingernails. There's a mole on her jaw, right here." She indicated to the spot on herself.

Dane was slumped against the opposite wall, arms folded as his back pressed into the wallpaper. His head had been down for the past twenty minutes, but he lifted it then, his lips thin and pale.

The woman's spirit moved through the table. Long fingers wrapped around either side of Dane's head as she bent to plunge her teeth into his throat.

As the silence stretched, Zoe glanced up, her pen poised over the replica family tree.

"Do you know her?" Keira pressed.

"Yes." Dane sighed and let his head drop again. "Filomena. My mother."

The frustration and anger had been a constant bubble in the pit of Keira's stomach, but it overflowed then, burning the insides of her chest. She turned away so she wouldn't have to watch the woman feed.

"I've got some good news and some bad news." Zoe rubbed her palm into one of her eyes, inadvertently smearing ink around it. "Good news, I don't think there's much more to do. Bad news, that's because we've basically filled in the entire family tree."

"What?" The stream of spirits had seemed constant, but Keira had been so absorbed in watching and identifying them that she hadn't tried to count how many passed through the room. She moved up behind Zoe and leaned over the back of her chair to examine the family tree. Almost every one of the dozens of names held a star next to it. Most of the question marks had been scratched out as the owners were identified.

"Yeah. I think the real challenge will be identifying anyone who *isn't* present."

Keira paced as she chewed that over. In her admittedly limited experience, she'd found lingering spirits were the exception, not the rule. Many of the graves in Blighty's cemetery were unoccupied. Most people preferred to move on.

Unfinished business can cause a person to stay behind. Is it possible that a whole family is tied down by one cause?

She thought it was. Just not in the traditional sense of unfinished business.

"Dane, you said your family took a lot of pride in their legacy."

"To a fault," he agreed. His lip twisted in disgust. "You may have heard that kings and queens used to believe that they had a divine right to rule, that they were physically *different* from the commoners."

"I've heard that," Mason said. "It's part of the cause behind major cases of inbreeding. They didn't want too much so-called impure blood entering the family line."

Dane flicked a hand toward the parchment. "That's similar to how my family thought—that the family line was somehow superior. They didn't believe they were better because of their money or their power. They thought they had money and power *because* they were inherently better."

Keira remembered the case of Emma Carthage. George Crispin, the patriarch of that time, had been enraged to learn his son had had an affair with a common girl. So enraged, in fact, that he'd been prepared to go to jail for murder rather than acknowledge that the relationship had resulted in a child.

Keira ran her tongue across the back of her teeth as she examined the spirits still in the room with them. A family that believed they were more than common mortals. A family that slavishly worshipped their own heritage, their own fame, their own estate.

It wasn't traditional unfinished business in the sense that they needed to conclude something or find closure.

It was more like...they couldn't let go of what they'd had. Perhaps a part of them knew that, when they passed into the next life, they would be the same as everyone else. There was no special, superior afterlife waiting for them. And they couldn't stomach that.

And so they clung to what they had once had, feeding off the heir, in the same way they had once been fed on. Their little family secret.

Out of the family tree, only a handful were not present. Keira skimmed over the names. George Crispin had died in jail. His son, Frank, had hanged himself in the old mill. Their ghosts would have both passed over without the chance to cling to the family estate. There were others, some who might have let go at the point of death, unwilling to become parasites. Others who, Keira suspected, were still in the house but hadn't shown themselves yet.

The lingering ghosts went all the way back to the first generations that had built their home in Blighty and established its industry with the mill. In those earliest generations, the burden would have been light, three or four ghosts that fed on the dozen children and nephews and nieces. They would have barely been noticed.

As time went on, the balance began to shift. The family line narrowed as children moved away or didn't marry. More ghosts, fewer sources of food. Even then, though, it was probably easy to ignore the effects. Maybe the family would have felt lethargic or had short tempers on bad days.

But the family had continued to narrow, and more generations of ghosts carved out their place in the house. Until it all came down to Dane.

One last descendant. A lineage spreading back hundreds of years. Dane was being crushed by the metaphorical weight of them.

At least three dozen ghosts. None of whom want to move on.

She thought of how exhausted she'd been after banishing the shade. How long would it take her to build enough energy to clear out even one of these ghosts? She could ask Mason and Zoe for help, borrowing energy from them like she had before, but that could only take her so far.

How long would it take to rid Dane of his parasites?

Years upon years. And that's if I neglect every other spirit I've promised to help, both in the cemetery and at the mill.

"Okay." Keira braced herself on the table as she stared down at the sprawling, interconnected list of names. "Okay, we can figure this out. We can…we can fix this. I think."

She still couldn't bring herself to look at Dane while his mother ate from him, but she could feel his gaze on her, silent but desperate.

"Does fixing this feel like something we can get done within, like, twenty minutes?" Zoe's smile was weary. "I realize this is a super-serious, life-altering situation that requires the most delicate of handling, but also I have work tomorrow and it's already one in the morning."

"It's *what*?" Keira turned to the wall behind her where a clock ticked faintly. Zoe was right. The hour hand was creeping past one. "When did it get so late?"

"My apologies." Dane pushed away from the wall he'd been leaning against. "I didn't mean to keep you here for so long. I'd offer to let you sleep in one of the guest rooms, but none of them are very habitable right now."

Is this it? We leave. He stays. Surrounded by a shroud of dead slowly sapping the life out of him. Am I really going to abandon him to them?

But what other choice do I have?

Keira took a sharp breath. Fresh hope thrummed through her. "You'll come with us."

Dane didn't speak but watched her warily.

"Ghosts have tethers," Keira explained, the words running together as excitement made her speak faster. "Usually either the place they died or the place they were buried. And, well, I'm assuming all of these ghosts died inside the house. Which means they're also tethered here. They can't leave. If we can get you far enough away, you'll be free of them."

"Is it that simple?" The hope had returned to his dark eyes. The prominent Adam's apple bobbed as he swallowed.

Keira rushed to gather up the copy of the family tree. Now that she had a plan, she was furiously eager to get them out of the house. "You'll stay at my cottage tonight. It's a little bit crispy around the edges and the cat snores, but I can promise you it's better than being here."

"I…I don't want to intrude…"

"You won't be. I'm already sleeping in a tent. We'll figure out something more permanent tomorrow." She was breathless and giddy as she turned toward the door. "Why didn't I think of this before? I can't remove the ghosts from you, but we can remove *you* from the *ghosts*."

"Ooh, like fishing him out of a pot of ghost soup and letting him drain," Zoe offered.

"That's a weird but surprisingly accurate analogy." She turned back to Dane. "Do you need to get anything before we leave?"

"No." His breathing was shallow and shuddering as he pulled his jacket over his shoulders. "I'm ready."

They moved through the house in single file, with Dane at the head of the group. He carried the lantern and it lit strips of the walls in flickering gold while the ghosts clung to him like cobwebs blowing in his wake. His footsteps formed a strange tempo as they crossed the foyer in long strides, under the watchful gaze of the myriad portraits.

Dane held the front door open as they slipped out, then stepped onto the porch himself. He made to close the massive wooden door but hesitated.

"Did you need to get something?" Keira asked.

"I don't have the keys to lock it." Then he clicked his tongue and shook his head. "As though there's anything here that I'd regret having stolen. No. Let's keep moving."

CHAPTER 10

DANE SNUFFED THE LANTERN and left it on the porch. Ribbons of moonlight rained through the jagged, dead branches as the four of them rushed through the overgrown, crumbling gardens.

The night air was bitingly cold. Keira's exhales snaked away from her as plumes of condensation, spiraling into the mist that was forming between the trees. Ahead, the ivy-covered gates loomed, still propped open from when they'd entered. They slipped through one at a time before Dane dragged the gate closed again. Then they turned toward town.

"How far away do we need to get?" Zoe asked, arms folded around her torso as she shivered in her ball gown.

"Not sure. A few minutes from the house, at least." Keira rubbed her hands in an effort to keep them warm. "I'll tell you when the ghosts start disappearing."

She'd seen the spirits' tethers in action a few times before. She'd visited a hospital with Adage where an older woman's ghost had tried to lead her to a van outside. The woman hadn't been able to travel to the stairs or elevators but instead led Keira through her room's window before vanishing once they reached the ground. Her tether had been three dozen meters at most.

The shade, on the other hand, had seen its sphere expand as it absorbed more energy. It had originally been limited to within a few feet of its tombstone before spilling out into the graveyard and even encroaching on the parsonage as it drew power.

That meant the stronger a ghost was, the farther it could travel. And these spirits, although not carrying the aggressive power of the shade, had spent their years eating from a captive prey. Keira guessed they might need to walk for a bit before the dead could no longer follow.

It wouldn't matter too much. The graveyard was far enough away that even the most powerful Crispin ghost wouldn't be able to reach it. In the meantime, Keira kept one eye on Dane's hunched form and the mist-like figures that clutched their arms around him.

"It's a nice night," Dane said unexpectedly. "There's a good moon to help us see our way."

"You like to take walks at night, don't you?" Zoe asked.

"When the insomnia sinks in, yes, it's one of the few things that helps." He glanced aside. "I avoid leaving my home during the day. Or straying too close to town. People stare."

Zoe's eyes narrowed. "Y'know, radical idea, but maybe they'd stare less if you didn't try to hide all the time."

"You're not shy to express your thoughts, are you?"

"I've been accused of many things but never shyness."

A huffing, scoffing noise escaped Dane, and it took Keira a second to realize he'd laughed. A small, tentative smile had begun to form on his sallow features.

Ahead, Keira could make out the rooflines marking the town's center. None of the lights were on and the buildings appeared uncomfortably cold, as though they'd been abandoned for years. Dead leaves skittered across the dirt road, tangling around her feet.

The spirits continued to stick to Dane. They were either stronger than Keira had expected or the continual feeding was artificially stretching their tethers.

They can't last much longer, surely. They'll have to snap back to their resting place soon, no matter how much energy they've stolen.

A glimmer of movement made her glance toward the trees lining the path. Mist coiled between the trunks and left a coating of dew over the bark. Keira could have sworn she'd seen something inside the trees, though. A pale figure, gone before her eyes could find it.

Keira tracked the space as they passed it by. She couldn't suppress the instinct to quicken her pace.

The mist was thickening around them, forming a lake of fog that they had to wade through. It clung to Keira's exposed skin and stuck loose strands of hair to her throat. When she swallowed, she tasted the icy droplets on her tongue.

No other sounds were audible above the crackle of dried leaves beneath their feet and their low, rough breathing. Another flicker of movement registered to her right, but it was gone the second she turned toward it.

"No one else saw that, did they?" Keira felt compelled to keep her voice to a whisper.

"Hm?" Zoe had her arms crossed and her shoulders hunched. "I can't see much of anything."

Keira couldn't blame her. As they passed under the shadows of the stores and the surrounding trees at the edge of town, the dappled moonlight began to play tricks on her eyes. She could no longer see more than forty paces through the fog. It was growing thicker…and faster than the night warranted.

Keira increased her speed again, her breathing turning raw. She thought she knew what was happening. The presence of ghosts could make an area feel cold and create mist where none had been before.

This was the first time she'd entered the town with her second sight engaged. She had no idea how many spirits might be lingering between the old stone buildings and on the worn sidewalks.

Ahead, the fountain marking the crossroads rose like a monument through the hazy white. Beyond it, figures flickered at the edges of Keira's vision. She pulled harder on the muscle that controlled her second sight and felt the headache burn behind her eyes. She'd badly overused it, but she couldn't afford to drop it yet.

She turned to see Dane. She'd been so preoccupied on the shapes around them that she hadn't been watching to see when the parasites lost their ability to cling to him. Even hunched, he created an imposing figure: his features were lost in the shadows and mist, but his black clothes and dark, shaggy hair created a wild silhouette. Surrounded by the old stone buildings and cobblestone streets, it was possible to imagine she'd fallen back in time.

The transparent, bony forms still hung from him, their eyes closed as they fed.

This shouldn't be possible. How can their tethers reach so far? Are they really that strong?

Keira ran a hand over her face. It came away damp with dew.

Something icy cold brushed against her back. It left the skin prickling like a low electric current had touched her, and hairs rose across her body.

She knew that sensation. A spirit had touched her. She turned to see the woman—the one who had laughed at Keira's attempts to banish her—glide past as she approached Dane.

"No," Keira whispered. She took a step back and turned, scanning the town's crossroads with increasing desperation. Faces stared back at her, rising out of the fog before fading again.

She'd assumed she was seeing ghosts who had died inside the town of Blighty—she was wrong. They were the Crispins, the same men and women she'd encountered inside the mansion. They'd followed her.

Not quite. They followed Dane.

A stab of defeat hit her hard enough to rob her breath.

"What is it?" Mason asked. He'd stopped close beside her, tentatively hopeful.

"I was wrong." The words tasted like poison on her tongue. "They aren't tethered to the estate. They're tethered to *Dane*."

She thought they must have been chained to the house at one point. Many of the spirits had been dead since before Dane was even born. But Dane was now the last living human in the house, and the spirits had been feeding from him for decades. Their tether had changed.

"So I'll never be free from them no matter how far I travel," Dane said.

Keira was helpless to do anything except nod miserably.

"I understand." Dane's dark eyes were unreadable. He turned away. "If it makes no difference where I spend the night, I may as well return to my home."

"I'm sorry." Keira didn't know what else to say. "I'll keep trying. There must be a way to get rid of them."

He didn't answer other than to raise one hand in farewell as he strode toward the shadows. The ethereal shapes in the mist moved to follow him, their flowing hair blending into the softly swirling fog.

As he disappeared behind the buildings, Keira finally let her second sight drop. The headache behind her eyes was a steady, aching thing, and she knew she'd feel its aftereffects the following morning. She frowned at the damp cobblestones as she focused on keeping her frustration under control.

"Well, damn." Zoe squinted up at the moon. "If my ancestors kept pestering me even after they'd died, I bet *I'd* be miserable too."

"It's definitely not helping," Mason agreed.

Zoe sent a sharp glance toward Keira. "Hey. Are you going to collapse into a heap of guilt-riddled despair if I let you out of my sight?"

"Nope," Keira said resolutely.

"Cool, because I have work in five hours and I'm so tired I think I could face-plant onto the road and not even wake when cars started driving over me come morning. I'm going to catch some shut-eye. I'll come by after work tomorrow, though, and we'll see if we can brainstorm this thing out."

"I'd like that." Keira tried to smile even though her face didn't want to form the right expression. "Thanks, Zo."

"Anytime. Here." She passed over the paper with the replicated family tree, then hiked her opera gloves farther up her arms. "Try to get some sleep. Both of you."

Zoe's shoes rang out against the road as she half jogged in the direction of her home. Keira shivered, then turned toward the path that would lead her to the cemetery. "Thank you too, Mason. And sorry for keeping you out so late."

"Good thing I don't have a curfew." There was a hint of laughter in his voice. "Let me walk you home."

She glanced up at him. His dark hair was growing heavy as the fog dampened it. His eyes were warm, though. He'd always been the steadiest person Keira knew. Being around him sometimes felt like holding on to an anchor in the middle of a storm, and she didn't like the idea of letting go of that security when she had so little else. But the cemetery was in the opposite direction of his house, and even if he didn't have work, he was still going to be missing sleep. She felt a small pang of regret as she said, "Thanks, but I think I need to be alone with my thoughts for a bit. Talk to you tomorrow, though?"

"Absolutely."

Keira turned away, then felt something warm and heavy land over her shoulders. Mason's jacket.

"You should keep—"

"My home's only a minute away. You've got the longer walk." He was backing away, looking cold in only his shirt but still smiling. "I'll pick it up tomorrow, all right?"

"All right." As Mason left, Keira dug her fingers into the gray wool jacket's lapels and pulled it tightly around herself. It dwarfed her, but it was warm and thick, and Keira couldn't stop herself from burying her face in the collar as she turned toward the cemetery.

Despite promising Zoe she wasn't going to collapse into a heap of guilt-riddled despair, she felt uncomfortably close to exactly that. She'd promised Dane she would help. She had no idea how she was going to do that. Or even where to start looking.

As Keira's pace quickened to a brisk walk, one thought surfaced: she wasn't entirely alone anymore when it came to matters relating to the dead.

She had an entire cemetery to help.

CHAPTER 11

"HM." KEIRA SQUINTED AS the early sun stung her eyes. She stood outside the cottage, still wearing the rumpled cat sweater from the night before, toothbrush gripped loosely in one hand and her mouth full of frothy toothpaste.

A steady headache thumped through her skull. She'd overtaxed the second sight. Keira gave the muscle a tentative pull and winced as the headache redoubled. A blur of ghosts flickered into view, then faded again as she let the sight relax.

Keira turned into the cottage, shuffling, her eyes squinted, and made her way to the bathroom, where she spat out the toothpaste and rinsed her mouth.

She'd been so tired when she'd arrived home that she'd assumed she would sleep until noon. Instead, she'd crawled out of her tent just after six, headachy and bleary and unable to stay still any longer.

Every time she closed her eyes, she saw the helpless resignation scrawled across Dane Crispin's face.

She dunked her face under the tap's cold water and rested there for a moment, letting the chill invade her head and cool the throbbing pain behind her eyes. When she resurfaced, blinking water out of her eyes and blindly reaching for a towel, she felt a fraction more human.

Daisy waited for her in the middle of the cottage's living space, huge amber eyes staring up at her imploringly.

"You want some food, huh?" Keira tied her hair back as she crossed to the kitchen. Daisy followed her, tail held high as she emitted faint, squeaky meows.

Keira served her up fresh food, then leaned her back against the counter while she ate a bowl of cereal and waited for her tea to steep. The day was overcast, and the biting cold from the night before had settled in. She'd left Mason's jacket draped over the back of the fireplace couch and eyed it as chills began to creep through her limbs. He wouldn't mind, she decided, and slung it over her shoulders, grateful for the way it hung down to her knees.

She made her tea stronger than normal, figuring she could do with whatever minute caffeine it gave her, then headed back outside. The muted light glared off damp gravestones and the low metal fences. She cupped the mug close to her chest for warmth as she squinted into the field of aging, crumbling gravestones.

Her second sight still ached when she pulled on it, but less than before. She guessed it would loosen up with some gentle use. Distant, pale shapes bled into view. None of the spirits were near her cottage that morning but scattered farther throughout the cemetery.

Keira's boots kicked frosty dew from the grass as she stepped between the graves. She strained to make out the spirits around her, putting names to the ones she knew.

She stopped near the graveyard's center. To her left and straight ahead, the forest's top was barely visible, rising above the mist like a watercolor painting against the gray sky. Shallow tingles prickled across Keira's skin. A warning that there were spirits nearby. That was exactly what she wanted.

"I need help," she said, speaking loudly enough that her voice would carry. "I need to practice sending spirits over to the next life. Is there anyone here who is ready to move on, who would be willing to help me?"

Wisps of condensation left her mouth with each word. She watched them coil away from her. Several of the distant spirits watched her, but none made any move to come closer.

Keira swallowed and adjusted her hold on her mug. None of the nearby ghosts were clear enough to see their expressions, only the vague outlines of their faces. The silence stretched.

A chill ran down her spine, like someone had dragged a frozen finger across the bones. She turned and found herself facing a tall, gaunt man. He looked like he was in his forties or fifties and wore plain, dusty farm clothes. One of his eyes was missing, and the lid was sewn shut over where it belonged. His hair might have been combed back during life, but strands had come free and hung across his sunken face.

"Hey," Keira said, smiling despite herself. "Are you volunteering?"

There was a second's pause, then he slowly nodded.

"Did you have any unfinished business that you can remember?"

Another pause, then he shook his head.

"That's good." Keira wet her lips. She hadn't thought to ask if any of the graveyard's denizens were ready to be released from earth before. Apparently, she should have. "Which grave's yours?"

The man's gait was slow and rocky as he led her a dozen paces away, to where a modest rectangle extended out of the earth. Keira crouched to read the faded stone. He'd died in 1925, just shy of his fiftieth birthday. "Solomon, huh? It's nice to meet you. I'm Keira, but I guess you might already know that."

There wasn't a reply. Keira was used to it by that point. Still crouched, she glanced up at the man beside her. He stared at the stone, some inscrutable emotion behind the blank, limp expression. Keira tried to guess what it was. Sadness? His slab was simple, no more than a foot high, and less elaborate than some of the others around him. He'd likely lived a modest life. The same could be said for a lot of Blighty's population around that time.

Keira cleared her throat and let her voice drop. "I could send you over right now if you wanted. But if you don't mind waiting a few days, I could really use some help practicing how to remove a stubborn ghost." She hesitated. "Raise one finger if you want to go now. Raise two if you want to help."

He was still and silent for so long that Keira began to wonder if he'd even heard her, then his hand came up. Two fingers were raised toward the sky.

"Thanks, Solomon," Keira said. She stood, leaving her mug on the soft ground near the grave. "This means a lot to me."

His eyes flicked toward her, then glanced away again. Keira had a sense that maybe this was what he'd been missing during life. A sense of purpose. To know that he was helping something larger than just himself.

"Right, here's what you need to do." Keira shook her hands out, trying to mentally prepare herself. "I'm going to reach into you and try to unravel your…well, whatever that thing is inside of you that's tying you to the earth. I need you to try to block me. Don't let me unravel it if possible. Not yet."

His one eye glanced at her again in a wordless acknowledgment.

"We might actually slip up and untether you before we mean to. Are you okay with that?"

A slow nod.

"Great. And, uh, if you decide you don't like this and want to stop, cross your hands, like this." She mimicked the motion, creating an X with her arms. "I'll understand what that means."

A final nod. Keira sucked in a deep breath and set her feet. "Okay. Get ready."

That last encouragement was as much for herself as for Solomon. She reached forward, aiming for his chest. His body gave no resistance as her fingertips passed through him, but she felt it just the same. It was like dipping her hand into ice.

Keira closed her eyes and focused. She found Solomon's thread immediately. It was tangled just to the side of his heart, at the center of his chest, the threads fizzing and bright and electric. Her sense of it was so perfect that she could see its shape in her mind's eye…including where a loose end extended from the knot. She found it with her fingertips. Icy-hot electricity zapped through her fingertips. When she'd tried this the night before, the Crispin woman had used the connection to suck Keira's own energy, but Solomon didn't try anything similar. Keira felt the energy flow out of her and back into her like a closed loop.

She tightened her hold on the thread and pulled. It refused to untangle. Instead, the knot tightened, becoming stubborn. Keira dug her fingers in tighter, but the more she pulled, the more it refused to budge. She let go and staggered back, releasing a breath.

Solomon swayed slightly. She wondered what that must have felt like for him to have someone reach into his chest and touch his essence.

"You okay?" She doubled over, hands braced on her knees as she collected herself. He nodded once. "Did it hurt at all?" A pause, then a slightly less certain shake of the head. It might not have been painful for him, but it probably wasn't the most comfortable experience. "Okay. You can still tap out if you want."

He chewed that over for a moment, then gently shook his head.

"Great." Keira straightened. "Ready for another round?"

The sun slowly rose and worked its way through the smothering mist as Keira and Solomon practiced in bouts. She'd encountered several hostile spirits before and none of the experiences had been especially fun. Solomon was different. He fought her, but he didn't try to hurt her.

That didn't stop it from being exhausting, though. She was already drained from the night before, and every attempt wore her down slightly more. Within an hour she was shaking and sweaty despite the cold morning.

Part of her had hoped there would be a secret trick to unraveling the thread. If one existed, she still hadn't found it. She'd tried teasing the thread out slowly, pulling it quickly, and picking at it in increments. Occasionally she got a small amount of give but never enough to undo the knot.

"Okay, great," Keira said, staggering away for what felt like the twentieth time that day. "I think I might need to call it quits for now. How're you doing?"

Solomon's features were less distinct than they'd been when they started. She could still make out the gaunt cheeks and wispy hair that drifted across his forehead, but his eyes and mouth had become vague and smudged. The exercise must have been wearing out his energy reserves too. He lifted one hand in a dismissive gesture, but Keira guessed he was about ready to be finished for the day too.

She picked up her cup from beside the grave and staggered to the nearest fence. The wood was rotting, with huge splinters running down its length as it sank into the soft earth, but Keira was still tired enough to risk resting against it as she caught her breath. She'd nearly finished her tea but drained the last cooled dregs then. Its caffeine had fueled her even less than she'd hoped.

There must be some way around this. Keira frowned at the long weeds around her ankles as she poked at the Dane problem for the hundredth time that morning. *Something I'm missing.*

Distant footfalls dragged her out of her reverie. She straightened, squinting against the glare, and saw two figures approaching from the cemetery's entrance. Two figures carrying…an enormous box? They each held one end, struggling under its weight as they made their way toward her cottage.

"I'll catch up with you later," she said to Solomon, but he'd already faded back into the ether. She took a deep breath and turned back to the approaching figures.

CHAPTER 12

KEIRA RECOGNIZED THE CLOSEST figure. Even with his burden, Mason's long gait was unmistakable. She couldn't see the person behind him, but as she jogged to meet them halfway, she realized they weren't carrying a box after all.

"The mattress!" She pressed a hand to her forehead. "I completely forgot."

"I don't blame you. The last twenty-four hours haven't exactly felt real." Mason was faintly breathless as he adjusted his grip. "I was going to bring it in my car, but it wouldn't fit. I'm lucky that Harry offered to help me carry it up here."

"I didn't offer," a muffled voice said. "I was volunteered against my will."

Keira leaned to the side to see around the mattress. Harry's face was squished against the fabric, crumpling one side of his disaffected glower and smudging the eyeliner he'd so carefully applied. "Hey, Harry. I'm guessing your mother did the volunteering."

"Just like she volunteered to bring me into this bleak, unfeeling world." His voice was as empty as his expression.

"Let's get this inside," Mason said. "It's heavier than it looks."

"Ah…yeah." Keira moved ahead to open the door. "Sorry, I meant to clean up for it. Can you just lean it against the wardrobe for now?"

Mason dropped his end, then pushed the mattress so it was propped against the wardrobe. Keira's old mattress was still on the bed, still sooty, with the old sheets and pillow bundled into a pile at its end. She had to admit, the thought of sleeping on the new, squishy-looking mattress was very appealing.

She cast a look toward the mantel clock. It was after midday. The morning had evaporated faster than she'd expected. "Have either of you eaten yet?"

Mason shrugged lightly. "I was going to pick up something on the way home."

Harry, for his part, had turned toward one of the windows that overlooked the cemetery. He stood as still as a statue, hands limp at his sides, his pale skin and black hair appearing all the starker in the cold light. "What is food except a shallow bid to delay our inevitable demise?"

"I'm taking that as a no." Keira crossed to the kitchen. "Let me get you something. It's the least I can do to thank you both for carrying that mattress all the way up the drive."

Mason joined her in the kitchen, and between the two of

them they put together drinks and a plate of sandwiches. Keira was overdue to go shopping; the sandwich bread was slightly stale, but she compensated by layering on extra butter. She made a note to try to get to the general store before it closed. She'd had the same mental note hovering in the back of her head for days.

Harry still hadn't moved from the window when Keira carried the sandwiches to the table. His sloping shoulders and limp hands betrayed no sense of emotion. She tried to read his expression, but it was hard when his fringe of black hair covered one eye. He was staring into the graveyard with an unnerving intensity, though.

An unsettling thought hit her. Watching him carefully, Keira asked, "Harry, can you see anything out there?"

"Ghosts, you mean?" His inflectionless voice held just a hint of moroseness. "No. But I like to cross my eyes and pretend I can."

"Oh." Keira almost laughed. For a second she'd thought that maybe she wasn't alone and that someone else in Blighty had a gift to see the dead. She didn't know whether to be relieved or disappointed that she couldn't ask her black-clad, melancholic friend for advice. His suggestions were rarely anything she wanted to implement, but it would have at least been *something*.

"I guess you figured out my secret," she said, sitting at the table and pulling one of the plates closer to herself.

"Secret?" He finally turned away from the window.

Even knowing that she didn't need to hide it from him, she still felt awkward putting it into words. "The...ghost thing."

"Oh. Yes." He approached the table and slunk into a chair of his own, with Mason taking up the third spot. "I didn't know it was supposed to be a secret. You live in a graveyard. It just makes sense."

Mason sent her a faintly skeptical glance. Keira doubted too many people would make the connection as quickly as Harry had.

"Dane invited us to his house last night," Mason said, taking up one of the sandwiches. "You told him about Keira's gift, and he wanted to see if she could help."

"Yes. Dane." Harry left his food and drink untouched. "I visit him often. Sometimes we play cards. Sometimes we just walk through the empty halls. It is the most fun I may ever have in this lifetime." He blinked. "He gave me the skull you took. I told him about that. He said he would look for another if I wanted. He's a good friend."

"Harry…" She cleared her throat. "I don't mind with Dane, since he needed help, but I'd be really grateful if you didn't tell anyone else about the whole ghost thing."

"Oh." He turned slowly, his sallow features flat. "I already told my mother."

"You…did?"

"She thought I was joking."

"I guess that's okay, then." Keira tried to imagine how the sweet, pince-nez wearing florist would react if she learned her son had been telling the truth. Polly Kennard did not strike her as the kind of person prepared to believe in ghosts. She supposed she was lucky that Harry's penchant for the dramatic and the macabre would help mask her secret if he *did* slip up. "Just keep it on the down low from now on. I could get in trouble if the wrong person hears about it."

"I understand." His gaze was unblinking. "A vow of secrecy. I've always wanted to be a part of one. We could cut open our palms and make a blood pact if you like."

"Oh, uh, I don't think we need to go that far."

His shoulders sagged a fraction. "No one ever wants to make a blood pact. We could invoke ancient spirits to hold us to our vow instead. I have some necromancy books at home. But I have to hide them behind my calculus homework; otherwise, my mother finds them and throws them out."

Keira was fighting against the urge to laugh. "I appreciate your dedication, but I'm cool to just take your word for it."

He stared into the distance for a second, as though this suggestion didn't make sense to him. Then he sighed, appearing faintly disappointed, and said, "Very well."

"Thanks, Harry. And thanks for being cool about all of this. It's nice to have people I can talk to."

"I would have thought you'd have plenty of that with the dead. The graves are silent. They will listen for hours." Harry took up one of the sandwiches and then, without another word, crossed to the door and left.

"Bye" was all Keira could manage as the door clicked closed behind the sallow man. She exhaled and leaned back in her chair. "I guess the dead must seem infinitely patient when you can't see them. Really, though, a lot of them are kind of prickly."

Mason chuckled. "Maybe that comes with the territory. I'm pretty sure I'd be in a bad mood too if I'd had to spend a century in a metaphorical waiting room and couldn't even choose my neighbors."

"True." Keira took a deep drink from the mug of tea Mason had made her. The ache still pulsed behind her eyes, but she was also conscious of how time was trickling away from her. Part of her knew it was unreasonable to expect results after half a day, but another part of her felt like every wasted minute was too much.

It was an emotion that was hard to put into words, but she knew Mason, at least, would understand. "I've been working with one of the ghosts to figure out how I can get rid of the Crispin spirits. I haven't made much progress. And...I feel like time might be running out."

Mason ran his fingers through his deep brown hair, pushing it away from his face. "I wasn't going to say anything."

She tilted her head toward him, one eyebrow raised.

He rolled his shoulders, looking uncomfortable. "You take responsibility—and guilt—for things too quickly. And I didn't want to apply more pressure when you were already working as hard as you could. But...I didn't like the way Dane was speaking last night."

"Like he was at the end of this tether," Keira said, knowing exactly what Mason meant. "Like...this is a final effort to fix things. And if this doesn't work..."

Keira had left her hand on the table, and Mason reached for it.

His warm fingers enveloped hers, heavy and solid and intimate all at once.

"You're not responsible for other people's choices," he said, and there was a deep conviction in his words. "Do you hear me, Keira? You can try to help people, and that's admirable, but you cannot shoulder responsibility if you're not able to save everyone. No number of lifelines will rescue someone who wants to drown."

She swallowed around a lump that had formed in her throat. "Okay, counterargument: if I try really, *really* hard—"

His smile was small and sad. "Keira."

"I know. I know you're right. But…" She took a slow breath and hated the way her voice caught. "It feels different because Dane has no one else. I'm the only person I know of who *can* fix this. I have to at least try."

"I understand how that feels."

His hand tightened over hers a fraction. It suddenly felt too warm and too close. Too intimate. Keira pulled her fingers out from under his as her face began to burn.

"Sorry," he said. "I didn't mean—"

"It's fine." She was already on her feet. Her body was hot in a way that felt uncomfortable under the layers of warming clothes. "I need to—I shouldn't waste time."

"Sure."

"I'm going to, uh…" She pulled the door open and felt the bracingly cold air cool her face. "Going to talk to the ghosts again. Solomon! Break's over, buddy."

She heard Mason follow her to the door, but she didn't look back.

She was afraid of what she might see in his face.

CHAPTER 13

KEIRA WASN'T THE ONLY living person in the graveyard that afternoon. Families came to visit loved ones, though most of them stayed by the parsonage, far enough away that they wouldn't be able to see Keira clearly.

There was one person who lingered close by, though. She'd assumed Harry had left for home, but he'd apparently taken his sandwich to eat among the dead. He now lay on his back, arms crossed over his chest, on top of one of the older grave sites. Dried weeds swayed about his body. She had the impression that he was willing the earth to open up and suck him down into the dark loam.

Keira ignored the increasing ache as she pulled on her second sight. A spirit stood beside the grave, pale but unmistakable, her hands on her hips and her jaw set. She saw Keira and gestured toward Harry as though to say *Can you believe this?*

Sorry, Keira mouthed.

Solomon was already waiting for her. He lingered beside his slab, his features still blurry. He didn't wait for her to speak but set his feet, indicating that he was ready to begin.

"I'm going to try something new this time," Keira said. She rolled her shoulders. "Brace yourself."

She still felt too hot and prickly from the conversation with Mason. Instead of trying to repress it, she let it rise through her like a tide, her breathing too fast and her heart racing.

Maybe this is what I need: emotions. The dead appear stronger when they're angry or upset. Maybe it will give me strength too.

She plunged her hand through Solomon's chest and felt for the threads there. He blocked her access immediately. Keira grit her teeth and pushed through, her fingertips finding the thread's end.

It had an inch of give in it. Keira pulled harder than she had before, letting the frustration and stress and confusion fuel her. It would feel good to untangle the knot. Cathartic. A way to let her own tangled emotions go.

But then the knot froze up again, growing tighter the harder Keira pulled. The fizzling electricity stung her fingertips. The anger redoubled, and instead of trying to undo the knot, Keira tried to snap the thread, but the fine, gossamer-thin strand was somehow the toughest material she had ever encountered.

When she staggered back, she felt angry tears on her face and swiped them away with her sleeve.

"Okay," she said, trying to bring her breathing back under control. "Okay, so…that didn't work. Let's try again."

The sun began its slow descent toward the horizon. Families came and went, though none came close enough that Keira felt compelled to leave her task. Harry was so still and so silent that she began to question whether he might have actually died. The spirit belonging to that grave had turned her back on him and stood with her arms crossed, silently sulking.

Keira didn't know how many times she'd tried to unravel the thread when a voice interrupted her, yelling, "Ahoy!"

She turned and squinted against the glaring light. Zoe had come up the drive without her noticing and stood near the cottage, her arms heavy with shopping bags.

Keira's head ached. It left her vision blurry at the edges and her mind slow and heavy. "I think we're done for today," she said to Solomon. "Thanks for the help. I'll see you tomorrow?"

He stared at her silently for a second, then faded from sight. Keira supposed that was as close to a yes as she could get from him. She wrapped her arms around her chest as she crossed through the long weeds to reach Zoe.

"Hey, Keira," Zoe said as she neared, then called, slightly louder, "Hey, Harry."

"Hello," he softly replied from his resting place.

"Oh, good, he's still alive," Keira murmured as she came up beside Zoe. "I was starting to worry. He helped Mason drop off a mattress and just…went to lie down in the cemetery, I guess."

"Eh, I get it. His mother can't put him to work in the store if he's, in quotes, helping a friend. He's making the most of this opportunity to get away from the flowers." Zoe's smile was wolfish. "Let's head in. It's freezing, and it looks like you have a fire going."

"I do?" Keira glanced up to the cottage's roof and saw that Zoe was right. A tendril of smoke wove out of the chimney.

"I'm assuming this one's a controlled fire at least." Zoe's arms were full of bags so she used her hip to bump the door open. "Otherwise I'd have to assume you were trying to burn down the cottage for the insurance money, which would be a terrible plan considering you don't actually have insurance. Hey, nerd."

That last part was directed toward Mason. He stood by the kitchenette, a towel slung over his shoulder.

Keira blinked. Her house looked like a house again. Not spotless but…considering it had been filled with smoke just days before, it was actually inhabitable. "You cleaned."

He shrugged, looking faintly embarrassed. "You're busy enough figuring out what to do with Dane's ghosts. I didn't have any plans for this afternoon, so I figured I could make myself useful."

Keira, faintly shocked, turned as she surveyed the space. There were still traces of the arson attempt hidden in the woods' grain and cracks in the stones, and Mason had piled unsalvageable pieces of furniture into a heap near the door, but her cottage was looking more like the space had when she'd first moved in.

"You'll still need some of the windows fixed," Mason continued. "I know a friend who can help with that. And some of the furniture will need to be replaced, but most of what you had was secondhand to begin with, and people throw out enough odds and ends that we should be able to fill the gaps without too much trouble."

"I don't know what to say. This is maybe the best thing that's happened to me all week." Keira turned to him and smiled. He smiled back, looking faintly embarrassed, then cleared his throat and took the towel off his shoulder. "Zoe. Anything new in your life?"

"Oh, you know. I'm running on about an hour of sleep. I caught my boss writing over the milk's expiration dates. Goth kid's trying to become one with the earth. The usual."

"Oh, the milk thing's kind of a worry, actually," he said.

"And super illegal. Maybe don't buy any milk from the store if it has text smudges on it." Zoe heaved the shopping bags into the kitchenette. "It gave me blackmail material to get all of this, though. Merry Christmas, Keira."

"It's definitely not Christmas yet." Keira frowned at the bulging bags. "And I should really pay for my own shopping."

"It's Christmas when I say it is. Also, I know how much you earn and I'm pretty sure a church mouse would take pity on you. Let's not look an expired milk horse in the mouth now."

Keira reached into the nearest bag and pulled out a can of cat food. "Honestly, I want to pretend I still have my pride, but I'm not in a position to turn any of this down. Thank you. Both of you. You've turned a kind of garbage day into a good one."

Zoe's eyes glittered with delight. "Wait till you hear the really good part. Not all of these bags are groceries. Despite being shackled by the job this capitalist society forced on me, I still managed to work a miracle."

She pulled open one of the bags with a flourish. It was full of books. Keira craned to read some of the spines, but the volumes near the top of the stack were all old, leather bound, and faded from age. "What...?"

"This is literally every book from within the library and my own not-so-modest collection that contains information on the supernatural or the afterlife." Zoe, beaming, pulled titles out with a dramatic flourish. "To be fair, a bunch of this will have about as much veracity as middle-aged dads talking about the biggest fish they ever caught, but I figure there have to be at least some grains of insight buried inside."

"Ooh." Keira picked up the closest book and wiped dust form its cloth cover. *Spirit Mediums and Medium Spirits* was heavy enough that she suspected she could break a toe if she accidentally dropped it. "This is great timing. I don't think I can practice any more for today. I won't say no to reading, though."

"I always wrote off these kinds of books as just hoaxes or wishful thinking." Mason took up a volume of his own, smiling. "I guess I can't do that anymore."

Zoe nodded, apparently satisfied. "It's settled, then. This is what we're doing for tonight. We'll divide up the pile and start skimming. When you find something that might be relevant, even if it's small, jot it down. We can compare notes at the end and see if anything vibes with how Keira works."

"Especially if it's about aggressive or uncooperative ghosts," Keira said. "I'm not having any problems with the friendly ones yet."

"Zo?" Mason raised one of the books she'd passed to him. "This one's on werewolves."

"Yeah, I got a bit carried away. But, hey, ghosts are real. Which means, statistically, we have a pretty good chance of encountering a werewolf in our lifetime."

"That's very much not how statistics work."

"Agree to disagree."

They pulled their chairs up to the fireplace, which was mercifully helping to ward off the chill. Zoe passed out pens and notepads, then they set to work.

The cottage fell still, with its silence only broken by the rustle of turning pages, the scratch of pens on paper, and the soft crackles and pops of the wood in the fireplace. Occasionally, one of them would get up to make drinks, add fuel to the fire, or stretch.

Keira's headache continued to burn at the back of her eyes. Her vision was going blurred, forcing her to strain to read the words on the page, which started to blend together. It was an onslaught of information, some of it seeming to be parroted from book to book, some of it coming from nowhere and with no explanation.

Keira was reading the same convoluted, run-on sentence for the third time when a slow, sonorous knock at her door jolted her out of the book. She glanced at the clock above the mantelpiece. It was nearly eleven. She almost never had visitors other than Zoe and Mason, and never that late at night. At least, not visitors with good intentions.

"Hello?" Keira called. "Adage?"

The door creaked open. With only the firelight and a lamp to illuminate the room, it was almost impossible to see the tall, thin figure in the opening. Keira had the impression of a face that was pale enough to belong to one of her ghosts, only part of it was missing, swallowed into a pit of darkness.

Then he sighed heavily, and Keira recognized Harry, his black fringe hiding part of his face.

"I need to go home now," he said, his voice flat. Then, as an aside, he added, "Your cat tried to eat me."

"Oh. Sorry." Keira glanced down. Daisy strode past Harry's legs and through the door, her tail held high, looking indescribably pleased with herself.

"I would have let her, but I have a curfew. Good night." Harry turned and slunk into the darkness. The door clicked closed behind him.

They sat in silence for several uncomfortable seconds, then Zoe whispered, "I can't believe he was out there the whole time."

"If I'd known, I would have invited him in." Keira grimaced. "It's cold tonight."

Mason rubbed at the back of his neck. "The only thing that got him moving was his curfew. Maybe he was actually happy out there."

Zoe laughed. "Harry? Happy? You know he resents that kind of slander."

Daisy strode toward them, all smugness, and Keira reached out to pat her as she passed. The small black cat considered the empty floor in front of the fireplace, then flopped over dramatically, exposing her stomach to the flames.

"I haven't crossed paths with her since breakfast," Keira said. "I'm surprised she's not hungry."

"I'm pretty sure Adage gives her bits of meat when he sees her," Mason said, admiring the cat fondly. "You'll have to keep an eye on that or she might overeat."

Zoe had been perusing a book the size of a brick but snapped it closed and dropped it onto the pile beside her. "I figure this is a good time to call it a night and go through our notes. Anyone find anything that stood out?"

"Let's see…" Mason flipped back through several pages written in a tight, neat hand. "The same themes came up multiple times. Burning sage. Salt. Iron and silver. Cleansings. Prayers."

"I had a lot of the same," Keira said. "The silver one surprised me. I thought that was for werewolves and vampires."

"It's all connected." Zoe nodded sagely. "Oh ye of little faith, you discounted the werewolf book too soon."

Mason made a noncommittal noise. "Well, another big theme was on how to *communicate* with ghosts. The older books usually talked about seances with candles and conduits and similar, but the newer ones usually just tell you to identify where you thought the ghost might be and speak to it directly. It's strange to think that ghost hunting has trends."

"I guess the communication part isn't the issue for you, huh?" Zoe asked.

"Not exactly," Keira said. "Except when they get stubborn and refuse to communicate back."

Zoe nodded. "These books aren't meant for actual legitimate

spirit mediums, I guess. They're for the average person who doesn't have much spiritual affinity. That's why old-timey seances were so elaborate—close the curtains, light the candles, put out bowls of food to attract the dead, sit in a circle around a table, touch hands. Some people think those rituals worked to lower the barrier between the living and the dead and allow occasional glimpses of the other side."

"Or the darkness and flickering candles made it easier for nervous participants to *imagine* they'd seen something," Mason added.

Zoe poked her tongue out at him. "Killjoy."

"What I'm really interested in is the ways to force the ghosts to move on," Keira said.

"Gotcha." Zoe flipped through her own stack of notes. Keira noted it was significantly thicker than either hers or Mason's. Zoe was a fast reader and an even faster writer. "Ghost eradication 101 has a bunch of common themes, like Mason said. Sage. Salt. Etcetera. I already knew about most of those and picked up what I could from the general store. It's all in the bags over there. The things I could get, anyway. For some bizarre reason, my boss never saw fit to stock dowsing rods in the store."

Keira couldn't stop herself from laughing. "You're amazing."

"Damn straight." Zoe's whole face bunched up as she grinned. "Figured you could give that stuff a try tomorrow. If they don't work, I found a lot of more esoteric suggestions too—rituals and circles and precious gems arranged just right. Maybe start with what's most common and work your way down the list, yeah?"

"That sounds like a plan." Keira kept her voice upbeat.

The books were thick with suggestions and anecdotes. None of them matched Keira's own experiences. They talked about ways to commune with the dead and ways to clear negative energy, but none of them mentioned unraveling threads or ghosts being tethered to their locations.

She didn't know what to think about that. Maybe it meant the books in Zoe's library were, like Mason had said, written by shams or simply repeating the advice the author had read elsewhere.

Or maybe Keira's way of communicating with the dead was unique. She didn't need a special situation for the ghosts to show themselves to her. She didn't need to rely on orbs in photographs or static in recordings. She just…had to open her second pair of eyes. And she didn't even know how she did *that* except it came as naturally as breathing.

Ghosts are real. And spirit mediums must be real as well, because as far as I'm aware, that's what I am. So why are my experiences so different?

She didn't like the answer that presented itself to her: she was alone. That, despite what other spirit mediums experienced, Keira's method of seeing ghosts was unique to her and only her.

Or at least, it was rare enough that not a single instance of it was mentioned in the hundreds of pages she and her friends had skimmed that evening.

"Keira?" Mason sat forward in his seat. Concern had pulled his eyebrows together as he watched her. "Something's bothering you."

"Just…" She made an effort to clear her face. "I don't like the way sage smells. And it sounds like I'll be burning a *lot* of it tomorrow."

"Sage bonfire," Zoe said, her face lighting up. "You could cleanse the whole town in one afternoon as long as the wind blew in the right direction."

"Hm." Mason didn't seem fully satisfied by her answer, but he didn't press her either. Keira was grateful when he changed the subject. "It's late, and none of us got enough sleep last night, so I'm suggesting we get some rest before we drop. I'm free tomorrow. How about you, Zo?"

"Day off." She grinned. "Sounds like we get to join in some of the ghost hunting."

"Good. We'll meet you back here in the morning, Keira. Before we go, though, let's get your old mattress out of here. You'll sleep better if you're not in a tent."

"You have no idea how good that sounds." Keira scratched around Daisy's head before standing. The cat's golden eyes peeked open a fraction, then gradually drooped closed again as she reached one paw toward the fireplace.

"We can drop the old mattress outside." Mason approached one end of the bed, while Keira reached for the other. "I'll take it to the dump on my next trip. Three, two, one—"

They heaved the old mattress up, blankets and all. It was heavier than Keira had expected. She scrunched up her face as soot and dust puffed out around them. They staggered toward the door, Mason leading the way. Keira was so occupied by their burden that it didn't register that Zoe had been speaking until she'd dropped the mattress onto the dirt outside her door. "Sorry, what was that?"

Zoe stood inside the cottage, staring at the now-empty bed frame. Her face had tightened with concern. "You might want to look at this."

CHAPTER 14

KEIRA CROSSED THE ROOM in three quick steps. She came to a halt at Zoe's side and followed her gaze toward the empty metal bed frame.

Mason had swept the floor when he cleared the room, but he'd missed the space beneath her bed. Dust gathered in the corners, along with the persistent traces of soot—and other objects.

In the center of the space, directly below where Keira had slept each night, was a symbol. Leaves and small sticks had been arranged to form a circular shape about the size of her head. Lines wove through the formation's center, segmenting it in ways that didn't line up but were somehow still symmetrical.

It struck Keira as the kind of thing she might find in an older, wilder world. A talisman. A rune. The kind of thing carved into trees or painted on stones with charcoal.

"What…" Mason had approached on Keira's other side. He

blinked at the figure, as though he didn't know what he was looking at.

"Do your best not to panic, but I think someone's tried to curse you," Zoe said. She shot Keira a brief glance. "It wasn't me. Just putting that out there."

Mason shook his head. "A curse? Zo, that's ridiculous—"

"Look at it!" Zoe flapped her hands out, exasperated. "I've seen a lot of weird stuff in my deep dives on the internet, and I can promise you this is *not* some potpourri arrangement. This is the kind of thing that *does* stuff. Bad stuff."

Even as Mason and Zoe became more agitated, Keira found she couldn't quite muster the energy to be upset. She blamed the lack of sleep. "D'you think Harry might have done it? Out of everyone I've met in Blighty, he's the most interested in this kind of thing."

"He wasn't here long enough today." Mason ran a hand across his face. "He was only inside for a minute, and we were with him the whole time. Unless he came some other day…?"

"Nah, Harry doesn't do weird stuff behind your back." Zoe rocked on her heels, her arms folded across her chest defensively. "I've known him his whole life and subterfuge is never his goal. He'll do weird stuff and then immediately tell you about it so you can admire it."

"I'm not sure who else it could be, then." Keira shrugged. "I doubt Dr. Kelsey is involved in these kinds of things, and Dane, for all his brooding atmosphere, is pretty well grounded in reality."

"Not to sound paranoid or anything, but Mason never said he wasn't responsible." Zoe leaned even closer, her eyes wide. "And anyone willing to sell their soul to the brainwashing camp called medical school can't be trusted."

Mason, frowning, shook his head without taking his eyes off the leaves and twigs. "Med school taught me a lot of things, but I can promise you occult rituals were not included. Except maybe around exam time—people become desperate around exams."

"We don't know how long it's been here," Keira said. "It might not have been intended for me. Blighty's old groundskeeper lived here a year before I did. Maybe it's something he set up—a protective rune or something."

Zoe crouched. One thumb ran across her lower lip as she peered at the arrangement, analyzing it in ways that Keira was too bone-tired to care about. "No. One of those leaves has spots of green left. It's fresh. Within the last week, I'd wager."

"Cool. Maybe I can just…sweep it up and go to sleep?"

Zoe's glare was furious. "Don't you care about this? Someone's actively trying to hurt you—"

"They can get in line."

"—and you don't even know what this symbol is supposed to do!"

Keira shrugged. "Whatever it is can't be worse than what's already going on."

"That's the thing, though." Zoe snapped her fingers as she rose from her crouch. "You've had awful luck recently. Your house was set on fire. Dr. Frankenstein over here has to stitch you up at least once a week. Maybe this curse is to blame. Maybe…it's trying to kill you."

Keira considered that for half a second. Her life, to the extent that she could remember it, had been a string of chaos. And Zoe was right: she'd gathered a collection of cuts, scrapes, and enemies during her time at Blighty.

But if anything, she considered herself lucky. She'd survived. She'd made friends. She'd found somewhere she could call a home. For all the bad that had happened, she'd never lost any of the things that mattered to her the most. "Maybe it's a good-luck charm."

"I love your optimism, always have, but no."

Mason continued to frown at the symbol. "There must be an explanation," he muttered.

Zoe turned on him. "Were you not listening when I brought up the whole curse thing?"

"No—I mean, I can't say I believe in curses, but that aside, *someone* put this here. Someone with access to the cottage. And the answer doesn't necessarily have to be sinister. Maybe you sleepwalk, Keira. Or maybe children found their way in here on a day you were out and built it as a game."

"If you find the type of children who would make something like this, kindly tell me so that I can avoid ever crossing paths with them."

"Oh!" Keira closed her eyes, rocking back on her feet. "I'm such an idiot."

Zoe clutched at her. "What? No, Keira, don't say that. It's just the curse trying to make you think badly about yourself!"

"No, really, genuinely, I should have figured this out the moment I saw it. I blame the sleep deprivation." Keira couldn't hide a grin. "It's turning my brain to mush."

Mason's glance was intense. Keira had the impression that, despite his staunch belief that curses weren't real, Zoe's worrying had started to fray at his certainty. "You know who's responsible?" Mason asked.

"Yep." Keira turned to stare at the small black cat beside the fireplace. "Hey, Daisy, we found your masterpiece."

Zoe's look of concern only deepened. "You're…saying…you think your cat…cursed you?"

"Something like that, sure."

"Maybe the curse really is sapping your intelligence," Zoe whispered, looking horrified. "Keira, quick, what's two plus two?"

"Three," Keira said, then ignored her friend's anguished wail. "No, seriously, it's fine. It's just Daze. She's been bringing in sticks and leaves over the last couple of weeks and always runs under the bed with them. I thought she was trying to build a nest or something. I kept meaning to clean them out but, well, the to-do list has been running long lately."

Both Zoe and Mason turned back toward the arrangement. Zoe's head tilted first one way and then the other, while Mason stood perfectly still, as they both scrutinized the design. Then Mason said, "I want to believe that theory. I remember seeing Daze run under the bed with something in her mouth before. But…well, the placements seem uncomfortably deliberate."

"Yeah." Zoe tilted her head one last time, her wide eyes giving Keira the impression of a curious owl. "I mean, it's not impossible for order to rise from chaos, but this thing is really, really symmetrical."

"I know." Keira narrowed her eyes at her black cat. Daisy lay on her back, her four paws curled above her body as she watched them through barely cracked lids. "It's not the only weird thing about her. She comes and goes when she likes even if the door's closed. She consistently finds me when I am lost. I don't think she's a normal cat."

Mason and Zoe turned once again, frowning as they stared at the small feline. Daisy showed no acknowledgment except to hiccup, which caused her tongue to poke out.

"I loathe being the skeptic in any scenario," Zoe said, "but have you ever actually met your cat?"

"I know, I know…"

"She has one single brain cell, and she puts it into long-term storage on occasion."

"I adore her," Mason added, "but I also have to agree with Zoe."

Daisy's eyes, barely visible under her almost-closed lids, had started drifting in different directions. Keira clamped down on her laughter. "For whatever reason, brain cells or not, she built this."

"Which raises more questions," Zoe said. "Why's your cat trying to curse you? Wait, is she, like, a witch's cat?"

"Well, I don't think I'm a witch." Keira turned back to the

formation. The twisting design inside the circle felt wild. Powerful. Dangerous. But not evil. "And I don't think this is a curse."

"Then what?"

She took a deep breath, then let her arms flop out at her side. "No idea. But Daisy built it for me, and I think that means it's important. Whatever it is. Hang on."

She crossed the room and retrieved her cell phone, which had been a gift from Zoe shortly after Keira arrived in town. As she unplugged it from its charger and returned to her companions, she flipped it open and tried to read the small, inch-tall screen. "Zoe, how does this take photos?"

"Great news: it doesn't."

Mason leaned forward to see her phone. "How many decades old is that thing?"

Keira squinted. "It has a pull-out antenna, so I'm going to guess...many."

"You can mock the phone all you like," Zoe said, "but it's designed to keep you safe. I bought that thing with cash, in a different city, while I wore a fake mustache. *No one* will be able to link it back to you."

"I guess that's good," Keira said, "if it keeps that organization, Artec, from finding out I'm here. Even if the battery only lasts an hour."

Mason rubbed the back of his neck. "It's good to be cautious, but come on, Zo. We can get her something a bit nicer."

"You're thinking smart technology." Zoe scoffed. "Smart

technology is a pretty bow put on top of a corporate spy machine. Do you want the government sending laser beams into your ear to burrow a hole straight through your squishy, malleable brain? Huh?"

That last question was directed to Keira. "Is...that a thing they can do?"

Zoe snapped her fingers. "No one's been able to prove they *can't*. No, you'll want to avoid smart technology. And you'll be thrilled to know your phone is as dumb as possible."

"I believe you," Keira said, deadpan. "So no photos."

"Oh, don't worry. Your amazing phone already has a built-in solution. There's a note-taking feature. What we need to do is type in ASCII letters and symbols in a strategic pattern to create a visual representation of the mark that is just as realistic—nay, *more* realistic than realism itself. You have the deluxe model, which means it can handle an amazing eighteen lines of text before its memory fills up and the whole phone turns into a brick."

Mason looked faintly pained. "I'm just going to take a photo with my phone instead, okay? I'll email it to you, Keira. Wait— do you have email?"

"Well, I don't have a computer, and my phone has two ringtones and one of them sounds like a truck backing up, so I'm going to say no."

"Gotcha." He aimed his phone at the pattern of sticks and leaves. The flash went off as he took the picture. "I'll print this out and bring you a copy later."

"Thanks." Keira pocketed her own phone. "I have no idea if I'll ever need it, but it'll be good to have just in case."

Mason glanced at the clock above the mantelpiece. "It's late. I'll help sweep this up, then we'd better head home."

"You know what? Leave the sweeping to me."

"Are you sure?"

"Yeah," Keira said. "Just help me get the mattress in place."

Mason nodded. He and Keira took opposite ends of the mattress he'd delivered earlier that day and heaved it onto the bed frame. The whole thing wobbled in a very appealing way as it flopped into place.

Zoe gave Keira a quick hug on the way to the door. "Stay safe, okay? If that cat *is* responsible, you might want to sleep with one eye open."

Keira couldn't repress a grin. "She's the size of a loaf of bread and weighs about as much. I can't say I'm especially frightened of her."

"Hm." Zoe leaned around Keira's shoulder to send a sharp glance at the cat. "Oy, listen up. You touch my friend, we all learn what cat stew tastes like. Got it?"

Daisy looked to be in the thrall of a dream. Her whiskers twitched as her tongue slowly drooped further out of her mouth.

"I'll pass on the message when she wakes up," Keira promised. "Have a good sleep, Zo. You too, Mason. Thank you both for the help today."

Mason raised a hand in farewell. "See you tomorrow."

Keira waited until their forms had faded into the thickening mist, then carefully closed the door. She stood with her back to it for a moment, listening to the pop of the fire as it broke down its last piece of wood into coals. One of Daisy's golden eyes slid open to watch Keira with an intent stare.

"You *were* awake, huh?" Keira tilted her head as she watched her cat. "So…what now? Do we talk? I mean, do you have any way to communicate? Besides sticks and leaves, obviously."

The golden eye closed languidly. Daisy squirmed around to expose new parts of her belly to the fire, then fell still.

"I guess we're going to bed instead." Keira inhaled deeply and held it for a moment. The headache thrummed quietly. "I definitely won't say no to that."

She'd told Mason and Zoe that she would sweep up the stick arrangement, but at that moment, it really didn't feel like much of a priority compared to how exhausted she was. Daisy wouldn't have created anything dangerous anyway. She dragged a clean blanket and quilt out of the closet, then draped them over the mattress before kicking off her shoes and slinking into bed fully clothed.

Keira was on the verge of falling into a deep sleep when she felt something small climb onto the mattress with her. Daisy's warm, wet tongue licked at Keira's arm twice, then the cat curled up, pressed against her back.

"G'night, Daze," Keira mumbled. "Things are going to be better tomorrow. I'm sure of it."

Daisy started to purr, and Keira had the distinct impression that her cat not only heard and understood but agreed.

CHAPTER 15

"I'M GOING TO TRY something new." Keira pushed her sweater sleeves up past her elbows. Ahead of her, Solomon watched silently. "I'm going to try drawing from your energy. I want you to try to stop me."

The idea had hit Keira that morning as she ate breakfast. Ghosts could sap energy from her. Maybe she could learn how to do the same in reverse: make them weaker until they were no longer able to stop her from untethering them.

Solomon lifted his chin a fraction, indicating he was ready. Keira plunged her hand into his chest.

Despite the chill, her body was coated in a sheen of sweat. They'd already been practicing for hours. To Keira's surprise, though, she wasn't yet flagging. The headache had eased overnight. She felt ready to fight.

Her fingertips prickled as they found the tangled thread.

Instead of trying to tug on it, though, Keira wrapped her whole hand around the knot and clenched it in her palm.

And now...draw from it.

She hesitated. The concept had seemed simple enough in theory, but in practice, she had no idea how she was meant to do that.

She tried to picture energy traveling along the thread and into her hand. She gripped the thread tighter.

I've taken energy before. From Mason and Zoe and Harry, during the fight with the shade.

Back then, though, she hadn't been trying. Her friends had simply touched her and she'd felt their energy run into her, like water trickling downhill.

It must be possible. Try again.

She tensed her muscles and clenched her teeth, willing the power to leave the thread. She tried pulling on the muscle behind her eyes to open her second sight wider. Perspiration ran from her forehead and dripped off her chin.

"Can you feel anything?" she asked Solomon. He stared at her silently for a moment, then slowly shook his head. "Well, damn."

So much of her ghost sight had been instinctual, but now Keira felt as though she was missing a piece of the puzzle. The energy was right there—she could feel it—but it flowed between her fingers and the thread with no real direction.

She adjusted her hold and squinted, willing the energy to drain into her with every fiber of her being.

Prickles caused the hairs on the back of her arm to rise. Keira took a sharp breath. Solomon stepped back, extracting himself from Keira's hand. She searched his face. It was hard to be certain, but she thought he might be a fraction less distinct than he'd been before.

"It worked," Keira murmured.

Solomon looked down at his chest, one hand brushing over his shirt in wonder. He'd felt it too.

"Again," she said, reaching forward. "Try to stop me."

She wasn't sure exactly what she'd done. As her fingers touched the thread, she tried her hardest to replicate the sensation she'd felt on the original transfer. For a moment it didn't seem to be working, but then a flush of prickles ran across her skin as she drew power.

Then, abruptly, the flow stopped. Solomon's brows were lowered and his hands clenched at his side. He was preventing the transfer, just like Keira had asked him to.

Keira strained harder, her fingertips trembling, her breathing ragged. A trace of energy flitted through her fingertips. She pulled more and received another pulse in return.

It works. I can draw energy from a spirit, even if they try to prevent me—as long as I fight for it.

Keira let go and staggered back. Her heart ran fast, the pulse pounding in her ears. Her clothes stuck to her body. But she felt stronger. It wasn't much, but the extra energy thrummed through her, tracing along her nerve endings.

"Okay." She struggled to find her voice. Solomon still stood ahead of her, but he was fainter. The outline of his gravestone was clearly visible behind him, and his features were once again becoming smudged and poorly defined. "Okay. Here. Can you take your energy back?"

She reached out and let her fingertips pass through his form. She waited, holding herself open, but the energy didn't leave her. Solomon stared at where her hand reached through his chest, then slowly looked up at her, unresponsive.

"Oh," Keira said, realization hitting her. "You don't know how."

The shade—and the spirits in Crispin house—all had to learn how to sap other people. Just like I myself had to learn. It's not something that comes naturally to ghosts.

That was a good thing, she realized. Spirits that could feed from the living were unnatural and dangerous. It wasn't a skill she should share with too many ghosts, no matter how friendly they were.

But it meant her practice with Solomon would have to be limited. He would regain energy the same way she did—by gradually absorbing it from the atmosphere—but that would take time. Days. Weeks, maybe. She'd have to keep any practice sessions short to prevent completely depleting him.

"Okay." Keira swiped her sleeve across her face to rub the moisture off it. "We'll take a break now. Thank you."

He dipped his head slowly in acknowledgment, then faded from sight, like a wisp of fog on a warm day.

Keira turned back to her cottage. Zoe and Mason sat on the fence, reading. Beside them was one of Zoe's shopping bags, its contents ravaged. Keira had spent the first part of that day using the trinkets to experiment on a very patient Solomon. She'd followed all of the advice she'd been able to gather from the books they'd studied the night before: she'd wafted burning sage through Solomon's body, she'd tossed salt over him and used it to form a circle around his gravestone, she'd poked him with silver teaspoons, she'd rung a string of bells, she'd scattered rice, and she'd poured Zoe's quasi–holy water across the space where he stood.

As far as she could tell, none of it had made any difference. The salt would probably keep Solomon's grave free from slugs for a while, and Keira now smelled like burnt sage, but that was it.

Neither Zoe nor Mason had been put off by the failures, though.

"Good work out there," Mason called as Keira neared.

Keira rolled her sleeves back down over her wrists. "Could you see much?"

"Well, no, but you looked intense. Have you had much luck?"

"Ehh…" She gestured vaguely. "Truthfully, I'd like to have more."

"It doesn't mean it's not going to work," Zoe said, looking up from her book. "We're kind of fudging the details on some of this stuff. Like, the sage is meant to be white and dried, but they didn't have any of that in the store, so I just got you the fresh green stuff. We can try again and do it properly next time."

"Thanks." Keira sat on the stone fence next to Zoe. "I'll keep trying. But…"

Zoe's gaze was uncomfortably perceptive. "You don't have much faith in it."

"A lot of what I know felt like second nature. Like muscle memory. But all of this—it feels completely foreign. I don't know." She shrugged. "I've figured out how to drain ghosts' energy, I think. A little."

"Nice. Will that be enough to take another stab at the leeches?"

"No. Not yet." Keira stared down at her hands. The skin looked pale around the fingertips. She'd spent too long holding them inside a freezing specter. "But it's a start."

"Some extra energy's got to help, if nothing else." A soft pinging noise came from Zoe's pocket. She pulled out her phone—a device surprisingly similar to Keira's, only plastered with a mixture of sparkly glitter stickers and goth decals. "I know that shade thing drained you pretty badly. Maybe this… can…"

She trailed off, staring at her phone. Her eyes narrowed as she read a message on the tiny screen. "Hey, anyone know of a suburb called Tarrow?"

Mason looked up, eyebrows raised. "Yes. That's not far from where I went to med school. About eight hours from here. Why?"

"Well, the whole witch-cat-curse-under-the-bed thing freaked me out pretty thoroughly, so I sent a drawing of the design to my network in case anyone had seen something like it before."

Keira took a sharp breath. "They had?"

"Maybe." She held up her cell phone. "This girl, Charlie, specializes in the occult and arcane and travels along ley lines searching for evidence of historical witch covens. She says she found something that looks remarkably similar in the woods outside Tarrow a few months ago."

"Covens, huh?" Keira sighed. "Maybe you were right about Daisy being a witch's cat."

Zoe winked. "I'm always right, one way or another. But I mean, even though Charlie's looking for the witchy stuff, it doesn't mean that's what she always finds. She noted the symbol as possibly significant but couldn't find much else in the area. So who knows?"

"Huh." Keira chewed on her lip as she thought. "And that's eight hours away, right?"

Mason was silent. He still held the book in both hands but no longer stared at the pages. Instead, his gaze was vacantly fixed on the gravestones ahead of them. The animation around his mouth and eyes that Keira had grown so fond of was missing. He looked shaken.

Zoe leaned forward, her eyebrows quirked. "Y'wanna go take a look at it?"

"It's just..." Keira squirmed. "I probably can't afford to start any new projects while Dane's waiting for help."

"Well, just like you said, it's not like we're having much success with this." Zoe tossed her book onto its pile. "That symbol's connected to you in some way or another. It might even help."

"Maybe. If I could get near it..." She'd had visions before. Touching an object associated with death could show her the victim's last moments. It was a reach to imagine anything like that would happen when she saw the symbol, but…the rune under her bed had to mean *something*. "If we do go, odds are we'll be looking at a dead end."

"Sure. Lots of things will be. But we're doing what all great scholars do on a regular basis: clutching at straws." Zoe shrugged. "Worst thing that happens is we lose a day or two and are no better off than we are now."

"True." Keira craned her neck to see Mason over Zoe's head. "What do you think?"

"Hm?" He startled, blinking quickly. Something passed through his expression but was gone before Keira could properly see it. "Sorry?"

She frowned, noticing the way his features seemed heavier, paler. "Mason? What's wrong?"

"Nothing." He flashed a smile. It didn't seem quite natural.

"You're a pack of liars, both of you," Zoe muttered. "I swear I could find you with an ax embedded in your head and you'd still try to tell me it was just a scratch."

"Ha." Mason seemed uneasy as his fingers ran along the edge of the book's binding. "No, it's… I wasn't expecting to go anywhere near my old university for a while, that's all."

"Oh." He'd always avoided talking about his time there. As far as Keira was aware, not even his family knew his reason for leaving. And as much as she worried about him, it also wasn't her place to pry. "Of course, we don't have to. Like I said, I'm busy with the Dane situation anyway."

Mason's glance was quick, and he didn't quite meet her eyes.

"No. It might be important to go. And maybe… It's sooner than I was expecting, but…"

"Mason?"

He stood abruptly, pushing his book back onto the stack. "Keira, I need to ask you a favor."

"Of course." She stood as well, and Zoe, eyes narrowed, began bundling their books back into her bag.

Mason opened his mouth, then closed it again. He still couldn't look her in the eyes. She hated that; she'd never seen Mason so withdrawn before. So…conflicted.

He wet his lips, then abruptly turned toward the house. "I need a drink first."

Keira and Zoe shared a glance as Mason vanished into the cottage. Then Zoe shrugged and picked up her bag of books, and they wordlessly followed.

CHAPTER 16

AS KEIRA PRESSED THROUGH the open doorway, she saw Mason was already in the kitchenette, staring at the softly rattling kettle while a mug and jar of instant coffee stood ahead of him.

"Oh," Zoe said, sounding disgruntled. "You meant *that* kind of drink. For a second I actually thought you were going to be interesting."

"It's probably for the best," Keira said. "I don't think I have any alcohol, unless Zo smuggled some in the shopping bags that I didn't see."

Mason sent them a wan smile over his shoulder. "Do you still like your tea black, Keira?"

"Sure, but let me make the drinks."

"No, please. I need a minute to think."

"Okay." Keira crossed to the chairs in front of the fireplace.

Daisy napped there, her tail twitching as she dreamed. Keira sat and laced her fingers together as she waited. After a moment Zoe sighed, then dropped her bag of books by the door and joined Keira on the chairs.

Mason was silent for nearly a full minute, then abruptly began to laugh. "Oh, I am *not* good at this."

"Good at what?" Keira asked.

"Admitting I've done something bad."

Zoe perked up. "Oh, so there's a chance you *are* interesting after all."

"Hm." Mason's smile faded as he stared down at the coffee cup. "Ever since I learned that you could see ghosts, Keira, I've wanted to ask for your help," he continued. "But I kept stopping myself before I could."

"What? Mason—"

The kettle turned off, and Mason poured water into the three cups he'd set up. His hand was shaking. "There were always more pressing problems. The shade. Then the burning cottage. Then Dane. You've been dealing with so much, and I didn't want to stack my own issues on top."

Keira felt herself turn cold. For all her time in Blighty, she'd never thought to ask her friends if they had any problems she could help with—past family members they wanted to say goodbye to. A quick check to make sure there were no spirits in their homes. Resolutions to old family mysteries.

There was a lot she could have done to repay their kindness, and she'd never thought to offer.

"You have a ghost problem," she said, speaking slowly. "And you thought I wouldn't make time to help?"

"I…" Mason cleared his throat. He finally dared to look over his shoulder at her. "You've been fighting just to stay alive ever since you arrived here. This seems so petty by comparison."

Keira didn't know whether to laugh or cry. "Come here." She reached a hand toward him. When he approached, she took the mugs out of his hands and propped them on the coffee table, then nudged him into the third chair. "Mason, you're being an idiot. *Such* an idiot. Tell me what's happening. Do you think you have a spirit in your home?" Keira caught herself. "No, wait, this started when Zoe mentioned Tarrow. This is something that happened while you were at university."

He dipped his head in a nod.

"Is it the reason you quit?"

Another nod. He worked his jaw. This was what had been eating at him, Keira realized. Consuming him from the inside out. And he'd been too afraid to ask for help.

"What do you need me to do?" she asked.

He took a deep, unsteady breath and held it for a beat before exhaling. "First, I need to tell you what happened. Why I left. And why I haven't gone back."

Zoe had been silent until then, but a wicked grin spread across her face. "We're finally unlocking your tragic backstory."

"Zo, please," Keira said, but Mason gave a shaky laugh.

"No, it's fine." His smile faded. "Sometimes you end up with ugly bits in your life. Things you'd give anything to go back and erase. But the past is immovable, and your choices are set in stone, and you just have to try to figure out how to live with what's been done. I have a few of those moments, I guess, but this is the bad one. It's something I never tell people about because I know it will change how they think about me. And I hate that. But…"

"No judgment here," Keira said. She kept her voice soft. "You were willing to be friends with a half-feral woman who'd run out of the forest with no memories. I'm sure I can live with whatever you did back then."

"Ha." His hands were still unsteady as he picked up his mug. "All right. Where do I start? When I was six, I broke my arm climbing a tree and had to get it treated at Cheltenham's hospital. There was a doctor there who seemed to have a knack for calming frightened kids. She was kind, and reassuring, and made me feel brave and strong as she wrapped my cast. That was the moment I decided I wanted to be a doctor too."

"I remember that cast," Zoe said. Her eyes had grown distant. "We weren't really friends back then, but you still let me draw bats on it."

"Yeah." For a second, Mason's smile was back: warm and steady, the way Keira had always known it. "It seemed like…becoming a doctor was a way to make a difference. To help people who were frightened. To heal, to repair, to give people another chance at life. It wouldn't change the world, not like inventing the cure to a disease would, but helping one life at a time and doing it every day…that adds up. I knew I would be happy as long as I could do that."

He stared into his mug. The black coffee swirled as he dipped a spoon into it, small bubbles gathering around the edges of the ceramic. "That became my only goal through high school. I aced my classes because I wanted to progress faster. I applied for courses that would fast-track me. And like I planned, I got my undergrad degree ahead of schedule and started med school."

"And became Blighty's brightest shooting star," Zoe said. "Escaping the grip of this dull little town to become a famous doctor."

"Yes." He grimaced. "I hate admitting it, but there was some ego at work too. I wanted to make people proud. I wanted to be *liked*. And that got worse once I moved to Ridgegrow University. It's one of the most prestigious medical schools in the area, and suddenly, it was no longer easy to be at the top of the class. People were competitive. And *smart*."

"He says that like no one in Blighty is smart," Zoe groused.

"Sorry, Zo. But it was a completely different atmosphere there. We were all fighting for the best placement, the best test results, the best reputations. And for a long time…" He flicked one hand out, a heavy frown darkening his eyes. "I thought I was thriving."

"You were top four in your class," Zoe said. "That sounds like thriving to me."

"Burnout can hit anyone," Keira said. "Sometimes people can look like they're thriving until they're not."

"A lot of people in my class *did* leave because of burnout," Mason agreed, "but I didn't. I loved my time in school. Loved studying. Loved the competitiveness. And that was the problem."

Keira tucked her feet under herself to keep them warm. "Yeah?"

"My goals were changing. Instead of wanting to help people, I wanted to be better than my classmates. Instead of wanting to make a difference, I wanted a perfect exam score."

"I think that's natural, though," Keira said. "If you're put in an environment that rewards certain behavior, that's the behavior you're more likely to prioritize."

"You're right." His eyes were still on his coffee. "But I could feel it changing me. And...I didn't try to stop it. One morning, I was walking across campus for an early exam. I heard a sound from behind the clock tower. Like someone yelling. The campus was often loud, and sometimes people would strike up games or tackle one another. But this was a different kind of sound. It seemed panicked. But it only lasted for a second."

He took a long, slow breath. His voice was growing tight. "I'd stayed up until four that morning studying and my head was full of numbers and symptoms and data sets for the exam. For half a second, I considered checking behind the tower to see what had made the noise...but that risked making me late. I decided it was nothing. I kept walking. The exam went well; all of that extra studying carried me through it. I barely noticed that the top student in the class was missing. It was only after the exam was over that they told us one of our classmates had been found dead."

"Oh," Keira whispered.

Shadows clung heavily around Mason's face. His eyes were

glassy and not quite focused on the drink in his hands. It seemed to take a lot of effort to keep speaking. "The police interviewed a lot of us. I had to tell them I'd heard a noise but kept walking. That was the most shameful moment of my life. I felt even worse when it was confirmed that the victim was Evan Radecki. He was a brilliant student—better than I was—and well-liked too. We weren't quite friends but we'd had study groups together several times. He always seemed so friendly and enthusiastic. He would have made a great doctor. Someone stabbed him eighteen times and left him to bleed out."

Zoe's eyes were bright in the fading light. "Did they find out who did it?"

"No. There were thousands of students at the university and no restrictions on visitors. Some people thought it was a jealous classmate, but that was hard to imagine; he was so likable. Others thought maybe an ex-partner had hired a hit, or he'd gotten tied up in the drug scene or maybe interrupted something he shouldn't have. For all we know, it could have been random—someone wandered onto campus and attacked the first vulnerable student they found. Tragedies don't always have a poetic twist to them." He grimaced, looking uncomfortable. "I stayed long enough to be at the memorial service, then I quit school and came back home."

"And never told anyone why," Zoe murmured. "Everyone thought you were just burnt out, you know."

"Yeah. My neighbors keep asking me when I'm going to go back. And I keep telling them, maybe someday." His mouth twisted, like he'd tasted something unpleasant. "Better than telling them what I did, anyway."

Keira leaned forward. "But…you didn't do anything wrong."

His glance was sharp. "I went into medical school to save lives. And then I kept walking while one was being taken less than twenty yards from me."

"You didn't know, though." Keira felt a hard note enter her voice. "If you'd realized someone was being attacked, would you have stopped?"

"Of course I would have—"

"Then you need to stop being so hard on yourself. You didn't *know*. It was a mistake, but not one you can be blamed for."

He sounded indescribably tired. "That's what the counselor said too. But the ultimate truth is that I wanted to get to my exam on time, and if I'd cared about that even slightly less, Evan would probably still be alive today."

Keira closed her eyes. She thought she understood how Mason felt. It had been such a tiny decision in the moment but one that was impossible to take back. And for someone like Mason, who based his identity on doing everything *right*, that was a hard thing to reconcile.

"You needed my help," she said, looking up. "Did you want to see if his ghost is still there?"

"Yes." Mason's voice had dropped to a hoarse whisper. "Since I found out that ghosts can remain trapped, I can't stop thinking about it. I…I want to know if he's moved on. If he has…maybe I can…"

"Of course." Keira filled her lungs, then let it out in a sigh. "Let's look for him. And if he hasn't moved on yet, I'll do everything in my power to make sure he does."

Mason sagged over his mug until Keira couldn't see his expression properly. "Thank you. Thank you so much."

She wanted to hug him. Instead, she said, "I can't believe you didn't tell me sooner."

"Ha." He shook his head. "I know you've been nervous about people finding out about your gift. And I understand that. You don't want to be exploited. And I...I didn't ever want you to feel that way around me."

"Hang all of that! Who's exploiting who? You've given me free medical care. We've gone trespassing together. You gave me an entire mattress! And even if you hadn't done any of that, you're still my best friend. And I want to be allowed to look after my friends."

"*He's* your best friend?" Zoe asked, one hand to her heart, looking mortally wounded.

"Dual best friend status," Keira conceded. "Seriously, though. I haven't been able to do much for either of you yet. I'm actually happy I get a chance to help. Let's go to the university tomorrow. Zoe, do you have work?"

"I'll call in sick." Her grin was wolfish. "We can take a look at that rune at the same time. It'll be the most productive of days."

"The university is about an hour from Tarrow," Mason said. "With an additional eight-hour drive each way, it might be hard to fit everything in. We can get the trip done in two days. I'll book some hotel rooms. Are you and Zo okay with sharing?"

149

"A hotel sounds good to me," Keira said. "But there's no point booking two. We can fit in one just fine."

"Are you sure? I don't mind getting a second room. You might appreciate the privacy."

Keira chuckled. "It won't be any different from that time you and Zo had a sleepover here. No, don't worry. I don't think any of us are going to be prudes about it."

"Neither of you has seen my fan fiction yet," Zoe said. "I think a prude would self-combust if they got within ten paces of me."

"I'll take your word on it." Mason nodded, rising. "Thank you. I'll pick Zoe up and then bring the car down to the base of the driveway tomorrow. Around nine?"

"That suits me just fine."

CHAPTER 17

KEIRA PICKED UP HER backpack from beside the stone fence outside her cottage. She traveled light: a change of clothes and her toothbrush were all she needed.

She'd asked Adage to watch Daisy, which he'd gladly agreed to. She'd also spoken to Solomon, asking he if would be patient enough to wait another few days for her return. Then she'd packed the backpack, locked up her cottage, and found she still had another few hours to burn before Mason was expected to arrive.

Keira spent that time in the cemetery. Starting with the tombstones that had spirits, she'd begun weeding around them, clearing away dead flowers and wiping moss off the stones. It was a relatively insignificant job in the larger scheme of things, but it still seemed important to Keira. A neglected grave struck her as an achingly sad sight; it was like saying the person inside the grave had been forgotten too. Many of the markers were so old that any close relatives were long gone. But as long as Keira was there, they didn't have to remain forgotten.

She finished gingerly pulling thistles out from around the elegant Victorian lady's monument just in time to meet Mason. She gathered her weeds, threw them into a pile past the forest's boundary, then picked up her backpack and began following the driveway to the main road.

Mason's car pulled into view as she reached the driveway's end. Keira checked the time on her phone. They were both a few minutes early. She found herself grinning at how predictable they were.

Mason reached across the passenger seat to open the door for her. Keira threw a glance into the back seat and found Zoe already lounging there, a gummy snake hanging from her teeth as she sent a message on her phone.

"You get to sit up front," Zoe said without preamble. "I get to pick the music and dole out the snacks. Deal?"

"Hello to you too," Keira said, tossing her backpack into the rear seats with Zoe before pulling her seat belt on. "Did you get the note to Dane okay?"

"Yeah. The gates were locked, but I reached through and jammed it onto a branch where he'd see. I wrote my number on it too, so he can call us if he needs to."

Keira nodded. She hadn't wanted to leave Blighty without telling Dane why she was leaving and when she'd be back, but he was almost uncomfortably hard to contact. He hadn't given her any phone number and she doubted he'd have an email address, so without many other options, she'd asked Zoe to leave him a note promising that she wasn't giving up on him.

Mason waited until she was settled, then turned back onto the road. He looked more like himself than he had the previous day. His smile was back in place, his hair tidy, his clothes comfortable but still professional. Keira had the distinct sense that this casual air came at a great effort.

"Are you doing okay?" she asked.

"Yes." He caught her watching him and cleared his throat. "No. I'm nervous. And desperately uncomfortable. But that's probably the best I could expect to be."

She reached across the space between them and lightly pressed his arm. He smiled at her, and this time it was with real warmth.

"'Scuse me," Zoe said, leaning through the gap in the seats to shove between them. "It's my job to put the music on. Can't leave us wallowing in our own thoughts for too long, can I?"

She plugged a USB into the dash before slinking back into her seat. There was silence for a second, then a deafening blend of untimed drums, screeching violins, and miserable wailing filled the car.

"What the—" Mason flinched but managed to avoid driving the car off the road.

"It's Harry's new album," Zoe called, nonchalantly fishing a pack of cotton balls out of the bags around her. "He's in that band, remember? Transcontinental death metal or whatever genre he claims it is."

"Post-transient death grunge," Keira called back. "This is what it sounds like, huh?"

"We're lucky. This album is *super* exclusive. Only two copies sold, and one of those was to his mum."

The furious drums abruptly faded out, leaving them in a brief reprieve of just the off-tune violin. Then a voice joined in, starting low but slowly building into the most awful scream Keira had ever heard. It sounded like a mountain lion being murdered. It stretched out longer and longer until Keira began to wonder just how much air Harry was capable of holding in his lungs.

"It's, uh, intense." Mason had to yell to be heard. "Did you want to try something else? I have a track of top one hundred hits—"

"True artists are never appreciated in their time," Zoe said, somehow remaining serene even as she stuffed cotton balls into her ears. "But by gosh we're going to appreciate this one."

"Fantastic," Mason managed, just as Harry's mangled voice broke into a chorus of "Death death death death *death death death death!*"

They passed out of Blighty's bounds and into the countryside surrounding it. Mason was a steady driver as he navigated the narrow mountain roads. Eventually they passed through Cheltenham, stopping briefly to pick up drinks before returning to the drive.

Zoe continued to play Harry's album, which seemed to never end and experimented with styles Keira hadn't even known existed. With no warning, a banjo was introduced around track eight. Another track was just sixteen minutes of Harry quietly sobbing into the microphone and those were sixteen of the most uncomfortable minutes of Keira's life. Despite repeated requests, Zoe refused to switch it off. "The man wants to express himself," she said. "Who are we to say he's not allowed?"

As the clock ticked past noon, they began to look for a place to get lunch. Zoe spotted it first. "Rest stop to the right. Lots of trucks are parked outside that diner. That means it's good. Truck drivers know the best places."

"Yeah?" Mason said, switching on the turn signal as he took the exit. "I like the sound of that."

The diner was old but painted in bright, barely matching colors. It was also bustling. As they pushed through two ancient, creaking glass doors, Keira tried to pull some money out of her backpack.

Mason waved her away. "You're doing me a favor," he insisted. "That means I get to pay for food."

Zoe, next to Keira, nudged her. "Meanwhile, I'm just a freeloader."

"You can be the emotional support," Mason said. "For both of us."

Keira couldn't stop herself from glancing around the diner as they entered. It was old, its furniture faded and its floorboards well-worn, but it had a comfortable feel, like a place that had more happy memories than sad ones.

They managed to get a seat near the window. The food arrived quickly and smelled amazing. "Told you," Zoe said as she picked up half of a toasted sandwich that was oozing with cheese. "Truck drivers know the *best* places."

"We're making good time," Mason said, picking at the plate of fries they were sharing while checking the map on his phone. "Tarrow is the closest destination. That's where Zoe's friend found the rune. We'll stop there first to make sure you have as much time with it as you need, Keira. Then we'll sleep at the hotel and continue on to the university tomorrow. Does that sound like a plan?"

"That works for me," she said.

Their server moved past, her dark, curling hair tied high on her head. As she checked their drinks she said, "Sounds like you're having a long trip. What brings you to this part of the country?"

Zoe grinned. "Ghosts."

"Oh?" Her eyes lit up. She leaned close over the table. "You know, we have a ghost of our own here."

"You do?" Zoe mirrored the motion by leaning toward her, toasted sandwich forgotten. "Tell me!"

"Don't worry, he's friendly." The server winked. "He's an old regular. Bob. Used to come in seven days a week. Always ordered the same thing—a salmon sandwich and a ginger beer. He was so reliable that we'd have his order ready before he even stepped through the door. Well, one evening when my coworker was leaving, she noticed Bob's car was still in the parking lot. He'd eaten his lunch, gone to drive home, and had a heart attack while still in park. It would have been over with quickly, the coroner said. But since then, we sometimes see Bob still here."

"Yeah?" Zoe whispered, enraptured.

"Never clearly." The server matched Zoe's conspiratorial whisper. "Sometimes you get a glimpse of him in a mirror. Sometimes you hear the sound of him clearing his throat. Or you swear you see him sitting at his old seat out of the corner of your eye, but when you turn, he's gone. It's lucky he was such a friendly person, because half the staff swear they would have left otherwise."

Keira couldn't help herself. She nodded to a stool at the bar. "He used to sit there, didn't he?"

The server inhaled sharply, her eyebrows rising. "You knew."

"Just a guess," Keira said, picking up her own sandwich. "That seat's the most worn."

"Hmm." The server glanced from Keira to the empty barstool and back, intrigue dancing behind her eyes. "What an odd thing to notice. Maybe you have a bit of a gift. That might be worth exploring, you know."

As the server left, Keira looked up again, her second sight held open. The man on the barstool, hazy and as pale as mist, raised a glass of ginger beer in Keira's direction, smiling.

She'd only seen one ghost interact with a spectral object before: the elderly Victorian woman and her elaborate walking cane. Otherwise, they seemed to have a small amount of control over the clothes they wore but very little else.

She guessed they might sometimes be able to manifest objects as well...but only objects so familiar that they existed almost as an extension of the person. For Bob, who had eaten every lunch there for years, the glass of ginger beer and the plate of salmon sandwich were likely always waiting for him.

Bob didn't appear to be waiting for help. He'd move on in his own time, Keira suspected. He just didn't want to say goodbye to such a familiar home. Not just yet.

They returned to the car and to the deafening notes of Harry screaming about how he wanted to crawl into a coffin and never come out again. They weren't on the road for long, though. That stretch of the highway must have been something of a local attraction because they passed multiple tourist traps, all in the form of large novelty sculptures off the side of the road, and Zoe begged them to stop at each one: World's Largest Prawn. World's Largest Banana. World's Second Largest Owl.

"I appreciate their honesty," Zoe said, stopped outside the owl. "I'm pretty sure the others were pure hyperbole. World's largest prawn? That thing was barely the size of a bus. I'm sure I could find a bigger one. This owl, though? It acknowledges that it's only number two. I trust it."

"Uh-huh." Mason took the requisite photo of them in front of the owl, then tucked his phone back into his pocket. "If you're done, we're still a couple of hours from Tarrow—"

"Don't get ahead of yourself. They have the World's Largest Grapes just up ahead, and I want to judge it for its unchecked hubris."

Their voices faded into the background as Keira froze. They'd pulled off the side of the road to pose with the owl, and traffic continued to move past at a steady pace. A white van whistled along the asphalt before fading into the distance. Its emblem had only been visible for a second, but it had sent shards of ice through Keira's limbs.

It was the emblem belonging to Artec, the organization that was hunting her.

Stay calm. They didn't see you.

At least, she didn't think they had. She'd been half shielded by Mason's car and the van had made no attempt to stop. She watched it until it disappeared over the crest of a hill in the distance.

She'd last seen a vehicle like that at Cheltenham's hospital, when she'd visited with Adage. If they were at Cheltenham, it made sense that they would be spread across the surrounding area as well. She would need to be careful.

"Keira?" Mason had noticed her distraction. He came up beside her, examining her face and then following her gaze toward the road. "Is something wrong?"

"I'm fine," she managed. "Just…nervous. What if the bunch of grapes is *too* large?"

"You're asking the right questions." Zoe threaded her arm through Keira's and gave her a squeeze. "Truly, how big can mankind make a bunch of grapes before the universe checks our unbridled ambition? We need to be reasonable or it'll be the Tower of Babel all over again."

Keira let Zoe escort her back into the car and ate the gummy snake that was pressed into her hand. Even Harry's distraught screams faded into the background, though, as she scanned the road ahead and behind them, looking for any more white vans, or any sign of the unpleasantly familiar logo. Even though they stopped at the grapes—which were insultingly underwhelming, according to Zoe—no vans came for her.

Still, Keira found herself breathing a little more easily once they turned off the freeway and into the narrower, calmer roads of Tarrow. Mason finally turned down the music as he followed his phone's instructions to reach the location Zoe had given them. Zoe's friend hadn't provided a street address but a set of coordinates. There was a reason for that, it turned out. The coordinates led to a sparse forest just outside of town.

"Are you sure we can trust your friend?" Mason asked, pulling his jacket on. They stood outside the car, parked off the edge of a road that ran alongside the forest. There were a few houses in the distance, but no other cars on the street. "In your expert opinion, what are the chances they're trying to lure people here to steal their organs?"

"Mm." Zoe considered that for a second. "Higher than zero. Charlie *did* mention that some of the rituals she wants to try someday involve murder."

"Great," Mason said, teeth bared in a tight grin.

"But she's currently in Ireland, according to the photos she's posting, so I figure we're safe." Zoe slung a scarf around her neck. "Ish."

"Ish is good enough for me," Keira said. She stepped through the closest row of trees and entered the woods.

CHAPTER 18

PINE NEEDLES CRUNCHED UNDER her feet as the forest's shade fell over her. A bird trilled somewhere to her left, then fell silent again. The woods were clearer than the overgrown brush around Blighty's cemetery. Pine trees stretched their branches high above her, and the cold air was still and heavy with the scent of sap and bark.

"It should be straight ahead," Mason said, consulting the coordinates on his phone. "Only a few minutes away."

Keira pressed forward, weaving between the trees. She always liked being in nature. It felt both freeing and comforting at once, and she breathed deeply as she rested her hand against the damp pine bark.

Ahead, the ground tended downhill. Keira followed it. There was something vaguely familiar about the landscape, like the memory of a photograph, and it itched at the back of her mind.

"Slow down!" Zoe called, slipping on the damp pine needles behind her. "There's no reason to rush. We still have daylight left."

Keira barely heard her, though. There was something up ahead, she was sure. Something significant. The trees were growing denser and the gaps between them grew darker, but she moved forward with a quiet certainty, knowing she was going in the right direction.

"Keira?" Mason had to break into a jog to keep pace with her. Zoe began to swear faintly as a pine branch slapped her in the face.

"I just need a minute…" The ground was tending downhill, leading into a hollow. Keira followed it. Fire was in her veins. Memories dug at her, so close that she felt like she could catch them in her hands if she just reached far enough.

Her breathing was quick and aching in her chest as she came to a halt in the center of the bowl-like clearing that was at least thirty feet wide. Trees formed a ring around its edge, a row of sentries, blocking out any sight of the world around her, their high branches latticing over her head.

"It should be close by," Mason said, carefully climbing into the basin with her. "We're at the right coordinates…"

"It's here." Keira didn't know how she knew, only that she did. She was as certain of this as she was sure that her name was Keira. The space felt both significant and strangely familiar.

The three of them stood together in the center of the ring, slowly turning to examine the trees around them. Then Zoe gasped: "Look!"

She pointed to one of the ancient pines framing the hollow. A faint outline was visible on the bark. Keira climbed the sloping forest floor to reach it and gently swiped spiderwebs out of the way.

Someone or something had painted an image on the trunk at chest height. It looked as though it had been made with ash or charcoal and painted by fingertip. The shape formed a circle with wild lines running through its center.

Mason held up his phone. Its screen displayed the photo of the rune from beneath Keira's bed, but Keira didn't even need to look at it to know they were identical.

"This is it," Zoe whispered.

"Yeah." Keira's breath misted ahead of her.

What does it mean, though? I feel as though there's something here that I'm supposed to find. But what?

She backed away from the tree, returning to the hollow's center. Leaves rustled over the forest floor as a cooling breeze buffeted them. Keira braced herself and pulled on her second sight. She was half afraid of what she might see, but as the veil over her eyes lifted, the clearing remained empty.

Empty of spirits at least.

Energy thrummed around her. It was slight—delicate enough to exist as just a whisper in the back of her mind unless she was paying attention to it—but definitely present. Keira raised her hands and imagined she could see it swirling around her fingers. She inhaled and felt it fill her lungs.

"That isn't the only one." She moved quickly, climbing the

hollow's opposite side, and ran her hands across the tree there. The rune had faded under months of rain and sun and wind, but traces of the distinct lines were still visible. Keira kept moving, touching each tree in turn and wiping moss and dew-coated spiderwebs away to reveal more of the symbols. Then she backed away, returning to the hollow's center. The trees surrounded her in a perfect circle. Their runes all directed at the nexus. At her.

"It's charcoal," she said, her eyes darting from tree to tree. "Made with a small fire here, in the basin's center, then painted on by hand."

Mason was looking at her strangely. Zoe was biting her lip, a smile fighting to break out.

"What?" she asked.

"*You* made these." Mason grinned, running his fingers through his hair as he gazed at the circle of runes around them.

"What?" she repeated, then blinked. "Oh. Wait. Did I?"

Something flickered through her mind. Not quite a memory but the reflection of a memory. Lights and shadows and sounds. Ragged breathing. Soot on her hands. Keira blinked and the images were gone, leaving her feeling slightly cold and lost.

"You knew where to find the clearing," Zoe said. "You knew there was more than one symbol. You know how they're made. Yeah, babe, I think this was you, sometime in your past life."

Keira felt shaky. She slowly lowered herself to the forest floor and pulled her knees up to her chest, her arms wrapped around them. After a second, Mason and Zoe sat on either side of her, shoulder to shoulder.

"Maybe Daisy is a witch's cat after all." Zoe gave her a friendly nudge. "At least it's not a curse. I mean, maybe it is, but I'm assuming you wouldn't want to go around cursing yourself. Do you have any idea what they actually do?"

"They concentrate energy," Keira said. She swallowed, and her throat ached. "You remember how I promised to sweep up the rune Daisy left under my bed? Well, I lied. And the following day, I felt better. A little bit stronger. That's what these do. They gather energy from the atmosphere and direct it into you."

She tilted her head to gaze across the clearing. She'd painted the rune on at least nine trees. "I must have needed the energy very badly when I did this."

"Do you remember making them?" Mason's voice was soft and careful.

Keira shook her head. "No. There was a flash, but…no. It's gone now."

"That's okay. Even just getting close to memories might be able to help. We still have at least an hour of sunlight. Why don't we stay here a bit?"

They sat in relative silence. At one point, Zoe flopped onto her back and began humming a tune that was weirdly reminiscent of one of the abominations from Harry's album. Mason gazed into the trees, apparently content to leave Keira with her thoughts. She was grateful. She didn't think she could explain what she was feeling, even to herself.

There was something bittersweet in the clearing. Desperation and hope. Zoe had said the runes had been there for at least a year; whatever had happened at that time hadn't been good. She waited, hoping flashes of the past would resurface again, but none did.

Even so, it was the most connected she'd ever felt to her prior self.

She'd sat in this exact place. Had touched the same trees. Had looked up at the same sky. It was disorienting to know how close she was to *finding* herself. The two versions of her identity were no longer separated by space but only by time.

Did I live nearby, or was I just passing through? Something must have happened to make me draw those symbols. Something major, something that left me shaken.

She wondered if she just spent long enough in the region, whether she might find more traces of herself.

Keira tilted her head back and closed her eyes, waiting to see if her subconscious could show her anything more. It had remembered this space well enough to lead her to it. She held herself open, seeing if she could detect any other kind of pull or path to follow.

There was nothing else. She released her held breath and relaxed again.

As the sun slid toward the horizon, the runes faded into the shadows lacing the trees. The basin began to fill with thin mist, swirling around Keira and her friends. She imagined they must look a bit like dumplings floating in a bowl of soup and a surprised laugh escaped her. Mason glanced toward her, his eyebrows raised.

"Okay," she said, standing and dusting her jeans off. "I'm ready to go."

"Ugh." Zoe rolled to her feet. "Every encounter I have with nature reinforces the belief that I am *not* a nature person."

"Thanks for enduring it," Keira said. "I think this has helped."

"We know one thing for certain at least," Mason said. He reached the top of the basin and offered a hand to help her out. "You were in this area at some point."

"Did these runes give you much power?" Zoe, grimacing, picked leaves out of her black hair.

"Some." Keira flexed her hands at her sides. It was hard to describe, but after days of feeling scraped thin, she finally seemed to be whole again. She'd noticed a strange effect, though: the longer she'd sat in the clearing, the slower the energy moved around her. "I don't think I can use it to, like, supercharge myself or anything. I think that rune gives you energy when you're low, but only fills you up to your normal level. If that makes sense?"

"I think it does," Mason said. "Like how putting a cold plate of food on the table won't heat it up, it will only bring it to room temperature."

"Exactly." Keira had been testing the rune's effects to see if they might let her solve Dane's problem, but it had become clear they wouldn't be enough on their own. Still. It was a useful trick to know for when she became drained.

Memories of Dane made something ache deep inside. She hoped he had found her note. She hoped he was doing okay, all things considered.

More than anything, she hoped she could figure out what she needed to do to save him, and soon.

The trees thinned ahead, and Keira squinted as the fading light cut across her eyes. The sun had nearly set and glinted off the roof of Mason's car, parked not far away.

"Let's get some dinner, then find our hotel," Mason said. "We have a lot of ground to cover tomorrow."

CHAPTER 19

THERE WERE, MERCIFULLY, NO more of Harry's musical stylings for the last stretch of their trip. Mason pulled into a hotel off the main road and collected their key while Zoe and Keira retrieved their luggage from the back of the car. Then the three of them climbed a flight of stairs to the second floor and shuffled into a cool room that smelled faintly of air freshener and lemony cleaning concoctions.

Mason found the light first, and the room was flooded with a yellow glow. Opposite, a curtained window overlooked the town. The center of the room was taken up by a couch and a small dining table. To the left was a door to the bathroom and a kitchenette, and to their right was a single queen-size bed with a muted gray quilt cover.

"Oh." A flush of color ran across Mason's neck as he lowered his luggage to the floor. "There must be a mistake.

I asked for three single beds. I'll call reception to see if they can change it."

"Don't you dare!" Zoe waved him away when he tried to move toward the telephone. "This is perfect. Oh, Mr. Toast would *love* this."

Keira frowned, trying to remember where she knew the name from. "Mr. Toast…isn't that the guy who's afraid of airplanes?"

"My rather paranoid insider contact, yes. We connected on a fan-fiction site. He is *obsessed* with enemies-to-lovers stories that involve having to unexpectedly share a bed." Zoe cackled. "No, Mason, I refuse to let you change our room. There's going to be *so* much dramatic tension tonight."

Mason sighed. "Well, you two can have fun with your enemies-to-lovers narrative. Just try to keep it quiet. I'll be sleeping on the couch."

"Yeah, that's kind of a problem." They'd picked up takeout on their drive to the hotel, and Keira piled it onto the small circular table in the room's center. "On account of my holding dual BFF status with both of you, if this is going to be a proper enemies-to-lovers scenario, you two will need to share the bed."

"Nope," Mason said in the same instant Zoe retorted, "No offense, Mason, I'd honestly rather eat a slug."

Keira grinned. "Well, we've got the enemies part of the equation down. Let's eat."

The town's lights blinked on outside their window. Doors opened and closed in the rooms around them, and a TV was playing somewhere in the distance. It was strangely comforting.

Keira and Zoe chatted. They pulled up the photos of the world's largest attractions they'd visited and argued over which ones deserved the title and which ones could have been bigger. Mason smiled and nodded along with the conversation, but he ate slowly and barely spoke. Keira knew he had to be preoccupied with thoughts of their final destination.

She wasn't the only person to notice how withdrawn he was.

"So, what are you hoping for?" Zoe asked Mason.

"Hm?" He looked up, abruptly pulled out of his reverie. "Hoping for…?"

"Tomorrow. At the university." Zoe twirled pasta around her fork. "Do you want there to be a ghost, or no?"

"I don't know."

"You've thought about it, though, haven't you?"

His smile was thin. "Of course I have."

"If there's a ghost, you get a chance to say goodbye. Or apologize if you want to. But then you'd have to live with the knowledge that what's-his-face—"

"Evan."

"Yeah, Evan. That he was trapped the whole time. If he's gone, you don't get the closure, but at least you know he was okay with moving on."

Mason had put down his fork. Keira shot Zoe a glare. She raised her eyebrows in response. "What? It's good to set expectations. It'll hurt him less if he thinks about it now."

"Still," Keira muttered.

"I *fear* the idea that he will still be there." Mason cleared his throat. "I don't know what I would say to him if he is. How can you possibly make something like that better?"

"You didn't kill him." Keira put all the conviction she felt into her voice. "If unfinished business has tethered him to earth, it will be because he wants to say something to his family, or he wants his killer caught. No rational person, least of all Evan, would blame you for his death."

"Yeah." Mason chuckled, then cleared his throat again. "I know. I just don't like knowing that I *could* have helped, if I'd just stopped for even a moment."

"Or you could have tried to help and gotten stabbed yourself." Zoe chewed on a long strand of pasta. "Or you could have chased off the killer but still been too late to save Evan. Or, or, or. If I've learned one thing about life, it's that there is never a *perfect* answer to any scenario. Not like a video game, where you have black-and-white choices. In life, everything gets messy eventually, no matter how carefully you try to control yourself."

Mason made a faint noise in the back of his throat. He stared at his half-eaten plate for a beat, then said, "Thanks, Zoe. That actually helps."

"Hmm." She sucked the last of the pasta strand into her mouth and swallowed it whole. "But I get it. It's hard to shake the *maybes*. I'm still trying to figure it out myself with—anyway."

Mason leaned forward a fraction. "With your mother?"

"Please, now's not the time for mom jokes."

"Sorry, I only meant—"

"Nah, I'm messing with you. You were right. It's about my mum." Zoe's face scrunched up into a fierce grin. "She's sick."

Keira's stomach turned cold. She'd known Zoe's mother was unwell, but Zoe spoke about it so infrequently that she'd accidentally let it fall to the back of her mind. She put her fork down. "I'm so sorry. I shouldn't have dragged you away from home."

"We can go back," Mason said, glancing to where they'd left their bags in the hallway. "Right now. We'll be home in the early hours of the morning."

Zoe flicked her fork as though to push the suggestion away. "Nope. Don't even think about it."

"But—"

"You know why I'm here tonight?" She shook her head. "No, dumb question, I want to go on a ghost-hunting adventure. Let me rephrase. Do you want to know why I pushed so hard for us to go looking for that rune in the first place? It's because it's impossible living in my home right now. Mum's sick but I don't know what with. She won't talk about it. And it's like this enormous thing looming over us every time I try to hang out with her, and it's driving a wedge between us."

Keira's stomach had turned to icy, uncomfortable knots. She didn't know what to say, but Zoe didn't let the silence last long either.

"She had tests but she won't tell me what the diagnosis was. She won't tell me if she's getting treatment. It's like she's trying to pretend it's not happening at all, and it scares me because what if she needs help that she's not getting? But the more I pry, the more she blocks me out, so I take every chance I can to get out of the house and focus on other things because it's the only way I feel like I can *breathe*."

She took a deep, gasping breath then. Her eyes were wet. She frowned down at her pasta as though it were personally responsible for everything that was happening. "So. Yeah. At least out here, I can feel like I'm doing something useful. Life at home kind of sucks right now."

Mason stared at her for a long beat, then stood and crossed the room to reach the phone.

"You'd better not be calling to change the beds," Zoe muttered at his back. "I like it the way it is."

"No." Mason's smile was gentle as he picked up the receiver. "But this hotel has room service. I can't stop life from sucking, but at least I can get us chocolate fudge brownies."

"Oh." Zoe's face brightened. "Oh *hell* yes. Extra ice cream, please."

They turned on the TV and sat on the floor, a towel draped between them to contain the three bowls of brownies and melting ice cream. A trivia game show played, and they all yelled answers at the screen between mouthfuls, their guesses getting more elaborate and more unfounded the further into the show they progressed.

Keira couldn't stop her mind from spinning through their conversation, though. Both Zoe and Mason were carrying their own burdens and were trying to cope with or hide what they felt in different ways.

She could help Mason, even if it was just in a small way. She could make sure Evan's spirit was at rest. It was probably less than he needed, but at least it was something.

Her heart ached just as much for Zoe, but there was so little she could do. Keira's throat grew tighter the more her mind swirled around what her friend had said. Zoe never talked about her personal life. It must have gotten bad to bring her to speak so candidly.

Zoe rested her head against Keira's shoulder. She smiled at the TV even as her eyes went glassy, and Keira guessed she must be feeling even more than what she'd admitted to. Keira was tempted to ask her about it but bit her tongue. She didn't think that was what Zoe needed at that moment. Instead, she looped her arm around Zoe's shoulders and pulled her closer.

When night grew deep enough that they were too tired to argue with the television any longer, Keira and Zoe curled up in the bed together while Mason, as promised, took a blanket and a spare pillow to the couch. Zoe tossed and turned for a long time before finally falling asleep. Keira, lying on her back and with moonlit shadows playing over the ceiling above her, stayed awake for far longer.

CHAPTER 20

DAWN SEEMED TO ARRIVE abruptly. Keira rolled over and saw Zoe had become hopelessly tangled in the sheets, her short black hair stuck around her mouth and her eyes. She'd reached toward Keira during the night, trying to draw her into a deathlike grip, and Keira'd had to extract herself carefully.

The couch was empty, the spare blanket neatly folded and the pillow put to one side. She craned her neck and spotted Mason on the balcony. His forearms were braced on the rail and his hands laced ahead of himself as he stared down at the town ahead of them.

Keira pulled a cardigan on over her top and then stepped through the sliding door.

Mason's smile was warm. "Good morning."

"Hey." She stopped at his side and rested her arms on the rail, like he had. The air was brisk and the faint scent of warm bread reached them from a bakery down the road. "Have you been up for long?"

His dark brown hair was still rumpled from sleep. "Only about ten minutes. I was tossing around whether to get us breakfast or whether to pick it up on the road. Ridgegrow University is only about forty minutes from here."

"Do you feel ready?" Even though Zoe was still inside the hotel room, Keira lowered her voice so she wouldn't disturb her. "Last night you said you were frightened that Evan might still be there."

"Yes. But after what Zoe said, I reexamined that. And I realized that I would prefer knowing that he was there over not knowing anything at all. It's the uncertainty that really hurts."

Keira nodded and let her gaze return to the streets around them. People were starting on early-morning errands, moving about and occasionally throwing greetings to neighbors. "I didn't realize things were so bad for Zoe," she murmured.

"I know Zoe's mother." Mason sighed. "She's a kind, sincere woman, and she loves Zoe dearly. But I can see that Zoe would want to talk about what's happening. And her mother *wouldn't*. It's a difficult situation to be in."

"I've been taking up so much of her time lately too," Keira said. She picked at a loose scrap of skin around her fingernail, working it free. "Days spent at my place. The camping trip. Now this. And she has a job on top of everything else—"

"Zoe's extraordinarily good at saying no when she doesn't want to do something," Mason said. "Like she said last night, she was the one who suggested this trip. She chooses to spend time with us. I think, in its own way, it helps her."

A heavy thudding noise came from the hotel room behind them. Keira and Mason turned to see the bed's blankets in disarray.

Without Keira to anchor her there, Zoe had rolled off the mattress. She sat up, squinting blearily, sheets tangled around her. Keira, grinning, opened the balcony's sliding door. "Good morning. Let me make you some coffee."

"Coffee. Yes." Zoe, still squinting, began to tug at the sheets that threatened to strangle her. "As strong as it comes."

Caffeine worked small miracles on Zoe. By the time Keira had packed her very modest backpack, Zoe had styled her hair, applied the dark eyeliner that had become her signature, and donned a surprisingly coordinated outfit for that day's outing, all somehow in the span of four minutes.

"Let's get an early start," she said, cheerfully kicking her own belongings back into the open suitcase on the floor. "We'll want to get there early enough that no one's awake yet."

"Morning classes will have started by the time we get there," Mason said, checking the clock. "Though you're probably right that no one in those classes will be even close to awake. At least it should be quiet around that part of campus. We just don't want to be there when lunchtime rolls around."

Zoe nodded. "Yeah. If we *do* need to deal with a ghost, I'm sure Keira would prefer not to have an audience watching."

"Ideally." Keira grimaced.

They were checked out and into the car within twenty minutes. Unlike the day before, Mason didn't need to look up directions on his phone. He apparently remembered the route to his old university well. They picked up bagels from a corner store on the way and ate them while driving.

Now that they were getting close to their destination, Keira's nerves had started to rise up. She wasn't afraid of meeting the ghost of Evan. But she was afraid of not being able to give Mason any closure. If Evan's ghost remained on campus, she'd need to try to clear him…and that might be easier said than done.

His killer had never been caught. If Evan's ghost lingered, that would be the most likely motivation: a desire for justice. And it would be near impossible to give him that, especially on the one-day deadline Keira had.

She kept stealing glances at Mason as he drove. His expression was set, though he looked pale. The fourth time she tried to covertly glance at him, he flashed a tight smile.

"I promise I'm fine." He slowed at an intersection and checked both ways before letting the car glide forward again. "Once you're there, just focus on what you do best. Whatever the outcome, I'll be grateful."

A turn off the main road led them to an enormous set of stone pillars with open gates. An ornate metal sign arching above the entrance advertised Ridgegrow University, with a Latin motto beneath.

"Great wisdom leads to great futures," Mason translated as they passed through the gates.

"Damn," Zoe muttered, watching manicured hedges and ancient, well-kept trees pass by their windows. "This place is Fancy with a capital F. Just how rich are you parents?"

He laughed. "Not rich at all. I had a scholarship."

"Of course you did."

Mason pulled into a parking lot that was nearly empty. Spreading trees that had to be hundreds of years old cast shade around them as they climbed out of the car. Keira shielded her eyes against the sun as she surveyed the buildings around them. Most were constructed from old stone. They were all several stories tall and elaborately designed.

Cobblestone paths led between buildings, with courtyards and benches spaced around. Everything was neatly maintained. Keira doubted she could find a blade of grass higher than two inches even if she had the entire morning to search. She had a sneaking suspicion the university applied those same rigidly high expectations to its students.

Mason's expression was hard to read, but Keira thought she saw a painfully bittersweet concoction of wistfulness, regret for what he'd once had and for what he might have become, and aching nostalgia. This had been his home for several years. And according to what he'd told her, he'd loved it there.

"Right," he said, blinking quickly as he seemed to realize that he was supposed to be guiding them. "Behind the clock tower. It's just over here."

They left the parking lot and set out along one of the cobblestone roads weaving between buildings. A handful of students passed them, many appearing fresh out of high school, with occasional older students mixed in. Conversations were energetic. Keira had been afraid she would stand out and instinctively hunched to make herself less noticeable, but almost no one glanced in their direction.

As they rounded the corner of what appeared to be a staff hall, they found an older, dark-skinned man in a vest walking in their direction. His round face brightened. He raised one hand, his beard bristling as he smiled. "Mason!"

"Professor." Mason managed a choked laugh and extended his hand as they neared each other. "How are you?"

"Busy as always. I swear the students get younger every year." The man clapped Mason on his shoulder. "Tell me you've come back. I've been missing you from my class."

"Ah, not yet. Just visiting a friend." Mason cleared his throat. "Professor, I'd like you to meet Keira and Zoe. Keira, Zoe, this is my favorite teacher, Professor Ayad."

"That's the kind of praise I like to hear," Ayad said. "And you're not even buttering me up for better grades. Very good. But I do hope you'll be back soon." He turned a smile on Keira and Zoe. "One of my best students. He's going to go far. Just as soon as he finishes his degree, that is."

"I'm just waiting for the right time," Mason said.

"Very well. But don't wait too long. We're holding a spot for you, but you won't want to fall behind." He gave Mason's shoulder another clap. "I'd best leave you. I have lecture notes to mangle into slides. Take care, now."

"You too, Professor." Mason raised a hand as the older man continued along the path. When he turned away, there was a trace of pain in his expression. "I didn't realize I'd missed him until then," he explained at Keira's curious look.

"Do you *want* to come back?" she asked.

He rolled his shoulders in a noncommittal shrug. "Maybe. When I feel like I'm not at risk of losing myself like I did before."

In Blighty, Mason continually spent time helping his neighbors: washing dogs, doing their shopping, repairing broken furniture, and spending time with them if he thought they were lonely. He'd turned up on Keira's doorstep the morning after she'd arrived at town, prepared to treat the cuts on her arm without so much as a question.

He said he thought he'd lost his direction while he was at school. That he'd let competitiveness and ego override his desire to improve the lives of the people around him.

She wondered how much of his helpful nature was his natural temperament and how much of it was a desperate, unspoken need to atone for imagined flaws.

"It's just over here," Mason said. Keira looked up and saw a massive stone clock tower. Four sides each held a clock face that must have been twice as tall as she was. Massive hands moved with each passing second, and even from their distance, Keira thought she could hear the mechanical ticks carried on the chilled air.

A door had been set into the clock tower, presumably for maintenance, but Mason led them past it and around the structure's corner. Stone walls had been built, to create a windbreak for a courtyard that spanned about twenty feet, that shielded it from sight from most of the other buildings around them. The stone floor had been laid in an elaborate geometric pattern, and two wooden seats were set at opposite sides of the courtyard. Planter boxes spilled over with miniature pines and flowering shrubs.

Mason came to a stop at the entrance to the courtyard. He thrust his hands into his jacket pockets, rocking on his feet uneasily.

"This is where it happened," he said. "I passed by on the clock tower's other side. Evan would have been following this path to the same exam hall when he was either lured or dragged into here. The school's admin scrubbed the blood off the stones the best they could, but I've heard people say you can still see traces if you look between the cracks."

Keira shivered. She hadn't needed Mason to tell her they'd arrived at their destination. The area had emotions attached to it. The quiet, uneasy prickling of a realm stained by death.

On the back wall of the courtyard was a small bronze plaque. Even from a distance, Keira could see the words imprinted on it: *In memory of Evan Radecki.* It seemed like an inadequate kind of memorial. The type of plaque the school might put up so no one could accuse them of not caring and yet small enough to be overlooked and soon forgotten. The school didn't want to be remembered as the place where a young man had been killed.

"Okay." Mason swallowed thickly. "I...I'll let you work. Tell me if you need me for anything."

He and Zoe took several steps back, giving Keira space. She

clenched her hands at her side, then reached for the muscle behind her eyes.

Her second sight opened. She blinked at the courtyard. The benches. The high stone walls. The plaque.

There were no spirits.

Keira took a slow, steadying breath, then pulled on the muscle harder, opening the sight as wide as she could. Then she spoke: "Evan Radecki. If you're here, please respond to me."

The world remained still and silent.

She waited, but there were no electric prickles. No drop in the temperature. No presences. Just the faint, distant stain of death on the ground, nothing more.

Keira let her second sight relax. She turned back to Mason. He stood just outside the alcove, tense and expectant. She shook her head.

"Evan isn't here. It's empty."

"Oh." His breath seemed to rush out of him like he was being deflated. He ran his hands across his face, and that was when Keira noticed his skin was damp with anxious sweat. She reached for him and took hold of his arm. He was clammy. She didn't know what else she could do to help, so she leaned her head against his shoulder. The muscles underneath her tightened, then relaxed, and Mason put his hand on her back in return.

"Thank you," he said.

"Yeah." Keira closed her eyes for a second, focusing on Mason's warmth, then took a breath and stepped back. "There's…uh, there's one other thing…"

He tilted his head slightly as he watched her. "Keira?"

She swallowed. "There's another place Evan might be. The graveyard where he's buried. From what I've encountered, ghosts either become tethered at the place they die or the place where their body is interred. If we wanted to be certain, I'd need to visit the graveyard as well."

"Right. Of course." He nodded, blinking rapidly. "I didn't think of that. But I should be able to find the address online. If it's not too far, we might still have time to visit it today."

"Already done." Zoe raised her phone in one hand, a crooked smile playing over her mouth. "I looked it up last night, just in case. It's actually on our way back to Blighty."

"Ha." Mason shook his head. "And you pretended you couldn't remember Evan's name."

"I can't appear *too* helpful or, heaven forbid, people will start asking me for help." Zoe tucked the phone back into her pocket. "His grave is at a cemetery only an hour and a half from Blighty. It's barely a detour. We can stop off there, make sure what's-his-face is well and thoroughly dead, and be home for dinner."

"You could be a *bit* more respectful," Mason said, half smiling.

"Honestly, I think I'd be miserable if people were too reverent toward me when I died." Zoe hitched her bag higher on her shoulder. "When I go, I want you to gather around my grave and tell absolutely outlandish stories about me. Tell people I waxed my eyebrows off and drew replacements two inches too high. Say I had a collection of creepy dolls and called them my babies. Swear on my grave that I liked to fill my bathtub with gravy and lie inside and pretend I was a turkey. Then, and only then, can my spirit truly be at rest."

Mason and Keira laughed as they turned away from the court-yard. Mason seemed to be relaxing now that they were leaving the alcove. Keira found she couldn't, though. The emotional residue continued to press on her. It was subtle, like a feather grazing across her back, but impossible to ignore.

The ground is tainted by death.

Keira came to a halt. Evan was gone, but he'd left an imprint when he'd died. And Keira's abilities sometimes allowed her to access imprints to see a flashback to the moment of death.

Evan's killer had never been caught.

Do you really want to do this?

She didn't. The visions were always painful. They filled her mind with images that embedded themselves. If she gave herself access to Evan's death, she would never be able to forget it.

And even if she saw who had killed him, it likely wouldn't do any good. The school held thousands of students. The killer would need some very distinctive feature like a tattoo or a scar if there was any chance of Mason identifying them based on Keira's description.

And that was assuming the killer was a student; they would have no hope if, like the police suspected, the murderer had walked in off the street.

The odds were impossibly slim no matter how she looked at them. But they weren't zero.

Both Mason and Zoe had stopped to watch her. Concern lingered around Mason's eyes. "Keira? Is…is it Evan?"

"No." She swallowed. "I just need a minute."

She didn't want to see Evan's death. But she thought she had to. It might be the last chance to get justice for Evan and his family.

Keira turned back to the alcove. Her palms were damp and her heart ran too fast. The emotional residue—the stain caused by death—radiated out of the ground. She didn't need to search between the bricks for flecks of red to find the place Evan had died. He'd been killed almost exactly in the center of the geometric pattern.

Keira knelt down beside it. If the vision still existed, she only needed skin contact to access it. There was a chance it was already gone, though. Not every death left a memory, and the pressure washing could very well have eradicated or weakened it.

Still, she had to try.

Keira set her jaw and reached her hands toward the stones. She touched the center of the pattern. Her vision flashed to white.

CHAPTER 21

KEIRA WAS STILL IN the courtyard. It was different, though, in subtle, uncomfortable ways.

The plants in the pots were a fraction smaller and a fraction more leafy. The stones looked older. Dirt and age had crusted over them and built up in the gaps between. They had not yet been pressure washed.

Ahead, the stone wall was bare. No plaque. No memorial. Not yet.

A figure stepped into Keira's view. He had an open, gentle face and tawny skin. A satchel was slung over one shoulder; it looked heavy with books. Everything about his appearance was understated but tidy. His shirt had been ironed and a light jacket matched the brown in his pants. His smile was warm but, Keira thought, held just a hint of hesitancy.

Evan Radecki.

He spoke, but the words were lost to Keira. She strained to read his lips. He was asking if she needed help, she thought.

No. Not me. He can't see me.

A second figure stood near her, wearing a striped jacket. Its hood had been pulled up. From Keira's angle she wasn't able to see the figure's face.

Her body turned cold. Dread, heavy and icy, filled her chest.

Quick. Focus. You only have once chance at this.

She strained forward, trying to see under the hood, but the scene swam around her. Evan had approached the figure. There was something like an apology in his face. *Empathy.* Mason had said he would have made a great doctor; it was very much like Mason to admire someone who contained so much kindness.

Still, Keira could not see under the hood to make out the stranger's face. The sun's angle was wrong, throwing his features into shadow.

The visions never lasted long. She only had seconds. Desperate, Keira darted her eyes across his form as she memorized as much as she could. He was a man but small. Only a little taller than Keira herself. She could see his hands: they were trembling. His skin was very pale. The jacket clung to angular shoulders that had been hunched.

The images swam again, leaving Keira reeling. Evan and the stranger were closer, Evan standing at the man's side, one hand gently placed on his shoulder. He was speaking, but there was no smile on his face any longer, just sadness.

Something silver glittered in the man's right hand. A pocket-knife, held carefully at his side.

Nausea rose in Keira. She would not be able to escape the next part of the scene, no matter how badly she wanted to. All she could do was try to stay focused and gather as much information about the stranger as she could. His jacket was cheap cotton, but his sneakers looked expensive. So did the pocketknife: pure silver. Something about the blade snagged at the back of Keira's mind, as though there was something important about it that she should recognize, but it slid away again before she could grasp it.

The image shifted once more. The stranger had thrown himself at Evan. They tumbled to the ground, the stranger on top, the blade plunging into Evan's chest and into his right lung. Evan's mouth opened, but the impact would have been sudden enough to knock the air out of him.

Mason would be on the clock tower's other side, Keira realized. If she'd had the ability to move, she could have craned to see over the courtyard walls and glimpsed him there, hesitating.

Instead, she had no choice except to watch the brutal attack before her. The images shifted erratically, blending in strange ways, as the red-slicked knife rose again and again. Evan fought back, his hands scrabbling at the stranger's jacket, but the knife wouldn't stop.

It lasted too long. Longer than Keira had imagined might be possible. She tried to close her eyes to block it out but the scene continued to play across the back of her eyelids. The killer's hoodie almost slipped away from his face, and for a second Keira thought she might be able to glimpse him properly, but then he pulled it back into place, leaving her with just the image of pale hair and the end of his nose.

The images shifted a final time. Evan lay still. His head rested back on the stones, and his eyes were open but unseeing. The killer rose and staggered away, clutching the knife in his blood-stained hands.

Keira had known this was how the vision would end, but she still felt her heart break as she stared down at Evan. He lay in a slowly widening pool of his own blood. The killer had cut his throat to finish the job: a jagged line ran from ear to ear. His limbs were limp, his gentle face slack. The satchel had burst open during the attack and textbooks scattered out of it, slowly soaking up the blood.

The killer's chest rose and fell quickly as he reached into one of the planters and pulled out a backpack. He fumbled to unzip it, then dropped the knife inside before tugging the hoodie over his head and bundling it up.

The murder had been planned. He'd worn the cheap hoodie to catch the blood spatter and had brought the backpack to hide the dirtied clothes as he walked back to whatever refuge he had. He wiped the hoodie across his hands in an attempt to clean them, then stuffed it into the backpack.

Keira was still at the wrong angle to see his face, though. His hair was blond, like she'd thought. Small ears poked out of the side of his head. But almost as though he knew she was there, he still wouldn't face her. He kept his back to her as he clutched the backpack to his chest and moved toward the courtyard's exit.

Turn around. Keira bored her eyes into the back of his head, willing him to react. *Let me see your face.*

He stopped in the courtyard's entrance. She imagined he was running through his itinerary a final time, making sure he hadn't forgotten anything, reassuring himself that he hadn't left any evidence at the scene.

Come on. Turn!

The vision was almost over. She could feel it fraying at its edges as it unraveled.

Please!

At the last second, the killer turned. He glanced down at Evan's body a final time, and Keira finally got a clear look at his face. Her heart froze.

The vision dissolved. In an instant she was back in the center of the courtyard, on her hands and knees, touching the place where Evan's body had laid.

A rushing noise filled Keira's ears. Her limbs had turned to water. She nearly pitched forward into the stones, except strong arms caught her.

"You're okay." Mason spoke gently into the back of her head. "You're back now. Just breathe."

Her throat ached. Her heart ran so fast that it felt as though it were bruising itself against her rib cage.

"Breathe," Mason repeated, and Keira realized she'd been holding her breath. She inhaled, and it ached as it traveled through her tight throat.

The dizziness abruptly morphed into nausea, and she heaved.

Mason pressed a hand to her back, comforting, as he waited for the queasiness to fade. In that moment, she wanted to be *anywhere* except in that courtyard.

"Can we leave? Please?" Keira asked.

"Of course." Mason adjusted his hold on her and then lifted, and somehow they both got to their feet.

Zoe came up on Keira's other side and threaded her arm through Keira's. "These time-hopping things really do a number on you, huh?"

"They're not the most fun I've ever had," she mumbled. The rushing was slowly fading from her ears, but she could still feel the uneasy prickling at her back. The stain of death. The stain of suffering. She wanted nothing more than to be away from it.

They emerged around the side of the clock tower. Mason supported part of her weight as he led them back toward the parking lot. The campus was growing busier; Keira could feel curious glances sent her way like lasers trained on her back. She pulled forward, quickening their pace, as her legs began to regain their stability.

The walk back to the car felt far longer than the first trip had. As Keira dropped into the passenger seat, she let herself slump forward to rest her head on the dashboard.

"Keira?" Mason climbed into the driver's seat beside her while Zoe squirmed in between the shopping bags at the back. "Are you feeling sick?"

"I'm fine." She forced herself to smile. "I'd just like to get away from the campus."

"We can do that." The car rumbled to life as he started the ignition. "Zoe, can you pass me a water bottle?"

"Boy, I did the snack shopping for this trip. I packed energy drinks, soft drinks, and a bottle of pure flavored syrup, but I can *guarantee* I did not pack any water."

"I knew you wouldn't, so I did. In the black bag." He caught the bottle she tossed to him and unscrewed the cap. "Here, this will help."

Keira accepted the drink. Her throat continued to ache but she forced herself to swallow some. "Thanks."

"I can't believe you packed water for a road trip," Zoe muttered. "A time specifically designed to indulge in all that is unhealthy, like Dionysus at a weekend-long party. What else did you bring? Salads? Vitamins? High fiber cereal?"

"Just the water," Mason said, steering them out of the parking lot and toward the main roads. He cleared his throat. "And granola bars."

"Utterly typical."

Keira was grateful that her friends didn't try to pry information out of her but let her sit as they coasted away from the university. Her mind wouldn't keep still; it kept looping around the same dozen impossible questions, all without answers.

She'd only seen the killer's face for a fraction of a second, but that had been all she'd needed. She thought she might be sick again.

"There's a park up ahead," Mason said. "We're a few minutes from campus. If you want to stop."

"Yeah."

Mason pulled off the street. The park was heavily shaded and mercifully quiet. In the distance, two mothers watched their children play together. A jogger ran laps along the path. Keira climbed out of the car, still clutching the water bottle, and crossed the lawn to reach a picnic table.

The wood was rough and cracked under her fingers, and grass grazed her ankles as she sat. Mason and Zoe slid into the table's opposite side. Then they waited, watching her with a mix of confusion and concern.

Keira took a slow breath as she fidgeted with the sticky edge of the bottle's label. She had to tell them. As little as she wanted to relive what she'd seen in the vision, she was past the point of being able to keep secrets from her friends. They deserved the truth. More than that, they *needed* the truth. Even if it hurt. "I know who killed Evan Radecki."

CHAPTER 22

"NO WAY," ZOE MUTTERED. Her eyes were huge.

Mason took a sharp breath. "You recognized them?"

Keira's mouth was too dry to do anything except nod.

He frowned, his eyes darting across the wooden table as he tried to make sense of what she was saying. "But today was your first time on campus. You've never met the other students. Who could you have—oh no. Please, not Professor Ayad."

"No." Keira managed a thin laugh. "No, it wasn't him."

"Thank mercy." Mason sagged a fraction with relief. "He was my favorite teacher. I would have hated to lose him."

"Especially after all that work you put into being a teacher's pet," Zoe added.

Mason ignored her as he leaned forward, closing the distance between himself and Keira. "If not him, then who?"

Keira was slowly shredding the label off the bottle. She didn't know how to lead into the next part. It was going to be ugly no matter how she approached it. "Gavin Kelsey was a student at Ridgegrow, wasn't he?" There was a second of terrible silence. Then Mason spoke, his voice thin. "Yes. You… Am I right in thinking you're trying to tell me…"

Keira could only nod.

She'd met Gavin Kelsey, the cruel and sarcastic son of Blighty's doctor, shortly after moving to the town. The encounter had left her deeply uncomfortable. And with good reason.

Her glimpse of the hooded man's face had only lasted for a fraction of a second, but it was all she'd needed. The blond hair. The icy-blue eyes. Gavin had gazed down at Evan's body with so much unbridled pride that she didn't think she could ever scrub the image from her mind.

"You're serious?" Zoe blinked. "Gavin? For real?"

Keira nodded again.

"Wow." Zoe leaned back, staring blankly at the trees above them. "I feel like I should be shocked right now. But honestly, he's always been a weasely little snake. He was a nightmare when he was little and gets worse every year."

"Gavin's father wanted him to be a doctor." Mason had grown pale. He looked shaken and stressed in a way Keira hadn't seen before. She pushed the water bottle over to him and he took it, grateful, and drank deeply. When he resurfaced, he said, "Dr. Kelsey paid his son's tuition into Ridgegrow. And…well. It wasn't much of a secret that Gavin Kelsey was only there because his father had made a sizable donation."

"He didn't finish school either, did he?" Keira remembered how, after Gavin had confronted her and her friends at the grocery store, Mason had mentioned that Gavin had been kicked out before the end of his first year.

"No. His grades were always precarious. Eventually the school expelled him for disruptive behavior. Even so…I didn't think he'd be capable of…"

"I'm honestly surprised you didn't at least consider him," Zoe said. "Weasel-snake that he is."

Mason lifted his shoulders into a shrug. "Honestly? It was easy to forget he was there. He enrolled two years after me and had different classes and different social circles. It's a big campus. I remember being surprised when I heard he'd gotten in, but otherwise, I almost never saw him. We only had one year where our time at Ridgegrow overlapped. But of course, that was the year Evan was killed."

Keira frowned. "Why would he target Evan, though? It's hard to imagine Gavin could have spent much time around him to build up a grudge."

"The thing is, I was well-liked in my class, but Evan was beloved by the whole school. It was no secret that he was the best student from any year. I could imagine Gavin viewing him as something like a physical manifestation of his own failures. Evan was everything Gavin wasn't: well-liked, capable, talented."

"And so Gavin used him to take out his frustrations," Keira muttered. Gavin Kelsey wasn't a large person, and he wasn't strong, but he liked to have control over others. It was rare he could get it, though; his own father, Dr. Kelsey, was severe to the point of being overbearing.

Anyone else with a stifling home environment might have developed anxiety or poured themselves into hobbies. Gavin, though, had developed a cruel streak.

"Maybe it was, like, a spur-of-the-moment frenzy," Zoe said.

"No." Keira grimaced. "Gavin had planned it. He'd hidden a backpack there to store his dirty clothes once he was done. He must have known Evan would be walking that way to reach the exam hall and was waiting to lure him into the courtyard…possibly with some request for help." She remembered the empathy on Evan's face as he spoke with Gavin. He'd tried to be kind.

"There's more." Keira took a deep breath to steady herself. She hadn't wanted to share this part with her friends, but there was no avoiding it now. "This isn't the only time Gavin's killed."

Mason ran a hand over his jaw.

Zoe's eyes widened. "What?"

"I accidentally touched him back in Blighty, and I saw something from his past. There was an older man standing on a bridge during winter. He made a joke about Gavin, and Gavin pushed the man over. He fell through the ice and didn't come up again."

There was a beat of perfect silence, then Zoe and Mason spoke in tandem: "Wilson."

"You knew him?"

"He stayed in Blighty for a couple of years," Mason said. "He didn't have a permanent home and picked up whatever odd jobs were available, but he seemed friendly and was a hard worker. He vanished one day, leaving his belongings behind, but a lot of people thought he'd simply moved on to a different town."

"They found his body the following spring," Zoe said. "In a thawing pond a couple of hours from Blighty. The rumors were that he'd gotten drunk and fallen into a river. Even then, no one could agree if it had happened inside Blighty or somewhere else. The police didn't take long to close the case. Wilson didn't have family or an estate, so they just stamped *accidental* on his file and moved on."

"I bet Gavin planned for that," Keira muttered. "He couldn't afford to have too many deaths connected to him, even tangentially. So he targeted Wilson because he knew his disappearance wouldn't draw as much attention."

For a moment, they were silent. Distant children shrieked with laughter as they played. Tree branches creaked overhead. The world felt almost too calm for what they were discussing.

"I need your advice," Keira said, and swallowed around the lump in her throat. "I need to know what to do about Gavin."

"That's a good question. He's killed twice." Mason ran a hand across his face. "Is he likely to try to kill again?"

Zoe slapped an open palm onto the table. "Of course he is! Have you never listened to a true crime podcast in your life?"

Keira didn't need any podcasts to have her answer. She already knew that Gavin wasn't done; she'd been his third intended victim. He'd stalked her late one night and attacked her at the edge of the stream.

During the flashback to Evan's death, something about the pocketknife had snagged in her mind as important. She now understood why. It was the same knife Gavin had used when he'd attacked her.

Just like with Wilson, he'd picked Keira as a target because he saw her as vulnerable. She had only just arrived in town. And Gavin had been happy to explain to her that nobody would worry much if she were to suddenly disappear. Most people would barely notice she was gone.

Only, Keira hadn't been as vulnerable as he'd imagined. She'd fought back. And she'd overpowered him. In that moment, pressing Gavin into the mud with her own knife to his throat, the idea of killing him had flashed through her mind. That impulse had horrified her…and left her frightened about what she might have been capable of in her life prior to Blighty.

Keira shook her head to purge the memories. "I can't go to the police. Even if they were willing to believe in psychic visions, I don't have any kind of personal ID or even a surname. I can't risk drawing attention to myself. It's why I never said anything about it to begin with."

"No," Mason agreed. "But you wouldn't necessarily need to. We could put in an anonymous tip instead."

"Do they have a DNA profile for Evan's killer?" Zoe asked him.

"I'm not sure. I didn't follow the investigation very closely."

"If they do, we might be able to solve this without Keira's name ever being raised," Zoe said. "Gavin just needs to have left something at the scene. It doesn't have to be much: a scrape of skin under Evan's fingernails, a drop of blood, even a hair would be enough. If that's the case, an anonymous tip might be enough to prompt the police to test him and get a match."

Memories of the vision flashed through Keira's mind. Evan had tried to fight back, but his hands had scrabbled at the hoodie, not Gavin's skin. She shook her head. "I don't think there'll be much. Maybe he dropped some hairs, but…"

"It's a public courtyard." Mason frowned. "I'm sure the forensics team were as thorough as they could be, but there's probably DNA from a hundred students there. Gavin could easily claim a stray hair came from a study session spent there."

"Huh. Yeah." Zoe frowned. "There would need to be a strong enough connection to convince a jury beyond reasonable doubt."

Mason took a breath. "There are other kinds of evidence. You said Gavin took things away from the courtyard, Keira."

"Right." Keira blinked. "The backpack. The hoodie. The knife. They were all soaked in Evan's blood."

"It's more than a year since Evan died," Mason continued. "I imagine Gavin would have long-since burned or thrown out the backpack and the clothes. But there's a chance he held on to the knife as a memento. He was probably smart enough to sterilize it, but the police can still match its length and shape to the stab wounds. Things like that count as evidence. It's not much, but it's *something*."

Keira closed her eyes. She remembered the night Gavin had attacked her at the stream. She pictured the glitter of silver as she knocked the pocketknife out of his hand. It had plunged into the river. And the night had been so dark, and Keira already so exhausted, that she doubted she could find which section of the river the fight had taken place at, even if she had a month to search it. "I don't think we're going to find the knife."

"Ah," Mason said.

They lapsed into silence. Keira chewed at her lip as she thought. Gavin wasn't especially intelligent—he definitely didn't have Mason's book smarts or Zoe's street smarts—but he was cunning. And that had been enough for him to be involved in two murders and one attempt, and with very little evidence left behind.

"Okay, I have a plan," Zoe said, leaning forward. "It involves an invitation to a fake party and sixteen circular saws."

"No," Mason said flatly.

"Come on, you don't even know what the plan is yet!"

"I'm not getting involved in a murder scheme."

"We're facing a classic trolley problem." Zoe steepled her hands ahead of herself. "Do you kill one person to save many, or do you let the train go clatter-clatter-splatter-splatter?"

Mason sighed and turned back to Keira. "We can put in an anonymous tip. At the very least it will put Gavin on the police's radar, if he's not already there."

"And then what?" Zoe asked. "We wait for him to kill someone else and hope there's more evidence next time?"

"We might not have much of a choice," Keira said. She frowned at the table. "I can't tell the police what I saw, and if he didn't leave any usable DNA, then everything we have against him is circumstantial."

"Maybe…" Mason had gone very still. "Maybe there's another option. You saw what happened, but you can't testify. You don't have an identity and you weren't on campus when the murder happened. But…I was there. I could come forward and say I was an eyewitness."

Keira stared at him. "What?"

"I was there at the time. The police have my statement that I was close enough to hear Evan's cry." Mason swallowed thickly. "I could go to the police and say I actually saw it happen but lied about it to protect Gavin. They would probably believe we were friends. We grew up in the same village, after all. I could say the guilt has gotten to be too much and I felt compelled to come forward with the truth."

Zoe pursed her lips. "It's a nice plan, but with a pretty big flaw. You're an atrocious liar. They'll know you're making it up."

"Not if I can tell them details that could only be known by someone who was there." Mason fixed his gaze on Keira. "The police routinely withhold key elements of a crime. It's how they winnow out attention-seekers from genuine confessions. I might not have seen the attack, but *you* did. And you can teach me what to say."

He was right. She could. When Mason had described the murder to her, he'd said Evan had been stabbed eighteen times. He hadn't mentioned the finishing blow: the cut throat, slit from ear to ear. Keira was fairly sure that was the key detail the police had withheld.

She'd seen that, along with everything else. The way Evan's books had spilled out of his satchel. The angle of his limbs. The smears of blood Gavin must have left on the plants when he retrieved his backpack. It would be more than enough to make the confession convincing.

She was the perfect eyewitness. Mason would become the mouthpiece.

"You know what the police will think?" Zoe looked uncomfortable. "They'll think you participated in the murder. Or, at the very least, that you knew it was going to happen. Even if you say you were trying to protect an old friend, they'll ask how it was possible for you to watch someone die and then continue on to the exam hall and calmly take the test without so much as a whisper."

"You're right." A pale sheen of perspiration had formed across Mason's face. "But I know how the police work. They can't prove I was involved, so they won't bring any charges against me as long as I act as their witness. They'd prefer to get what they think is half of a conviction than reach for a hundred percent and lose it all."

"Mason…" His fingers rested limply around the half-empty water bottle. Keira reached across the picnic table to wrap her hand around one of his. "It's not just what the police will think. If you say you were present at the murder, you'll never be allowed back to Ridgegrow. Or any other school. And people will talk. Even people in Blighty who know you and like you. They'll turn."

"I know." There was a desperate kind of fear in his eyes as he met her gaze. "But this has to be my responsibility. I heard Evan cry out as he was being killed, and I kept walking. Maybe…this is how I make things right. This is how I fix it all."

CHAPTER 23

KEIRA FELT COLD, BUT it was nothing compared to how icy Mason's hand was. He was fully prepared to lose everything to bring Gavin to justice. It would cost him the respect of his peers, his future, even his dignity.

And the very thought of it left Keira aching.

Mason shouldered more guilt than he'd ever deserved. He was one of the few truly good people Keira had ever met; he gave his time and energy freely, and he took responsibility for things that should never have been his. It killed her to think that he would lose so much. And he was only facing that future because of Keira.

Except for Keira, they never would have traveled to Ridgegrow. Except for Keira, they never would have found out what Gavin had done. And except for Keira, Mason never would have been in a place to step forward as a witness.

Keira knew that she was a hiccup in the natural order of things. She reached through the veil between the living and the dead. She shifted fate in ways it was never supposed to bend. Her very existence was an aberration.

And she felt a quiet certainty that the only way her role in the world could be forgiven was if she always strived to use it for good. To fix old wrongs; to guide the dead to their rightful resting place. To repair what had been broken.

She wouldn't—*couldn't*—use her gifts to harm the people she loved.

Keira stood. "You need me to give you details about the murder to make your confession convincing."

Mason rose as well. He was pale and his hands were unsteady, but he set his jaw. He was ready. "Yes."

"Then I'm not telling you a thing." Keira turned and began striding toward the car.

"What?" It took him a second to catch what she meant, then he began jogging after her. "Keira, stop!"

"Nope." She refused to slow as she crossed the field.

Mason came up beside her, walking sideways so that he could face her. "What do you mean, *nope*?"

"I'm making my own trolley problem. How did Zoe put it? Clatter-clatter, splatter-splatter."

Mason choked on thin laughter. "You can't be serious. This might be our one chance—"

"Then I guess we're going to blow it." Keira raised her eyebrows at him.

They had reached the car. She tried to open the door but Mason reached around her and pushed it back closed.

"I'm pretty sure you're trying to help me, but this isn't your choice to make." He took a slow breath. "Evan was my friend. Ridgegrow was my school. This has to be my decision."

"Just like I get to decide how and when to use my gift." Again, she tried to open the door. Again, Mason gently closed it on her. She turned so her back was pressed against the door. Mason loomed over her. All trace of laughter had faded from his face. "Keira, please listen to me. There's more at stake than just our own feelings. This might be the only way we can get justice for Evan and bring closure to his family. And it may be the only way to keep Gavin from hurting anyone ever again."

"I know." They were only inches apart. Keira could feel the heat from his body and see the flecks of color running through his dark eyes. He looked so serious. So sad.

She couldn't help herself. She leaned up and bumped the tip of her nose against his.

Mason reeled back, stunned, and Keira took the chance to open the door and climb inside. She carefully closed the door again before Mason could collect himself.

Mason sighed and ran a hand through his hair. He rounded the car and opened the driver's side but didn't get in. "Please, Keira. I *need* to do this. I won't be able to sleep at night otherwise."

"I hear chamomile tea is good for that."

He groaned and rested his head against the car.

"You reprobates left your water on the picnic table!" Zoe

yelled, jogging up behind them. She hurled the bottle through the open car door. "Littering is a crime, Mason!"

He ignored her and instead turned toward Keira. "I know how focused you get when you set your mind to something. It's one of the things I admire about you. But at least let us talk about this."

"Sure." She pulled her seat belt on. "We have, what, eight hours until we're back at Blighty? That should be plenty."

Mason narrowed his eyes at her. He considered for a second, then nodded and reluctantly climbed into the driver's seat.

"You act so high and mighty about murder but then you waltz about desecrating the environment," Zoe crowed as she crawled into the back seat. "Shame! *Shame!* Criminal scum!"

He only sighed again as he turned the engine on.

They were quiet for the first few minutes as Mason navigated out of the park and turned them toward the roads that would eventually lead to Blighty.

Keira felt calmer than she'd expected. Something like a weight had been lifted from her when she told the truth about Gavin. The only thing she regretted was that she was now sharing her anxiety with her friends. If she could take that back, she would in a heartbeat…but it felt good to no longer be alone.

She felt calm about the decision not to share the vision with Mason too. He would hate it, but she refused to give him the ammunition he needed to sacrifice himself.

The only thing she *didn't* feel comfortable about was Gavin. She wasn't going to let Mason confess to something he hadn't done, even if it was in service of a greater good. But that left them back at square one with the doctor's son.

Mason was the first to break the silence. "You probably think I'm trying to be a martyr." He glanced at Keira before fixing his eyes back on the road. "But I promise I'm not. If we can come up with another strategy—anything at all, even if the odds of success are slim—I'll gladly take that instead."

"We always have Zoe's plan B," Keira said. "The one with the sixteen circular saws."

Zoe leaned forward to poke her head through the gap between the front seats. Her eyes were uncomfortably bright. "I know where to find some that are *real* rusty."

"Yeah, I think I'm going to nix any plans of murder," Mason said. "We need to be realistic. None of us have the stomach for it."

That was true, Keira conceded. She'd come close to it when she'd had Gavin trapped on the riverbank, her knife to his throat. Every fiber of her being shuddered at the memory.

"Don't underestimate my stomach," Zoe said, sliding back into the rear seats. "You might get all squeamish around blood but I… No, actually, I get squeamish around blood too."

"It's a very normal reaction," Mason conceded. They were shifting back onto the freeway. "Assuming we scratch any plan that involves homicide, we still have upward of eight hours until we get home. That's a good amount of time to work through the Gavin situation and see what we can come up with. And"—he cast another tentative glance at Keira—"if we can't find a better solution by the time we get home…"

"Nope," she said, picking at a rough corner of her thumbnail.

"You're really not going to budge, are you?"

"Also nope." Keira tilted to catch Zoe's eye through the rearview mirror. "You're on my side here, right?"

"Oh, yes, absolutely." Zoe was chewing on a comically long string of licorice. "Let him suffer. It's good for his moral fiber."

Mason groaned.

"We still have the option to send in an anonymous tip," Keira said. "Like Zoe said, it might be enough for the police to connect him to the murder."

"If he left enough DNA at the scene for them to get a profile," Zoe said, checking caveats off on her fingers. "If they think the tip is credible enough to pursue. If he doesn't try to argue that his DNA was incidental."

"Yeah." Keira sighed. "It's a long shot at best."

"And a slow one. Even if the police take our tip seriously, it could be months before they get around to following it up. There likely aren't many man-hours being dedicated to Evan's case now that more than a year has passed."

"Hm." Keira leaned her head against the window. Buildings and trees flickered past, creating a soft blur as her eyes unfocused. She felt at peace when it came to withholding information from Mason. She did *not* feel that same peace about the Gavin situation.

"He's an opportunistic killer," Keira said. "He wants to hurt people who he thinks have wronged or embarrassed him. But more than that, he looks for vulnerable people."

"Like you," Mason noted, and there was something sharp in his eyes that made Keira believe he suspected more than she'd ever let on.

"He knows not to mess with me," she said. "I'm more worried about making sure he doesn't try it with anyone else. Is there anyone in town who would make an easy target for him?"

"Yes. Too many people, unfortunately." Mason's gaze had turned dark. "Isolated people, like Dane Crispin. Some of the elderly population. Even people like Zoe could potentially be at risk."

"I'd like to see him try," Zoe muttered.

"My point is, if you were to disappear, the police would likely treat you as a runaway. And that's all Gavin cares about: not having too many active investigations that can be connected to him."

Keira's own run-in with Gavin had occurred just recently. She thought it was enough to frighten him. Maybe not forever, but long enough to buy them some time.

On the other hand...it was Gavin. From what she'd seen, being humiliated or feeling weak were two of the things that could prompt him to lash out. Maybe she'd inadvertently pushed him closer to the edge.

"Here." Zoe reached forward to slot a USB into the car's dash. "I've got some mood music to help us think."

"I thought we'd finished Harry's tape," Mason said, grimacing as the first strains of their friend's screaming rocked through the car.

"We did. The first one. That was *Death Murder Death*. This

is one of his older tapes, *All We Want Is Death*. I find you really need to experience them both to fully appreciate the breadth of his genius."

They let the music wash over them. To Keira's surprise, it actually seemed to help. The steady rush of countryside around them and the ceaseless, off-tempo drums seemed to focus her mind and blur out external distractions.

Every few minutes one of them would reach for the stereo and turn the volume down to suggest a new idea.

"We could plant listening devices in his room," Zoe suggested at one point. "Get a confession on tape."

Mason only shook his head. "It wouldn't be admissible in court. And that's assuming he gloats, out loud, about his crimes while sitting in his bedroom."

"I could easily see him wanting to monologue like a villain," Zoe said.

"What if *I* wore a listening device?" Keira asked. "I could confront him about it. Try to get him to admit something."

"You run into the same laws, unfortunately. Illegally obtained evidence can't be used in court."

They lapsed back into reflection as Harry's music flowed around them. Keira was the next to break their silence. "What if we claimed he'd confessed to us? I can't risk getting on the police's radar, but you and Zoe together might make a convincing pair of witnesses, and it saves you from the ugliness of pretending you hid knowledge of a crime for more than a year."

Mason adjusted his grip on the wheel. "It's an option. But if

Gavin denies it—which he will—it becomes a case of he said, she said. Or he could claim he was lying for attention. Or any of a dozen other excuses. Without other evidence, it would never get to court."

They continued batting back options for nearly two hours. By the time they pulled into the same rest stop they'd eaten at the day before, they were no closer to having a workable plan.

Their original waitress was tending a different section but passed by them when she saw them. "Catch many ghosts, then?" she asked Keira.

She smiled. "Not as many as I was expecting, to be honest."

"Oh well." The server chuckled. "There's always next time."

Over by the bar, Bob lifted his drink to salute her.

They ate lunch quickly, still debating, in hushed voices so patrons at other tables weren't as likely to hear, then got a box of hot fries for takeout, to eat on the second stretch of their drive.

"The problem with any kind of elaborate plan is that it leaves Gavin out in the community and unsupervised," Zoe said as Mason turned their car back onto the road. "That's risky."

"We can't keep him under surveillance." Keira took a fry from the box perched between them and broke it in half. "There are only three of us. It would be impossible to watch him around the clock, every day of the week. At least, not without having a nervous breakdown from it."

"Especially not if it goes on for months," Zoe added. "Let alone years. But what about spreading rumors about him to other people in town? We wouldn't need any kind of legal proof to make people wary of Gavin. Fifty sets of eyes, even just eyes watching him out of curiosity, is better than three."

"That's more likely to provoke him, I think." Keira chewed on her lip as she considered it. "It could make him feel cornered. Paranoid. It might force him to lash out."

"Actually…" Zoe picked up a fry and pointed it at Keira. "Why don't we lean into that? Set up one of us as bait. Not you, since it needs to be someone who can file a report with the police. And not Mason, since he's big enough to give Gavin second thoughts. It could be me, though."

Mason was looking uncomfortable. "I don't think I like this plan."

"But you said it yourself—I'm part of that demographic Gavin's looking for. Someone he considers weaker than himself. Someone who would probably be filed as a runaway if I vanished. And Gavin already *loathes* me. I'd just need to push enough of his buttons to provoke an attack—and, trust me, I'm *very* good at pushing buttons—and we can get him for attempted murder."

"There's only one problem with that," Mason said. "The part about the attempted murder."

"You guys would be waiting in the wings to stop him before he got too far. We wouldn't let him *actually* hurt me."

"But there's still a chance he would." Mason shook his head. "No matter how cautious we were, there is still no way to guarantee a scenario like that would be safe. And even if we did manage to pull it off flawlessly, the end result is likely to be less than a year of jail time. A provoked, spur-of-the-moment outburst that leaves no injuries is considered much less serious than a premeditated attack."

"Ugh." Zoe scowled as she shoved the fry into her mouth. "The legal system sucks."

"It does, though maybe not for those exact reasons." Mason sighed. "All of these ideas are far more complicated and risky than the original plan of letting me act as a witness."

"I'm still not budging," Keira said, and Mason sent her a rueful smile in response.

"We could probably drive the whole Kelsey family out of town if we tried hard enough," Zoe continued, picking at where food had gotten stuck between her teeth. "But that's not exactly going to help, is it? It'd just make Gavin some other town's problem, and that hardly seems fair."

"Agreed." Keira glanced into the rearview mirror to meet Zoe's gaze. Beyond her friend's head, through the back window, she saw a white van farther down the road.

Mason started talking about ethics, though Keira barely heard his words.

She couldn't drag her eyes away from the white van. It had a small emblem in the center of its hood. It was too far away for her to make out the details clearly, but her stomach turned into icy, aching knots at the sight of it.

It's them.

CHAPTER 24

KEIRA DUG HER FINGERTIPS into the fabric seat sides, as though bracing for a collision.

"Keira?" Mason had noticed the change in her posture. He watched her from the corner of his eye. "Did something happen?"

She wasn't sure she had enough breath to speak. "The van behind us. I think it's them. Artec."

Zoe swore quietly.

"Keep still, both of you." Mason glanced into the rearview mirror. "Keira, do you think they've seen you?"

Her muscles were locked into place. "I don't know."

Mason reached for the mirror and covered it with his hand to block the reflection. Then he tilted it, angling it toward the ceiling so Keira could no longer watch the van and, more importantly, the occupants in the van wouldn't be able to see her. "Don't turn your head," he said, his voice soft but tense. "Stay facing forward. They won't be able to get a clear look at you. I'll take the next turnoff."

Behind Keira, Zoe's breathing had grown quick. Like Keira, she was sitting completely still, afraid of moving in case it drew attention. "The more important question is if they recognize this car."

"They shouldn't." Mason frowned. "Unless they've been watching us without our knowing."

"I saw another of them yesterday," Keira said. Her grip on the seat tightened. She knew it was safer to have the mirror turned away, but not being able to see the van felt so much worse. "They drove past while we were stopped to look at the oversized owl. I didn't think they'd seen me, but maybe…"

"Don't panic." Mason's gentle, calm voice was betrayed by white knuckles gripping the steering wheel. "It might be a coincidence. Artec's headquarters could be somewhere in this region, and they send out vans regularly."

"He's right," Zoe said. "If they were truly trying to follow you, I'd think they would do it covertly, not while covered in their company branding."

That was true. But it didn't help quell the rising panic in Keira's chest.

Everything about that symbol was bad. She felt it in her blood, in her nerve endings, in the subliminal part of her mind. She needed to get away from it. And fast.

A turnoff appeared ahead. Mason put on his indicators. "This will give us some answers," he said. "Depending on whether they follow us or not."

"What happens if they do?" Zoe asked. Keira could feel her eyes boring into the back of her head. "Do we lead them on a high-speed chase or…?"

Mason cleared his throat. "To be honest, I've never gone very far over the speed limit in my life. But I'm prepared to try."

"We are involved in a life-or-death situation," Zoe whispered, "and you are still somehow the most boring person I know."

"Thank you."

They glided into the off-ramp to exit the freeway. "Cover your face," Mason said to Keira. She raised a hand and pretended to fidget with her hair as she used it as a shield.

"I think they're staying on the freeway," Zoe said.

Mason shifted slightly forward in his seat, putting himself between Keira and the van. Their car slowed as the road peeled them away from the freeway.

Through her fingers, Keira glimpsed it: the white van, cruising comfortably along the freeway. The symbol, black on the van's white paint, stood out clearly on the side panel. Its leaf design twisted in a hexagonal pattern. Bile rose in the back of her throat as clammy sweat pearled across her skin.

But the distance between them was increasing, and the van stayed straight ahead on the freeway.

Mason released a held breath and his grip on the wheel relaxed a fraction. "Okay. That's a good sign, I think."

"They didn't try to look at us as they passed," Zoe said. She slumped back into her seat. "I was watching. I figured, if they knew you were in the car, they'd at least turn their head to glance at you. But they didn't."

"Okay." The queasiness still wouldn't dissipate, but Keira forced a smile. "Thank you."

A service station had been built close to the exit, and Mason let the car coast into it before pulling into one of the empty parking spots. He turned the engine off, then swiped the back of his hand across his own face.

"So," Zoe said, still slumped in her seat. "That just leaves us the question: What are the odds that we see two vans in two days? How close exactly are we to Artec's headquarters?"

"We could look up businesses in the area," Mason suggested. "There might be a commercial area or a business park nearby. It might help us narrow our search."

"Or, here's an idea: We could get back on the freeway. Try to catch up to the van. Then we could follow it and find out where it goes."

"No," Keira said quickly. Her skin prickled uncomfortably, and she ran her hands across her forearms as though she were brushing invisible cobwebs off. "We absolutely cannot do that."

"Keira's right. They may not have noticed us, but we don't want to risk changing that by tailing them."

"They have their logo on the vans." Zoe frowned. "But not the business name. That's kind of weird, huh? If you go to the effort to advertise your company on your vehicle, wouldn't you want to tell people who you are?"

"True," Mason said. "No phone number. No website. Not

even a slogan. You either recognize them by the logo, or you don't recognize them at all."

Zoe shuffled back in her seat. "I shouldn't be surprised. Everything about them is shady, shady, shady."

A truck trundled past them slowly, pulling into a bay to refuel. Keira focused on her breathing and getting it back to a more comfortable pace. Mason ruffled his hair back out of his face then asked, "What would you like to do, Keira? Would it help to stay here awhile?"

"No. Thanks. It might be good to get back on the road." She rubbed itchy palms on her jeans. "I don't think I'll feel properly safe until we're home."

"I can understand that." Mason started the car again. "We're only a couple of hours away now."

Keira still couldn't quite relax as they returned to the road. Nor could she keep her eyes off the vehicles around them. She kept flicking her eyes from the now-corrected rearview mirror to the lanes on either side, half believing that at any moment another van might emerge from the traffic like a shark out of deep water.

"Music?" Zoe offered. She'd leaned forward to be closer to Keira. "I won't even put on Harry's third album. Promise."

"Thanks, but I'm good."

Zoe cleared her throat. "This is probably awful timing, considering how we all want to get home, but did you still want to stop at the cemetery where Evan is buried?"

"Oh." Between the Gavin situation and the white van, Keira had completely forgotten. Evan's spirit hadn't been at the campus, but there was still a chance he'd become tethered at his final resting spot, his grave. A small chance…but a chance nonetheless.

She glanced at Mason. He gave her a soft smile in return. "It's okay. Let's just go home."

Home was somewhere Keira very badly wanted to be at that moment. Blighty felt like a different world: smaller, safer, hidden away. A place where white vans and men with skull-like masks would never find her.

But if she didn't follow through, she knew there would always be the what-if lingering over them. Especially Mason. He would always wonder. And with Keira's life as precarious as it was, she couldn't guarantee that she'd get another chance to travel out of town anytime soon.

"No," she said, and put some conviction into the words. "Let's finish this off properly. We'll go to the cemetery. Do you know the way, Zoe?"

"Yep, I gotcha. It's only an hour from Blighty and won't even make our trip that much longer. Take the next exit, Mason."

They left the freeway shortly before it would have connected them to Cheltenham and wove through several smaller roads that branched from town to town. Keira found the quieter roads easier; there were fewer cars to watch. Although she kept a close eye on the vehicles behind them, none tailed them for more than a few minutes at a time.

The area felt nice. Farmland was interspersed with wooded, untamed areas, and they passed over several rivers. At least one of them, Keira was certain, had to be the same river that wove through Blighty. She tried not to think about it too much.

"It's just up ahead," Zoe said. "Should be on our right. Pleasant Grove or something just as trite. It's one of the main cemeteries for the area; it shouldn't be hard to find."

"Mm. Looks like we've already found it." Mason nodded to their right, where a high brick wall fenced a large area off from view.

The bricks looked fresh and neat. Their bright coppery color contrasted hard with the evergreen trees and bare, deciduous branches visible over their top. Keira was so used to Blighty Cemetery's graceful aging that she'd almost forgotten it was possible for cemeteries to be modern.

The wall was too high to see over and seemed to stretch forever. Trees and shrubs had been planted between it and the road as a screen, and they were all neatly maintained. Mason let the car coast forward until the bricks began to turn inward in a smooth arc that invited them into the cemetery.

The two fences curved toward one another until they ran parallel on either side of the drive and ended in a tall, square steel gate. The frame was high enough that a small truck could travel through. The gates themselves were opened, welcoming visitors into a view of tightly maintained, gently rolling lawns and a neat parking area.

"Stop," Keira said. Mason pulled off the side of the road into the narrow strip of grass between it and the brick fence. The open gateway stood ahead, and Keira slowly climbed out of the car without tearing her eyes from it.

The iron was clean and shone in the day's cold light. The gates themselves held straight bars that twisted into a geometric pattern in the middle. The archway above them, although narrow, mimicked the pattern. Only, in its center, it held an emblem.

An emblem that was strikingly, horrifyingly familiar.

CHAPTER 25

"YOU'RE KIDDING." ZOE KEPT her voice to a whisper as she climbed out of the car behind Keira. They both stared up at the archway and the too-familiar logo presented there.

Mason joined them, running his fingers through his hair, his eyes tight with concern. "This is really it."

Keira couldn't breathe.

Get out of here, the voice in the back of her head whispered. *This is a bad place. A dangerous place. You can't be caught here.*

They'd found it, though. The source of the people who had been hunting Keira. The people who were so desperate to catch her that they had brought out helicopters to scour a mountain range for her. The people with the skull masks and the massive, unnatural, snarling dogs.

And they'd stumbled on it by accident.

"It's so simple," Zoe muttered. "A cemetery. Why didn't I think of this before? It's so obvious it almost feels like a bad joke."

Keira managed to draw a thin breath and felt it ache as it passed the lump in her throat.

Mason lightly touched her arm, and she flinched. He drew back. "Sorry. I just wanted to ask—should we leave?"

Yes, her mind responded. Keira's tongue refused to move. She couldn't take her eyes off the sharp, polished gates.

"We can't leave yet, can we?" Zoe said. "Not when we've finally found them. The cemetery where Evan was buried of all places. I still can't get over this. How did I not think to look into death-related industries before?"

An engine rumbled somewhere in the distance. Keira's pulse jumped as adrenaline coursed through her veins. She darted back, desperate for some kind of cover. Her shoulder blades hit the brick wall. It was shockingly cold compared to its warm hues.

Mason and Zoe glanced at each other, then moved to follow Keira and pressed against the brick to either side.

The engine was only a soft rumbling purr but growing louder. Keira wanted to sink into the earth. To crawl behind some plant. To find shelter of any kind, but there was none around save for their own car a few feet away.

An SUV emerged from the gates. Faint pop music floated through the slightly opened windows. A graying man was fighting to get directions on his phone while his sunglass-wearing wife drove. In the back seats, a girl in pigtails stared out the window at Keira and her friends. She blinked twice, then gave them a gap-toothed smile. Keira, still hunched against the brick wall, could only stare back.

Just visitors. Not Artec's people. Not yet. But they'll find you soon enough unless you leave.

"Okay," Zoe said, slowly relaxing as the car turned onto the main road. "It's a cemetery. People visit cemeteries. Makes sense."

"We need to go," Keira whispered.

"We'll leave right now." Mason already had his keys in hand. "Hop in."

"Wait, wait for a moment!" Zoe snagged at Keira's sleeve. "Don't you want to at least learn a bit about this place? We can't just ditch it the moment we find it."

Mason had hesitated at his car's open door. "We can look the cemetery up online once we get back to Blighty. It might be smart to keep our distance until we know what we're dealing with."

Zoe sighed as the energy drained out of her. "I hate it when you're right."

"Wait." Keira couldn't stop her voice from shaking. And she couldn't tear her eyes away from the symbol above the gate. Her mind was screaming at her to go, and go quickly, but she knew that she might not get a chance like this again.

I can afford one or two minutes. As long as I'm fast. As long as I'm careful.

Mason leaned on the car, silently waiting.

She ran her tongue over dry lips. "We came here to make sure Evan hadn't left a ghost behind. And I still want to do that."

"You're sure?"

"Yes."

Mason searched her face for a second, then nodded. "Okay.

But let's move the car into the parking lot first; we'll attract less attention that way."

Keira couldn't stop herself from being as rigid as a statue as they coasted back onto the driveway. One hand clutched the seat while her other held on to the door handle, as though she might need to bolt out at a second's notice.

They passed beneath the steel gates. Keira gasped. Even though she was sitting, she felt like she'd missed a step in a stairwell and had plunged into an endless abyss below. Sensations rushed through her in a wave as she scrambled to put up her mental defenses against them.

It's a cemetery. A big one, too, with a lot of recent graves. It's going to be more active than Blighty's ever was.

The land's emotional imprint was one of the worst she'd ever felt, though—worse than Cheltenham Hospital and stronger than the abandoned mill in Blighty. And the latter had almost brought her to her knees. She squeezed her eyes closed as her grip on the door handle tightened.

"Keira?" Mason's voice sounded like it came from far away.

"I'm fine." She hoped she wasn't slurring the words as badly as she thought she was. "Keep driving."

She felt as though she were tipping over the edge of a roller coaster into a free fall, only the sensation never stopped. Her skin prickled. Her mind felt as though it were being zapped with small electrical charges. She fought to push against the sensations, to numb herself to them, and it helped a little. As the car came to a halt, she opened her eyes and saw they'd stopped in a secluded part of the parking lot.

"Are you sure—" Mason started, but Keira cut across him.

"Yep." She shoved the car door open. *Two minutes. Find the grave. Check it. Get the hell out of here.*

Her only prior experience with graveyards came from Blighty's. It was old and, although it sprawled deep into the forest, limited. Few new lots were added there each year. The passage of time had helped to diffuse its emotions into the atmosphere until Keira barely felt them at all.

This cemetery—Pleasant Grove, Zoe had called it—was recent, and it was being filled fast as it took placements from all of the surrounding towns. She hadn't been prepared for how strong it would feel. How *raw*. Her mental defenses were being worn down as fast as she could replace them.

"No sign of security cameras," Zoe said, turning slowly, her keen eyes darting over their surroundings. "No guards that I can see. And there are plenty of other cars in the parking lot. Ours should blend in well."

Keira had promised herself she would be cautious while she was in Artec's domain, but she could barely see clearly, let alone think. She was grateful Zoe knew what to look for in her place.

"Hang on." Zoe popped open the car's trunk and rummaged through her luggage. She brought out a fluffy black scarf and passed it to Keira. "Put this on and wrap it up high. You can use it to hide your face a bit."

"Thanks." She coiled it around her neck, bunching it over her chin and up to her nose to conceal them. It wasn't a perfect disguise, but it was something. "How far to Evan's grave?"

"It's close." Zoe flipped open her phone to check notes she'd written for herself. "In a section to our left. I'll lead."

Mason stayed close to Keira as they crossed from the parking lot to one of the paved pathways. She could feel concern radiating from him and was grateful that he didn't pepper her with questions. She found herself leaning toward him. He was one of the few things near her that felt truly solid and steady.

Bad ground. Bad air. She blinked hard and folded her arms across her chest, fighting back against the emotions that were chipping their way into her mind.

Pleasant Grove wouldn't feel like an uncomfortable place for visitors, she thought. A lot of care had gone into making it soothing and pleasing, like the name suggested. Trees—still young but beginning to spread—were surrounded by tidy shrub arrangements. Modern signposts stood at intersections. Park benches had been spaced about for visitors to rest at.

Still, there was something uncomfortable and artificial about the place. The graves were all too similar and too clean. They stood in neat rows with the grass surrounding them perfectly trimmed. None of them tilted. None of them were cracked or grew lichen. There were no massive monuments like at Blighty's cemetery; here, the stones were all the same shape and size, only differentiated by the names and dates carved into them in neat, clear letters.

It left Keira's skin crawling in a way she didn't fully understand.

None of the plants felt truly alive either. They were immaculately maintained. The hedges were cut into sharp walls.

Shrubs were rounded. None of them had been allowed to spill from the perfect, symmetrical arrangements. The area should have felt lush and green, but instead struck her as harshly artificial.

Other visitors passed them on the footpath. The graveyard was busier than Blighty's ever had been; none of the graves here were old enough to be truly forgotten. Keira forced herself to lift her eyes to take in the scope of the place. It seemed to stretch on forever, divided into blocks by those angular hedges and signposts. Dizziness crashed over her. She put her head down. Mason found her hand and wrapped his own around it. She squeezed back, immensely grateful.

Zoe turned off the footpath and led them between the rows of identical graves. The lines were straight and predictable; unlike in Blighty Keira didn't have to try hard to avoid walking over any of the dead.

She'd lost all relativity. She didn't know where in the cemetery they were or how far they'd come. The ocean of harsh green grass and rigid, identical stones seemed to surround them. Her breathing was growing labored.

"Here," Zoe said, stopping next to a stone that looked no different from any other. They'd found themselves in a corner of the graveyard; one of the artificially sharp hedges created a wall ahead and to their left. It afforded them some privacy from the rest of the cemetery at least.

Keira blinked. The words carved into the gravestone floated into focus. *Evan James Radecki.*

"Okay." She swayed. Mason still held her hand, and she pressed it one final time before letting go and stepping forward.

This was the part she'd been dreading. She would have to dismantle the mental barriers. She would have to open her second sight and, in the process, open herself to the emotions and sensations that came with it.

Do it quickly. If you're lucky, his ghost won't be here. You can leave. And never come back.

Her mouth was dry. He heart pounded and filled her ears with a faint whistling. She clenched her hands at her sides and took a final deep, unsteady breath, then pulled on the muscle behind her eyes.

The undead world floated into sight. Keira didn't have enough breath left to whisper, let alone scream.

CHAPTER 26

HER BLOOD TURNED TO ice in her veins. She tried to step back but it was like her legs had become roots, grounding her to earth that was thrumming with twisted, broken energy. She couldn't even blink as her eyes fixed on the specter ahead of her.

Evan stood on his grave, almost seeming to sprout out of the lush lawn. He looked nothing like the Evan she'd seen at the campus, though. The gentle face and bright eyes were gone. He'd been replaced with something that didn't even look human.

His form was a mass of writhing smoke. Strands of storm-cloud gray, so dark that it was almost black, flowed like ethereal ribbons twisting over one another to create the impression of a human form.

Keira's mind had emptied as pure fear sparked through her. She knew what she was facing, and the very name left her cold to the bone.

A shade. Formed from a spirit that has been so twisted by negative emotions that it becomes something else entirely. Something dangerous.

She'd seen a shade before: the spirit from inside the forest, buried in Gerald Barge's grave. It had been corrupted by an unyielding desire for revenge. It consumed everything in its path, ghosts and the living alike, and as it ate, its strength and sphere of influence grew.

This shade was so close that Keira could have reached forward and brushed her fingertips across the writhing mass. That was too close. Far, far too close. Shades could bite, and their clawlike fingertips could scrape across skin. Any contact led to angry-looking burns that took time to heal. She didn't take her eyes off it as she reached for Mason and Zoe and pushed them behind her.

It's not trying to reach me, though. It could, but it's not.

She could make out the edges of a human form. The head rising above sloped shoulders. Two empty pits where the eyes belonged. They were fixed on her. A dark gash of a mouth opened into a howling scream.

"You're kinda freaking out right now," Zoe said from over Keira's shoulder, her voice tight. "Should I freak out too? Is this a freak-out-worthy situation right now?"

Keira didn't have enough moisture left in her mouth to answer, even if she'd known what to say.

The empty, pitlike eyes bored into her. The howling mouth gaped, fading in and out of sight as its form swirled. But it didn't lunge forward.

Almost as though something's stopping it...

She looked down. Dark chains ran over the shade's body. They wrapped around its torso, viciously tight, pinning its arms to its chest. More snaked around its legs. Their ends vanished into the soil, blending through the unruffled grass.

"What..." The word tried to choke her. She backed up another step, pushing Zoe and Mason back with her.

The chains seemed to be made of the same substance as the shade itself. They'd blended into its form so well that Keira hadn't even been able to see them until she looked closely. They shifted as the shade's form tried to break free, and Keira imagined that, if she'd been able to hear the spectral world, she would have heard rattling like something out of a nightmare.

The shade snarled, its jaws gnashing as it tried to follow her. It was pinned in place, though. Almost as though someone had found a method to contain it there. As though someone had deliberately trapped it in place.

Did I...? Is it possible...?

Evan had died well before Keira lost her memories and arrived in Blighty. Back then, she would have been acting with the full breadth of her knowledge, not the scraps she'd managed to clutch together since. Maybe *she'd* done this. She could have identified the shade and used something—possibly a rune, like the one used to concentrate energy—to pin it in place.

And she'd done it in this graveyard, owned by the corporation that now hated her.

Hated her for...meddling with its graves?

The theory collapsed at the end. The corporation had sent hunting dogs after her. They'd tried to *shoot* her. Business owners didn't do that to someone who had, at most, performed mild vandalism.

Because that was all it would look like to anyone who couldn't see the spirit world: a rune, perhaps, scribbled on the earth where the chains now vanished.

She crept forward again, leaving Zoe and Mason bewildered behind her. The shade twisted, its mouth gaping, as it fought to escape its binds. They were tight enough that there wasn't even an inch of give.

Spectral chains, pinning it to its own grave.

In every instance before, Keira had felt some familiarity with her own work. That was how she'd found the threads inside spirit's chests. How she recognized what a shade was. How she'd known the rune under her bed wasn't malicious. There was an itch of familiarity there, guiding her hands.

She felt nothing of the sort when she looked at the chains. There was something like a memory there…but not a familiarity. Not a sense of how she could conjure something similar in the future. Instead, the sight of the chains left her with a sense of slick, horrified dread.

Someone had pinned this ghost in place, but it hadn't been her.

"Keira?" Mason kept his voice soft. "Evan… He's here, isn't he?"

She wasn't sure how she was supposed to explain that yes, he was, and it was somehow the least of their problems.

A prickling kind of unease ran across her back. It was a feeling she associated with being watched. Mouth dry, Keira turned.

Mason and Zoe waited just a step behind her. And beyond them, a dark, twisting figure.

Shivers ran through Keira in waves. Another shade stood just inches from Mason's back. Its open jaws twisted as it tried to reach him.

She grabbed Mason's and Zoe's arms and pulled them closer to get them out of reach. The specter threw its head back in a silent, frustrated howl.

It wasn't the only set of eyes on them, though. Keira had been facing Evan's grave, which had been set in a corner, bordered on both sides by the shrub wall. She hadn't seen the others. But they were there.

Everywhere.

Hundreds of sootlike figures surrounded them. Each was anchored onto its own grave, strapped in place by the ethereal chains. And they seemed to stretch on forever.

"Hey, bestie." Zoe patted her wrist. "I'm sure whatever you're going through right now is utterly wild, but you're pinching *really* hard."

Keira glanced down at where she gripped her friends' wrists. Her knuckles were white. It still took effort to release them. She didn't like the idea that they were blind to the maze of danger around them. "Don't move until I say so."

She didn't know what would happen to her friends if they accidentally walked into one of the specters. Could they be bitten? Burned? Drained of their energy? None of the visitors seemed to feel anything, but would Mason and Zoe be more vulnerable after spending so much time around Keira and sharing their energy with her? She didn't know, and she didn't want to find out.

I can't see a single normal ghost. Only shades. What the hell happened to them?

Keira craned to see over the hedges at her side. More sections of the cemetery branched out as far as she could see. All populated by the dark, writhing shapes. As far as she could tell, every single grave was occupied by one of the wraiths.

Shades were supposed to be rare. For the hundreds of spirits she'd encountered in Blighty's cemetery and mill, she'd only found one of the twisted creatures. They weren't easy to create. Their unfinished business had to be tied to some powerful negative emotion: fury or a desire for revenge or pure, bleak hatred. And it had to be left to fester for years or even decades, slowly corrupting them from the inside out.

Is there something bad about the land? Something that turns them rotten? No…not even that makes sense. Not all ghosts linger after death. Even if there were something wrong with the earth, there should still be empty graves, spirits who passed over at the point of death.

Her eyes darted from identical headstone to identical headstone. Each one had a matching specter. Spaced in perfect alignment, the rows of graves created unsettlingly straight lines. She couldn't find even a single gap among the dark figures, no matter how far her eyes searched.

This wasn't accidental. Whoever created this graveyard created the shades as well. Deliberately. Methodically. They knew what they were doing. And they understood the consequences.

Keira's eyes continued to flick from section to section. The cemetery was only recent, but it already held hundreds upon hundreds of graves. Hundreds upon hundreds of shades. All twisting to face her, as though they could sense her presence. Hundreds of gaping mouths screaming wordlessly.

And in among them, visitors strolled. Some pushed strollers. Some had come alone. Some carried flowers or other small gifts. They smiled softly and talked in hushed tones as they visited their lost loved ones, blind to the voiceless horrors surrounding them.

Keira's frantic gaze landed on one person that stood out from the others. He wore gray overalls and a matching cap, and carried a bucket with gloves and weeds poking over the top. A grounds-keeper. He'd fallen still, his expression cold, as he gazed at Keira. One hand reached into a pocket. He pulled out a walkie-talkie.

CHAPTER 27

KEIRA TURNED AWAY, HER heart hammering an uncomfortable tune against her ribs as she adjusted the scarf to cover more of her face. She could still feel the groundskeeper's eyes on her back. She imagined him bringing the walkie-talkie to his mouth and speaking in a quiet voice so as not to disturb the other visitors.

"Walk with me," she whispered to Zoe and Mason. "Don't get too close to any of the graves."

"Y'gonna explain what's going on?" Zoe at least kept her own voice to a matching whisper, even as impatience bled into her words.

"Later. I think I've been seen."

"Who—" Zoe made to glance behind them, but Keira yanked on her sleeve to keep her facing forward.

"Don't let him see your face."

Keira kept her eyes wide, scanning their periphery, counting the visitors around them. Watching to see if any turned in her direction. If they pulled out their own communication devices.

The parking lot seemed impossibly far away. No matter how quickly she walked, it wasn't fast enough.

They knew she was there. The alarm had already been raised. How long did that give her? Two minutes? Less?

Around her, the writhing shades twisted in their shackles to follow her progress. Like fields of hideous seaweed, weightless and swaying in water Keira could neither feel nor see. Their arms were all locked at their sides, their clawed hands twitching. Hollowed-out eyeholes tracked her, unblinking. Gaping mouths howled.

In the distance, Keira could make out the edges of the gates they'd entered through. It still seemed so far away. She quickened her pace as much as she could without breaking into an outright run.

A distant rumble of engines set her nerves on fire. Even as she watched, the front of a large white van appeared outside the gates. The familiar logo was emblazoned on it in shimmering silver. They were already there. And they were blocking her exit.

Keira pulled to a halt. One of the shades at her side twisted toward her, jaws gnashing. Keira risked glancing behind herself and saw the groundskeeper rounding one of the hedges as he loped toward her, walkie-talkie held to his mouth, ice in his expression.

Think. Think! What other exits are there? How else can you get out?

The cemetery was broad, with many segments to it. The driveway ran in an irregular loop around it, leading to multiple parking lots around the extremities. As far as Keira could tell, though, there were no other entrances. Even if there were, they would likely be blocked within seconds.

Zoe's voice squeaked at her side. "Keira, not to panic you, but, uh…"

Keira followed her gaze. Men in dark suits were jogging between the graves. Some grazed up against the shades, though they didn't acknowledge them. One pulled something small and black from his pocket. A Taser. They weren't prepared to shoot her in front of the visiting guests, but anything short of that was acceptable.

Think!

The cemetery's walls were at least a foot higher than her head. The only handholds were the channels of cement between the bricks. No trees grew near enough to the wall to help her scale them. It was like they had been designed to be impenetrable. As though they'd expected they might one day be able to trap her inside. Keira was faster and stronger than she looked, but she still doubted she could climb the walls on her own.

But I'm not alone, am I?

"Here," she hissed, darting off to the right. Zoe and Mason followed. Keira no longer tried to disguise her retreat as a walk but bolted between the rows of gravestones, leaping past the shades. One of the men in suits yelled something behind her. They still had a lot of ground to catch up, though, and Keira was already at the wall.

"Mason, give me a boost," she barked.

He didn't hesitate but crouched to hold her legs, then heaved her upward. Keira threw her arms out and grabbed the wall's top, then shimmied up the rest of the way. The wall was just thick enough for her to balance on her stomach, and she twisted around, hooking her legs over either side to hold herself in place. "Zoe next," she said.

"Zoe what?" was all Zoe managed before Mason crouched and lifted her. She squeaked as her head rose past the wall's top, and Keira grabbed under her arms to pull her up.

"Use your thighs to hold on," she muttered as Zoe scrambled onto the narrow perch. "Don't let yourself fall back in. We still need to get Mason."

The men were almost upon them. One pulled something silver from his pocket. *A knife?* She didn't get a chance to see it clearly. The man threw it with startling precision. Keira raised her left hand to block her face and felt the blade slice through her forearm, just above the wrist. Specks of hot blood hit her jaw and neck.

"Keira!" Mason, ash pale, stared up at her with wide eyes.

Pain radiated from the cut skin. Her fingers still moved, though. That meant the tendons and muscles were mostly intact. And that was all she needed.

"Arms up," Keira called. "*Jump.*"

For the third time, he followed her instructions and leaped. Keira grabbed one arm while Zoe fumbled to catch the other. They hung there for a second, attempting to hold Mason's weight as his feet scrabbled at the wall. Pain roared through the sliced skin and up to her elbow. She closed her mind to it. There was too much at stake to let her grasp loosen, even when trails of blood ran over her fingertips and down Mason's arm.

Just don't let go.

Keira tipped herself backward, toward the outside world. Zoe gasped as she realized what they were doing, then squeezed her eyes closed as they used their weight to pull Mason over.

Shrubs grew close against the wall and gave some token effort at cushioning them. Keira crashed through them first, then felt two shock waves as Mason and Zoe impacted next to her.

"Ow," Zoe muttered, and Keira was fairly sure she'd share the sentiment once she had a moment to assess her own bruises and cuts. That would have to come later. Right then, they had seconds until the suit-wearing figures closed in around them like a net.

"Up," she barked, grabbing at her friends and dragging them with her. A park had been built opposite the cemetery. They staggered across the road and toward the picnic tables, Keira leading the way. Her eyes kept moving, glancing from houses to trees to cars, as her subconscious ran the calculations she needed to stay alive.

Too far. Not enough cover. No exits.

Her gaze fixed on a row of houses behind the park. One of the closer homes had a shoulder-height, solid metal fence. Its front gate hung open a crack.

We might be able to make it. If we're fast.

Keira aimed for it. The ground vanished under her as she flew across the park, still holding on to her friends. Voices yelled somewhere behind them. The black-suited men had tried to follow over the fence. Failed. They were going back to the gates.

"Slow down," Zoe gasped, but Keira only tightened her grip on Zoe's sleeve. She couldn't afford to lose them. They either all made it out of this, or none of them did.

The gate looked rusty, like it was prepared to screech if they moved it. The gap would still be wide enough, though, as long as they went through single file. They were right on the threshold when Mason balked. "I think this is trespass—"

Keira didn't give him a chance to finish. She shoved him through, making him stagger, then dragged Zoe in behind her.

Thick shrubs, more unruly than the kind Pleasant Grove allowed inside its walls, grew dense and wild in a narrow garden bed. Keira pulled her friends into it. The three of them crouched, their backs to the metal fence, half-hidden among the greenery.

Only then did Keira spare a glance to the rest of the yard. A balding, middle-aged man stood at a flaming grill just ten feet away. He wore an apron with *Hot Food, Hotter Cook* emblazoned on it in a bright-pink font and held his tongs poised over a row of char-riddled sausages on the grill. A boy, no older than eleven or twelve, stood at his side and held a plate with a slice of bread. They both stared at Keira and her friends, dumbstruck.

Keira made eye contact with them, then lifted a finger and pressed it to her lips. At her side, Mason whispered, "Oh, I'm so incredibly sorry about all of this."

They couldn't afford to make noise. Keira clamped a hand over Mason's mouth and felt his hot and panicked breath against her fingers. A second later, footsteps thundered along the pathway on the other side of the fence.

Keira pressed her back tight against the metal, her own heart pounding like a fist in her chest. She tilted her head up just as long, pale fingers slipped over the edge of the metal. One of the men was looking into the yard. Keira, scarcely daring to breathe, pulled her feet in closer to herself.

The suited man had to be staring at the father and son. He hadn't leaned over far enough to spot Keira. The fingers hung there for a second, then they retreated, sliding back out of view. The footsteps rang out on the sidewalk as he continued his search.

Ahead, the father's eyes flicked from the flecks of blood on Keira's face to the fence and back. He clicked his tongs, then cleared his throat, stuck in a spiral of uncertainty. His son only stared.

"Are you…in trouble?" the man ventured.

"Yes." Keira tilted her head, listening for sounds from the road behind them. It seemed empty. It wouldn't stay that way for long. She pulled the scarf over her head and wrapped it tightly around the cut on her forearm, hiding the dripping wound. "We're going to take the back exit."

She lurched to her feet, dragging Zoe and Mason with her. A carport ran along the house's side. Beyond it, another fence separated them from the neighbor's yard. Keira aimed for it.

"Sorry," Mason said again as they ran past the grilling father and son. His apology was lost under Zoe's contribution of, "Dinner looks great!"

The grill's crackle faded behind them as they reached the backyard. Their path was simple: a tree grew near to the fence and its branches looked sturdy enough to carry their weight. Keira swung herself up and over, landing squarely in the flower bed on the other side.

"Oh, hell to the no," Zoe muttered behind her. Keira craned to look at her friends over the barrier. Zoe glared back. "One fence was plenty for me. I might have wanted to be a gymnast as a child, but I promise you that dream was firmly abandoned by the time I was twelve."

"Come on," Keira hissed, reaching over to help Zoe. "You can complain as much as you want later, but we're kind of short on time here."

Even with the tree to help them, it took longer than Keira was comfortable with to get all three of them over. The grilling father had approached his carport and watched them with helpless bewilderment, tongs still held up at his side as though he might need them as a weapon. Keira flashed him a tight smile as they disappeared into his neighbor's yard.

If there was any small mercy, it was that the house they'd arrived at seemed empty. Keira kept her head down as she jogged toward the property's front and the street that waited there. She turned left on the sidewalk, hanging close to the fences as she navigated the narrow suburban streets.

The grilling father would most likely admit to seeing them if the men in suits came back to question him. That would be okay, though. Keira had a head start now, and the more distance she put between them and the cemetery, the harder they would be to find, even if there were witnesses along the way.

Mason and Zoe were already flagging, though. She'd made them run too fast, too far. Keira's skin itched with the sense that every lost second was a risk they couldn't afford, but she let their pace drop as they crossed the street.

Brief flashes of familiarity sparked through her. She knew these houses. Memories teased at the edges of her mind, tantalizing, only to vanish before she could grip them properly. She'd been along this road before, though, she was certain. Moving on instinct, she turned right.

Sewers, her subconscious whispered. On cue, she spotted them: a drainage ditch at the end of the street held a large metal grate. Thin, waterlogged trees grew out of the soil around it, shielding it from easy view. Keira dropped into the ditch, water splashing across her shoes, and pulled at the grate. It was loose, just like her subconscious had expected it to be.

Lines of slimy moss hung across the grating and a faint but persistent drip echoed from farther along the concrete tunnel. It wasn't tall enough to stand in, but they could move at a crouch. Keira slipped inside and felt the chilled air gust across her exposed skin.

"Okay, into the sewers, I guess," Zoe squeaked. "That's totally safe. And hygienic. And normal."

"Shh," Keira whispered. She stepped to one side, beckoning,

and after an uncertain glance toward each other, both Mason and Zoe followed her into the ditch. The space was tight and they brushed against her as they passed.

Keira waited until all three of them were inside the drain, then pulled the grate back in place, covering their path. She squeezed past Mason's hunched form, then crept deeper into the tunnel.

The light faded within feet, leaving Keira blind in the dark, cramped passageway. The smell wasn't as bad as she'd feared, just damp and earthy, telling her the space was laden with moss. The water running around her boots seemed clear.

"Bend to the right," Keira whispered as her outstretched hand found a wall ahead. Even though she was blind, she still had a surprisingly good idea of the path. She'd traveled along this tunnel before—possibly more than once.

Three sets of sloshing footsteps mingled with their rough breathing. Keira followed the bend in the tunnel, then another, her path guided by one hand stretched before her and the other tracing the damp ceiling above. Finally, after the second turn, she judged they were far enough hidden to risk some light. "Mason, Zo, do either of you have matches or anything?"

"Hang on." Mason fumbled in his pockets, then there was a faint click as their passageway was lit by a microlight on his key chain.

To their left was a mesh ledge used to cover a smaller side pipe. It was just high enough for them to sit on awkwardly, and Keira did just that, sighing as she was able to straighten her back.

"I think we're okay now," Keira said, relaxing as much as

possible without letting her clothes graze against the slimy walls. Mason sat to her right and Zoe to her left, Mason aiming his light at the ceiling and the tendrils of dripping gunk suspended there. "They shouldn't be able to find us in here. We just need to stay still and quiet for a bit until their search moves on."

"Cool," Zoe said. "Fantastic." She closed her eyes. "I think I'm gonna be sick."

CHAPTER 28

"HEY, YOU'RE OKAY." KEIRA carefully patted Zoe's shoulder. "We're safe now."

"You just forced me to jog for, like, an hour—"

"It was ten minutes, tops."

"And it's nearly killed me." Zoe pressed a hand to a stitch in her side. Her breathing was ragged, Keira realized. So was Mason's. Keira was faring a little better, but her limbs still felt shaky and her lungs were aching.

"Sorry." Keira managed an apologetic smile. "We should be able to rest for a while now."

"You can *really* move when you want to," Mason said. He sounded faintly impressed.

"Like a bat out of hell," Zoe agreed.

"We still cut it close." Keira felt her smile fade. "I'm really sorry. We should have left the moment we saw the logo on the gate. That was more danger than I ever wanted to put either of you in."

"We're not the ones who got hurt." Mason tucked the flashlight between his knees to hold it steady. "Let me see your arm."

Keira had pushed the pain so far into the back of her mind that it had almost been possible to forget it. She extended her left arm toward Mason, and he carefully unwrapped the scarf from it. She squinted her eyes closed as he examined the cut. It was only two inches long, but it seeped blood unrelentingly.

"My first aid kit's back at the car," Mason muttered. "There's not much I can do until I get it back. In the meantime, we'll need to apply pressure and hold it above your heart to stop the bleeding."

"Sure." Keira retied Zoe's scarf around it, squeezing as tightly as she could tolerate, then pressed the arm against her chest, holding the cut at shoulder height. "Zo, can you do me a favor?"

"I'm pretty sure you just saved my life, so, yeah, sure."

"Cool. I got some blood spatter on my face and it's going to draw too much attention if I keep walking around like this. Can you see it well enough to get it off?"

"Can do." Zoe dipped the corner of her sleeve into the shallow running water and used it to dab at Keira's face, careful to avoid any open cuts. "They *really* wanted to hurt you, huh?" Zoe said.

"Yeah. I think…" She cleared her throat. It was the first time Keira had had a chance to actually process what she'd seen inside Pleasant Grove and what it meant. "I think they're desperate to stop me."

"Why?" Zoe finished cleaning Keira's face and unwittingly leaned her head back against the wall. Slimy water trickled through her short hair as she squinted one eye at Keira. "What makes you so dangerous to them?"

"I can see what they've done." Very briefly, Keira recounted the horrors she'd uncovered. The rows upon rows of shades, all chained to their graves. Each one planted there with unyielding precision. Not a single one allowed free.

"Oh," Zoe whispered, her eyes glassy as she stared into the concrete wall opposite.

Mason held his hand over his mouth, his eyes tight as he hunched forward. He was taller than both Keira and Zoe, and still had to crouch slightly, even when sitting down. "I had no idea. It just felt like a normal cemetery to me…"

"Me too," Zoe said. "The gardeners were a bit too pedantic for my tastes, and the gravestones were kinda ugly, but if you'd asked me to guess what kind of messed-up junk was going on, I'd have no clue."

"No. I don't think anyone does."

"Except for you," Zoe added, and Keira nodded mutely.

"We guessed you might have taken on some kind of whistle-blower role," Mason said, tilting his head. "I guess this is confirmation that we were right."

A keen light entered Zoe's eyes as her exhaustion faded under blossoming excitement. "They're desperate to keep people from finding out about the shades, and you're the only one who can break that secret open."

"Can I, though?" Keira asked. She adjusted her grip on the scarf tied around her arm. Her fingers were slick with sweat and the tunnel's humidity. "You two believe me because you know me well enough to trust what I say. But what if I'd gone up to one of the families visiting the cemetery and tried to explain that their beloved relative had been robbed of their freedom after death? How many would believe me?"

"That's a good point," Mason muttered. "The world is already skeptical about ghosts and the afterlife. You'd first need to convince them that spirits exist before you could even begin to talk about what's happening in the graveyard. Even if you found a way to get them evidence—photos, video, anything of the sort—that's easily discounted as editing tricks. I don't know that the people at that cemetery are especially worried about you becoming a whistleblower."

"But they want to stop me from doing *something*," Keira muttered. A strange thought bubbled free, and she found herself chuckling.

Zoe raised her eyebrows as Keira's chuckles grew into full laughter. "What?"

Keira only shook her head, biting down on her lip to silence herself. As soon as she got her laughter under control, she said, "This has backfired on them *so* badly."

"Yeah?" Mason asked.

"I don't think they know about my amnesia. If they'd just, y'know, *left me alone*, I would have caused zero problems for them. I wouldn't even know they existed! But they've hunted me, and that's forced me to figure out who they are, and now I'm doing my best to find out what they *don't* want me to do so that I can do exactly that."

"Ha." Mason grinned, shaking his head. "You're right. They have no idea how many problems they've made for themselves."

"And I bet I *was* a problem for them in my past life," Keira said. "That's why they're so twitchy. Why all of their efforts to catch me are so overblown. Because whatever I knew or whatever I could do, it was really, really bad news for them."

"And now you just need to figure out what it is again," Mason said.

"I know so much more than I did before." Keira tilted her head as she listed points. "We know they own that cemetery. We know they've found a way to turn spirits into shades. And we know they've deliberately locked the shades there…for…"

Zoe frowned. "That's the question, huh? What are they actually doing with all of those ghosts?"

Keira thought back to the rows upon rows of dark, twisting specters. Chained in place, howling.

What do they want with them? What could anyone *want with them?* It was a question she didn't know how to answer. The only shade she'd met before was a force of destruction; he consumed and consumed with very little care as to what or how. He couldn't create, only extinguish.

"Hang on, I can figure this out. I'm the queen of deciphering bonkers schemes from tiny scraps of evidence, after all." Zoe frowned, running one finger across her jaw as she thought.

"Maybe they're planning to use a shade army to take over the country. If the shades get strong enough, they can start sapping energy from regular humans, right? Imagine sending an army of shades into, like, congress and watching all of the politicians collapse from some deadly force they can't see. You could literally supplant the government in an afternoon."

"That feels very… supervillain-ish," Mason said.

"The only reason we don't yet have comic-accurate supervillains is because the costumes look goofy in real life. Trust me, if people could do it, they would."

Mason, cast in the unsteady shadows of his light, only looked dubious.

"Mock me if you like," Zoe said, "but don't discredit it. Using an army of the undead to take over the world would be a total power move and everyone knows it."

"Sorry, but I'm hyperaware that this is coming from the woman who believes the world is flat."

"Pshaw." Zoe flicked a hand. "No. Only fools believe in a flat earth. It's all about turtle world these days."

"I'm sorry, are you talking about—"

"World. On the back of a giant turtle. Turtle is trying to eat an equally giant lettuce leaf. Get with the program, Mason."

He sighed.

Keira found her eyes tracing over the edges of moss patches, looking for patterns. The tunnel's green and gray tones were muted by their dull light, and shapes seemed to dance in her peripheral vision. "Supervillain overtones aside, it's possible that the shades could be used as a weapon of some sort. I just can't see *how*. Their tethers grow longer as they gain more power, but they would still be limited to the area surrounding the cemetery. It might be worthwhile finding out what businesses are nearby, though."

"There aren't any, as far as I'm aware," Zoe said, shrugging. "I took a look at the area when I was getting directions to it. It's in a dead spot in between suburbs, probably because the land was cheap there. There are houses around, but not any business districts or even major shopping malls within a ten-minute drive."

"Huh." Keira frowned. "So they're probably not intended to be used as a weapon. We're back at square one, then: What's their purpose?"

For a second, they were surrounded by the heavy, echoing silence of the tunnel, interrupted only by the background drips.

"Maybe there's a more pressing question," Zoe said. "*What's next?* I mean for us, here and now. Do we have a plan? Are we just going to stay down here and become sewer people? As thrilling as the concept is at first glance, I don't want to spend the rest of my life eating moss."

"The car's back at the cemetery," Mason said, frowning. "We can't risk you going anywhere near it, Keira, but maybe I could slip in and—"

"No." Keira was surprised by the spike of fear that pulsed through her at the thought. "We don't know how good a look they got at you and Zoe. They might not recognize you. But the alternative is still too much of a risk. If I send you back in alone, I'll have no way to help you if things go bad."

She was relieved when Mason didn't argue. He was strong and clever and capable, but he wasn't experienced at fighting, and she knew he didn't stand a chance against the men in suits if they surrounded him.

"So…" He cleared his throat. "Does that mean we have to leave the car there?"

"For the moment." Keira rose, bending her head so it wouldn't scrape the ceiling, then turned to continue their passage down the tunnel. "Let's keep moving. We've sat long enough that the search has probably passed us by, but I still want to put some more distance between us and the cemetery. We'll have to try to get the car back, though, and soon. If it stays in the parking lot for too long, they'll make the connection and will get your details from the plates."

The shallow water sloshed as Mason's shoes cut through it. "We have a small layer of protection there, at least. It's registered under my mother's name and at a different address. It won't lead them to Blighty. At least, not immediately."

"Good." Keira closed her eyes, faint relief running through her. "That'll buy us a bit more time. And I think I have a way to get your car back tonight. I just need to get somewhere with better reception."

Keira followed the winding drain with her path lit by Mason's key chain light. She had no conscious memories of the space, but her feet seemed to know where to carry her. She turned her mind off and let her subconscious lead her around bends and down a side shoot, eventually arriving at another grate that gave way under pressure.

The sun had set while they were underground. Tinges of crimson highlighted the horizon but would soon be gone. Clouds were gathering. Unless she was wrong, they were due for rain that night.

Keira stepped back and let her friends follow her out before shoving her shoulder against the grate and forcing it closed again. They'd emerged at the edge of the suburb. House lights twinkled behind them and to their right. Somewhere to the left was the freeway they would need to follow back to Blighty. Ahead looked like a scrappy forest.

Keira climbed out of the ditch and into long, unmown grass as she fished her mobile from her pocket. She selected Adage's number and held the phone to her ear. It didn't even ring before going to voicemail.

"Sorry, I can't come to the phone right now." Adage's voice was warm and friendly. "Leave a message, or try calling me back a bit later."

Keira ended the call without waiting for the beep. "He's not answering."

"Ah." Mason grimaced. "I should have guessed he wouldn't. One of his parishioners, Mrs. Mullion, is in the hospital. A stroke, they think. She doesn't have much family. He's probably visiting her, and he keeps his phone off when he's making compassionate calls."

Keira chewed on her lip. "I was hoping he'd be able to come and retrieve your car for us. He'd be perfect; Artec's employees wouldn't recognize him. Is there anyone else who might help? What about Harry?"

"He doesn't have his license." Zoe shook her head. "You could try his mum maybe. Polly's fond enough of you that she'd probably drive an hour to pick you up. With some grumbling."

"I don't want to risk it." Polly was sweet, but a little too inclined to gossip. Keira needed someone who was familiar with her situation and who would know what not to say if they were stopped at the cemetery's gates. "What about Dane?"

"I don't think he has a car," Mason said. "Whenever he leaves his estate, it's on foot."

"My mum doesn't drive either," Zoe said. "Otherwise she would come. And your family's out of town, Mason."

He nodded.

"That's okay," Keira said. "I'll keep trying Adage."

A drop of rain hit her back. Mason squinted up at the sky, feeling the impending storm, then turned toward the town behind them. A red neon sign was barely visible between the trees. "It looks like there's a motel close by. Why don't we get somewhere dry while we wait?"

CHAPTER 29

KEIRA WAS UNCOMFORTABLY AWARE of how close they were to the cemetery. The hike through the underground drain had put some distance between her and the field of chained shades, but not as much as she needed to feel truly safe.

Do you ever feel safe, though? No matter how far you are from Artec, can you ever stop flinching when you hear someone at your door?

That would change, she decided. She could give them a name now. She knew where they resided. And she'd gotten a glimpse at some of the secrets they were so desperate to hide.

They would come to fear her as much as she had feared them.

"This motel better have a shower," Zoe muttered. "I smell like drain water and my teeth taste gross because I tried to eat some of the moss."

"Why would you do that?" Mason asked, incredulous.

"I wanted to see what it would taste like! The answer is bad, by the way. *Very* bad."

They were hiking through the overgrown field outside the motel. The structure had positioned itself at the edge of town, trying to capture traffic from the highway, but in the decades since being built, trees and vines had grown up around its chain-link perimeter and shielded it from view. It felt strangely secretive, like it was the kind of place you weren't meant to find.

The front reception stood ahead of the accommodation. Lights from its windows ran across the cracked parking lot. Even though night had set in, there were only two cars present. The rooms themselves were spread out either side of the reception in a long row, probably no more than a dozen of them and all single-story. The smooth walls were only interrupted by identical windows and metal doors. A sign had been erected outside the parking lot and loomed high above their heads, its writing a glowing neon red: *Motel. Vacancies.*

The *T* in Motel flickered, burning itself into Keira's retinas. She had to turn away. The motel was old, painted in a dated beige shade that had discolored from years of rain and grime. Small cracks ran through the concrete walls.

"Hell yeah," Zoe said, looking on the motel with pride. "This is *exactly* the kind of place you'd go to when you want to find bedbugs."

"We could wait in the forest instead," Keira offered, then indicated vaguely toward the overcast sky and the flecks of rain hitting their backs. "It might be a bit damp, but…"

"Absolutely not! I've never stayed somewhere with bedbugs before. I want to know what it's like."

"You have a zest for life that very few people could hope to rival," Mason said drily.

They approached the reception. The windows had bars over them, and the front door squeaked as Keira pushed it open. Its inside was comfortable, if small. The reception desk was cluttered with papers and small pots bearing succulent plants. Two seats had been placed by the door, making the space feel more cramped than it might have otherwise.

An older woman stood behind the desk, dark brown hair curling about her head and crease lines running around her mouth and eyes. They crinkled as she smiled. "Oh, look at that. It's been a while since I've seen you."

Keira felt her mouth turn dry. Her fingers itched, urging her to back out of the door, to leave.

The woman didn't seem to notice her discomfort as she shuffled her stack of papers. "Sarah, isn't it? How many nights this time? I can give you a discount if you stay more than ten."

Sarah was the pseudonym she'd used in her prior life. She'd heard the men from Artec refer to her by the same name.

I've been here before. I've stayed here before. For more than a short amount of time, apparently.

Sharp, cutting curiosity hit Keira. She wanted to lean across the counter and beg the woman to tell her everything she knew. To ask what days she'd stayed and for how long. Whether she'd let slip any clues about what she'd been doing.

All of that was too dangerous to risk. She needed to stay quiet. Stay forgettable. Interesting people were talked about, and if the woman who ran the motel talked to the wrong people, it could mean something very bad. She was abruptly aware that, even though Zoe had cleaned the flecks of blood off her face, there were still dots of it on her clothes.

If she was smart, she wouldn't even stay at that motel, but would get back outside and keep moving until her legs gave out. She could feel Mason and Zoe's eyes on her as they waited to follow her lead. Behind her, distant thunder rumbled. Keira might be able to spend the night outside in a storm. She didn't think her companions would be so comfortable in the wilderness and cold.

Keira, her mouth dry, managed, "Just one night, please."

"All right." The woman—her name tag said Mel—put her papers aside as she began fishing through the keys behind the counter. "Did you want the same room as last time?"

"Yes. Please."

"We can do that. How would you like to pay?"

Mason shifted forward. He'd already brought out his card. Keira grabbed his wrist before he could pass it to Mel.

"I want to pay," she said, her voice a little too hoarse and too sharp. She licked her lips. "You paid for the last motel. It's my turn."

His eyes crinkled up with faint laughter. "It's fine, honestly—"

"No, it's not; I want to pay this time. I just need to get my bag. Come on."

She didn't let go of Mason's wrist as she dragged him to the door. Zoe, faintly bemused, sent a quick smile to Mel, then followed them outside.

Cold drops of rain landed across them. It wasn't until they were halfway across the parking lot that Keira relaxed her hold on Mason.

"I really don't mind—" he started, faintly confused.

"Good." Keira drew a quick breath and then let it out. "You'll need to be fine with paying because I don't have any money. But you can't pay with a card. Using your card gives them your real name."

"Oh." He blinked.

"Pay in cash," Keira said. "And give her a fake name when she asks."

"Right. I'll need to find an ATM."

"Over there," Zoe said, pointing. Across the road was a small general store and a pub. Nestled between them was a dull, blocky machine offering instant withdrawals.

Zoe and Keira followed Mason across the road. Keira fought to keep her posture relaxed. She knew the woman, Mel, was watching her through the motel windows.

Be invisible. Be discreet.

That was growing harder with every passing minute. Mason retrieved the cash, then excused himself and dipped into the convenience store next door. He was only gone for a few minutes, but they felt like an eternity. When he returned he carried several heavy shopping bags.

"Food," he said at Keira's glance. "I don't think this motel has room service, and we'll be able to think better if we're not hungry."

The rain had grown heavier by the time they crossed back to the motel. Keira hunched against it while keeping her eyes on the road in case any of the white vans cruised by.

Back inside, Mason approached the desk again, his smile almost natural. "Well, I won the argument after all. I get to pay."

"Wonderful," Mel said, her tone dry, as she took the notes Mason passed to her. "What name should I put the room under?"

"Name?" He cleared his throat, glancing at Keira. "John."

"Mm-hm." Her gaze was shrewd. "I'll need a surname too."

"Uh… Johnson."

Mel lifted her head from her ledger, eyes squinted. "Your name is John Johnson?"

"Yes." Mason had lost a shade of color. His hands, held at his side, twitched. "I was named after my father," he said weakly.

In the corner of her eyes, Keira saw Zoe staring at Mason with incredulous horror.

"John Johnson, son of John Johnson," Mel said, her mouth twisted as she jotted the details down. "You have Room 108. It's outside, to the right. Laundromat is behind the reception if you need it. Checkout at ten. Here's your key."

Mason mutely took the key from Mel, then walked stiffly to the door.

"Amazing," Zoe whispered as they stepped back into the carpark. "Truly a spectacular performance, Mason. No one will suspect a thing."

"I'm so sorry," he said, looking horrified. "I'm not used to lying. I panicked."

Keira nudged his shoulder. "It's fine. You didn't give her a real name, and that's the only thing that matters. We're only here until we can get through to Adage. That hopefully won't be long."

"You should have let me book the room," Zoe said. "I have six aliases, all with their own backstories and family trees, ready to whip out at a moment's notice. This could have been the time to shine for Adelaide Fairbrook, daughter of fugitive circus clowns who are on the run from a vengeance-fueled fire-eater."

"Somehow I prefer John Johnson," Keira said, and couldn't quite muffle her laughter.

Mason juggled the shopping bags to one arm as he fit the key into Room 108's lock. It threatened to jam, and Mason had to put his shoulder into it to get it to open. He found the light and turned it on as they all shuffled inside.

CHAPTER 30

THE ROOM WAS VERY different from the motel they'd stayed at the night before. It was darker and colder. The walls were painted in the same off-yellow shade as the building's outside, which only served to highlight all of the scuffs and scrapes left across it.

A double bed was squeezed against one wall, with a night-stand bearing a small TV opposite. Mason opened the door to the bathroom. It was narrow and many of its moss-green tiles were cracked.

"Yeah," Zoe said, looking incredibly pleased as she gazed at the space. "Guaranteed chance of bedbugs. Maybe some lice too if we're lucky."

"We probably won't be here long enough to get to know either very well." Mason dropped his bags of shopping onto the double bed.

Zoe was admiring a very small painting of a lopsided pear on one wall. It was the room's only decoration. "It sounds like *you* had plenty of time with them, Keira."

"Apparently." She hadn't moved from the entryway. As her eyes shifted from the scuffed wooden floor to the doors that didn't fit quite right in their frames and then to the lumpy bed, flashes of memories resurfaced. They were pale and distorted, like poorly remembered dreams. Tantalizing but insubstantial. "Pretty sure the potential bedbugs were less of an attraction for me, though. I stayed here because it was cheap. And because it was close to the cemetery."

Mason sat on the edge of the bed and began sorting through the bags of shopping. He hadn't been completely truthful, Keira saw. There was more than just food inside: he'd bought bottles of antiseptic, cotton swabs, a tiny sewing kit, and bandages.

"It's not as good as my full kit," he admitted, patting the space on the bed next to himself. "But it will do in a pinch."

Keira's skin crawled from being inside the room. She wasn't sure she wanted to sit. The memories swirling around her held emotions. Some felt good. Hope. Determination. But just as many, if not more, were bad. Fear. Stress. Anger. Pressure built up behind her eyes like unshed tears, but she couldn't tell what it was coming from.

Mason waited for her, patient. She ran her tongue across her dry lips. Her arm ached. She could ignore it, but the longer she pushed it to the back of her head, the more it wore her down. And it would be good to be slightly less compromised if they needed to leave quickly.

"Okay," she said, and sat.

"At least I'll be able to see it properly this time." Mason carefully unwound the scarf. His brows were heavy as he held her arm in his lap and examined it. His long, dexterous fingers moved around the edge of the cut, exploring. "It doesn't seem too deep, thankfully. But you'll need some stitches."

"A fresh addition to my collection," Keira said, and grinned.

Zoe flopped onto the bed next to them, her legs kicked out and her arms cast wide. She sighed wistfully. "You could bring a blacklight into this place and watch it light up like Vegas."

"Ew," Keira and Mason said in tandem.

"See, neither of you will develop strong immune systems with that kind of attitude." Zoe rolled over to reach the shopping bags. "What did you get us for dinner? Oh. Oh, no, you didn't."

"What?" Keira craned to see inside the bags.

"He bought toothbrushes. And granola bars." Zoe pulled out a handful of silver wrappers. "I can't believe you bought granola bars *twice* on the same road trip."

Mason, still focused on Keira's arm, didn't seem bothered by the needling. "The sugar content stops them from being an actual health food, but they're hard to beat when you need quick energy and don't have—"

Zoe, pure disgust plastered over her face, attempted to shove a still-wrapped granola bar into Mason's mouth midsentence.

"Hey," Keira said before it could break out into a full war. "Why don't you try Adage again?"

"Yeah, good thought." Zoe tossed the bar toward the trash

can in the room's corner, ignoring Mason's bitter complaint. She flipped through the numbers in her phone, selected one, and held the phone up to her ear. She listened for a moment, then ended the call. "Still voicemail. Which sounds like there's time for me to have a shower. And order us some pizza."

"I didn't *only* buy granola bars," Mason said as Zoe snagged one of the toothbrushes. She ignored him and disappeared into the bathroom, already clicking through buttons on her phone as she placed an order.

Mason shrugged, then turned back to his work. He left Keira's arm resting on a towel in his lap as he opened a bottle of antiseptic. "This will sting. Sorry."

"Ha. Don't worry about it." She turned her head away and squeezed her eyes closed. As promised, it burned like a nightmare. Keira pushed her thoughts elsewhere.

I stayed here before.

She should search the room. There didn't appear to be many places where her past self might have hidden clues to her purpose, but it was an opportunity she still shouldn't miss.

The longer I stray from Blighty, the more traces of myself I find.

The runes in the forest. The white vans. The cemetery, and now the hotel. All snapshots of who she once was.

She thought if she could just spend a little while longer in these familiar places—just look at them in the right way or wait until the shadows were at the perfect angle—she might remember everything.

The idea was painfully tantalizing. But it also held impossible danger. Blighty had sheltered her. Out here, she was vulnerable. And the longer she stayed, the greater risk she was of discovery.

"There," Mason said.

Keira snapped back to the present. He was tying off the bandages over her forearm. A small pile of cotton swabs, tinged red, sat beside him, along with a discarded needle, thread, and scissors. "You're finished?"

"Yes, all done. I bought some painkillers too. Nothing strong, but it should take the worst of the sting out. Here." He reached into the bag and passed her a small box of tablets and a bottle of water. Keira accepted them but made no move to take them. The sight of the gauze and sharp odor of antiseptic had sparked a memory.

Antiseptic. Bleach. Clean white walls and cold tiles.

"The hospital."

"What was that?" Mason watched her out of the corner of his eye as he packed the dirty gauze and thread into a spare bag.

"Adage took me to Cheltenham Hospital when one of his parishioners passed away. That's where I first saw one of the white vans."

The bathroom door creaked open. Zoe emerged, wearing the same clothes but tousling a towel through her damp hair. "Yeah, and you went missing for like two straight days and came back looking half-feral. I remember."

Keira chewed on the corner of her thumb, thinking furiously. "I remember feeling strange when I walked through it. The place was saturated with emotions—fear, suffering, and death. But there were almost no ghosts."

The entire time she'd been there, she'd only encountered two: Brody McCormack, the parishioner Adage had asked her to look for, and an older woman who had led Keira to the white van.

She stood, her heart beating too fast, and began to pace. "Brody's spirit had stayed, but when I asked him if he had any unfinished business, he said he didn't. He couldn't understand why he was still there. I assumed it just happened sometimes… there are ghosts in my own cemetery that don't know why they didn't pass over too. But Brody *wanted* to move on. He was frightened. He looked almost…"

She turned. Zoe and Mason were watching her. Under the motel's dim light, their eyes almost seemed to glow. Zoe slightly inclined her head, encouraging Keira to continue.

"Trapped," she finished. "He looked trapped."

The older woman's face resurfaced in her mind's eye. She'd been frightened as well. But her fear hadn't come from uncertainty about the future, like Brody. She knew something. She'd *seen* something. And she was desperate for Keira's help…

"The van was there," Keira said. Her legs felt weak. She leaned her back against the wall, her arms crossed over her chest. Her breathing came too fast. "To take bodies from the hospital's morgue. To bring them to the cemetery. They can do something—something that tethers the spirit with the body and makes it impossible to escape."

"That explains why Brody couldn't move on without your help," Zoe murmured.

"And it's why there were so few ghosts in the hospital. They weren't given any choice to linger there." Keira's throat was dry. "Artec is harvesting them."

The thought took a second to sink in, but once it did, it was like a cold, prickly insect burrowing under her skin. Keira had originally believed that the shades were a side effect of the cemetery, that Artec had begun as a funeral home or graveyard and had, at some point, figured out how to make the shades appear.

Now, it felt almost the other way around. The construction and maintenance of a cemetery was simply to have an excuse to take in dead bodies. It was an expensive prerequisite that unlocked access to hospitals across the country—and the ghosts they produced.

She'd been able to move Brody McCormack's spirit onto the next life. She hadn't been able to do the same for the older woman. They'd only just made it to the parking lot when the woman, at the limit of her tether, had vanished. From there, Keira's world had become consumed with the need to flee from the white van and from the driver who recognized her.

The woman, most likely, was now a part of Pleasant Grove. Chained there, like so many other innocent souls, condemned to writhe and scream without voice for an eternity.

Keira doubled over as sudden queasiness impacted her. Mason was at her side in a heartbeat, holding her up, one hand on her back. "What's wrong?"

She shook her head. Tears burned her eyes. Her heart was like a drum inside her head, incessant, unstoppable.

I thought shades were inherently malevolent. The one in the forest certainly was. But those spirits…an entire cemetery of them… were just average people. Parents. Friends. Some of them might have feared death. Some of them might have been ready for it. No one truly knows what waits on the other side, but none of them would have imagined this *fate.*

Clammy sweat covered her face. She pulled away from Mason and began pacing again. Furious, sizzling energy filled her limbs, and it felt impossible to keep still.

The air was stifling. She crossed to the room's only window and pulled the curtain aside to see if she could open it and let some freshness in. The outside world was heavy with darkness. A single spotlight illuminated the empty parking lot. To her right, she was able to see the reception. Its own window, shielded with bars, revealed a woman's profile. Mel. She seemed very still, and Keira had the strange impression that she was staring back. She let the curtain drop.

"I still don't know why they're holding entire fields of shades," Keira said, "but at least I know why they want so badly to stop me."

"Oh?" Zoe's bright eyes locked on her. "Yeah?"

"Yeah. Because I'm going to bring the whole thing down." She clenched and unclenched her hands at her sides. "I'm setting those shades free."

"Hell yeah." Zoe pumped a fist. "We're going to start a rebellion! Who cares that you haven't even figured out how to get rid of Dane's ghosts yet. We're gonna topple the whole system! Somehow."

"Yes, viva la revolution," Mason said more gently. "But, Keira, I thought shades were dangerous. Gerald Barge was. Wouldn't setting the shades free have the potential to hurt people?"

"Like opening the lions' cages at the zoo," Zoe said, gleeful. "And it's going to be glorious."

Keira licked her dry lips. "Maybe. But they were never supposed to be shades to begin with."

She thought of Brody McCormack, rescued at the last moment. He'd seemed anxious. Frightened. He'd been intended for the cemetery too, and Keira hadn't sensed a scrap of maliciousness in him.

They hadn't died with anger or hunger in their hearts. If they were dangerous now, it was only because the organization had twisted them to be that way. They deserved to have what death offered to all and what the cemetery had denied them: peace.

There was a good chance that Mason was right and that unleashing the shades would cause untold harm. But she still had to try.

And—Keira was now certain—this had been her role in her past life. It was what Artec was so desperate to stop. She was here to free the dead.

A faint sound floated through the window at her back. Engines. It was different from the traffic that flowed along the main highway; that stayed at a consistent pitch, growing closer and then fading again in an unvaried rumble.

These vehicles were moving more slowly. As though they were

trying to keep their engines quiet. As though they didn't want her to hear them.

Run, her subconscious whispered.

Keira's pulse was in her throat. She pulled the curtain back to see the outside world. Mel stood silent and stony-faced at the reception's window, staring toward Keira. One of her hands rested on top of the phone's receiver.

To the left and the right, cars closed in around the parking lot, all of them circling the spotlight, trying to stay invisible.

I'm going to free the dead.

This is why they came for me before.

And it's why they're coming for me now.

CHAPTER 31

"WE NEED TO GO." Keira's hands shook as she backed away from the window.

"What?" Zoe had been systematically throwing out the granola bars but lifted her head. "What's happening?"

"They're outside." There was no escaping through the front door. Vans had filled the parking lot to either side of their room; no matter how quick Keira was, the men in suits would close around her like a net.

Think!

The door was locked. That wouldn't hold them, though. Mel would give them a spare key. She'd felt no shame in calling Artec, which meant she wouldn't hesitate to go further. Keira only had a half second to wonder whether Mel had betrayed her before. She'd seemed surprised to see Keira back.

There was no time to follow that thread further. Keira scanned the small room with a growing sense of futility. No balcony. No windows that didn't look out into the same parking lot that was now swarming with Artec's employees.

Zoe was speaking, but Keira barely heard the words. "It's probably just the pizza. It should be arriving right about now. Hope you like anchovies because—"

She tuned her friend's voice out. Underneath Zoe's chatter and the rumble of highway traffic, she could hear their footsteps closing in. They were trying to be silent, but their boots were thick and heavy. A few more seconds and they would be at the door.

Think!

She darted into the bathroom. There was a window there that looked out into the motel's rear. A chain-link fence and thick vines were barely visible through the heavy night. Keira pulled the sliding glass out of its frame and propped it against the shower, then hesitated. The window was narrow. Keira herself would be able to squirm out with some contortions, but Mason would be too broad. She wasted a few precious seconds feeling around the frame to see if there might be some way to widen it, but there was no kind of give she could find.

She moved back into the motel's main room with three short paces. Her breathing was ragged. Zoe still held a half smile on her face, as though the worst thing about to come through the door was anchovies, though it was wavering. Mason was as still as a statue, his eyes darting between the doorway and Keira. He'd heard the footsteps.

There has to be a way. I always look for exits when I enter a new room. I wouldn't have stayed here before if this place didn't have an escape.

Her eyes flicked to the bed, to the TV, to the painting of the lopsided pear, and then up. Toward the small, discreet square hatch in the beige paint above them. The ceiling access.

That was it. That was their way out. A chair propped in the room's corner would give her just enough height to reach it. Except, they were out of time. The door's handle rattled as someone fit a key into it.

Keira couldn't breathe. She had no weapon. No time. No options.

Then a new set of footsteps approached: light, fast, slightly lilting, as though the stranger was skipping. It was followed by the shockingly chipper voice of a young woman. "Hiya, which of you ordered the pizzas?"

There was an incredible, painful silence. Keira could imagine the suited figures just outside the door, frozen in place. She sent up a quick prayer of thanks, then dragged the chair underneath the ceiling access as silently as she could and jumped onto it. She had to bend at an angle to keep her head from hitting the ceiling.

"Pizzas?" the teen tried again, still a little too cheerful. "I have one large pepperoni and one large supreme with double anchovies and double pineapple which…okay, it's not my place to judge, but *yikes*."

Using the cover of the deliverywoman's voice, Keira pushed on the hatch. Tiny flecks of paint landed on her shoulders as the board moved up and inward. Keira reached her arms through the opening and pulled herself up.

The ceiling was clogged with clumping dust. Crisscrossing support beams formed the only solid surface, with the gaps between them filled with cheap pink insulation. The stench of mildew filled Keira's nose. She still didn't hesitate as she crawled fully inside the hatch, the cut on her arm burning, and braced herself on two of the support beams. She turned around to help Zoe, who'd climbed onto the chair after her.

"So, yeah, which of you wants to take these?" the delivery-woman asked. Keira thought she could hear her shuffling the boxes as she grew uneasy. "'Cause, yeah, I got a few more deliveries to make, so…"

"Someone get rid of her," a voice hissed.

Below them, Mason silently pointed toward the bags of shopping, asking if he should bring them. She shook her head. The plastic would rustle too much. They'd leave as they'd arrived: empty-handed. Zoe was through the hatch, and Mason quickly took her place on the chair.

"Give me the damn pizzas," another man muttered, followed by the faint thumps of two boxes being thrown into the parking lot.

"Wow," the woman said. "I'm not gonna give you a refund, if that's what you want."

"Get out of here." The key clattered in the lock. Keira hauled on Mason, dragging him through the opening. His kicking feet scraped the chair back an inch. He scrambled into their hiding place just as the door unlocked.

Keira bit her tongue. Mason had landed on top of her, pressing her back into the wooden beam, but neither of them dared to breathe, let alone move, as the motel's door slammed open.

Light flooded through the hatch like a spotlight. When she craned toward it, Keira had a bird's-eye view of the space below. Five men in dark outfits filed into the room. They all held their hands over something strapped to their hips. Concealed guns, she was certain. They fanned out, two bending to look under the double bed, another two circling around the chair as they aimed for the bathroom. Still more figures were visible outside the door, barricading any possible escape.

"She took the window out of its frame," one of the men barked from the bathroom. That drew the others toward him, passing out of Keira's line of sight.

They hadn't seen the open hatch. The second they looked up, though…

She gently nudged Mason to move off her, which he did. One of the support beams creaked under his weight. They both flinched, their eyes meeting in silent terror, but the sound had gone unnoticed as the men examined the bathroom window.

"The fly screen's intact…"

"She's not here."

"How'd she get out, then?"

Keira crept forward and slowly, carefully pushed the square cover back over the opening. It scraped as it fell into place, and once again Keira flinched. Heavy footsteps echoed below her as the men crisscrossed the tiny room. The shopping bags rustled as someone dug through them.

"Did she leave before we got here?"

"Receptionist said she was watching the door the whole time."

"She could be lying to get the reward."

Oh. There was a bounty on Keira's head, then. The tang of mildew and dust tainted her tongue and dried out her lungs. She blinked furiously as tears stung the corners of her eyes.

In the dark, a hand found hers. Zoe's. She squeezed, grateful for the contact.

"Fan out," one of the deeper voices called. The leader, Keira presumed. "Search around the motel. Look in other rooms. Take the keys from reception, by force if you need to. Remember, she has two companions this time. Keep watch for them. You, stay here. Make sure she's not hiding somewhere in the room."

"Sure, in case she crawled into the walls somehow."

Keira swallowed, her heart hammering. The glib comment was close enough to the truth that she was afraid it would make the commander look at the room with fresh eyes. Instead, she heard a faint grunt as the loose-tongued man took a hit to his chest.

"Keep your eyes open," the commander snapped. His footsteps traveled through the beams and reverberated against Keira's back as he left.

His voice was familiar, she thought. Not from her life before—though she had no doubt she would have known him then too—but from the night she'd first woken in Blighty. When

Adage had learned she was being followed, he'd hidden her in his wardrobe. A man with a very similar voice had then knocked on the door and attempted to get information from Adage. The pastor had been clever enough to play dumb, something Keira suspected had saved her life.

Behind her, Mason let out a soft, shaky exhale. Zoe's hand was sweaty as it squeezed Keira's again.

They had a momentary reprieve. But it wouldn't last for long. The suited men would return once they couldn't find her elsewhere and take a more critical look at the room. They only needed to question why the chair was positioned in the center of the floor to put the clues together and look toward the ceiling.

That gave them only a few precious minutes to find a way out. They couldn't stay in the ceiling. But if they tried to leave, they'd be spotted.

Keira ran a tongue across her teeth and tasted dust. She turned toward Mason and Zoe. Keira couldn't see her friends; she could only tell where they were by the heat from their bodies and their soft, muffled breathing.

"Does anyone have a scrap of paper and a pen?" she asked.

They shuffled as they patted down their pockets.

"Paper," Zoe said, blindly passing a slip to Keira.

"I don't have a pen, but I have a light," Mason said.

She took his key chain and carefully clicked the microlight on. It was just enough to let her see her companions, flat on their fronts, braced on the support beams. Their faces were pale and covered in dust and sweat. She suspected she didn't look much better.

Keira examined the slip of paper. Zoe had used it to write down the cemetery's address. It would serve her purpose, though, as long as she could find something to write on it with.

She glanced up. A collection of small objects were clustered in the center of one of the pink insulation blocks nearby, like a strange bird's nest. Keira, frowning, crept toward it and raised the light.

The bundle included a box of matches. A couple of newspaper clippings, tied together with an elastic. A small piece of natural charcoal, likely taken from a firepit. A roll of money totaling around a hundred dollars.

Of course.

She'd stayed in that motel room before. Which meant she'd thought about her exit options before. She'd explored the ceiling cavity and used it to store items she didn't want to lose. This little nest of trinkets were her emergency supplies, and she was immeasurably grateful to find them.

Doors slammed below them. Keira flinched. The suited men were searching the motel's other rooms. Indignant shouts rang out as the few other occupants were disturbed. It wouldn't take Artec's people more than a few minutes to clear the other rooms and return back to hers, Keira thought.

She took up the piece of charcoal. She'd likely used it to draw runes underneath the bed. Now, though, it would serve an even more vital purpose.

She tore one side off the scrap of paper, making sure to get a blank part that didn't carry any of the cemetery's address. It was small, which meant her message needed to be equally tight. She rubbed the charcoal on one of the support beams to get a sharp point and began scratching.

John—meet me at the overpass. S.

It wasn't much. But it would have to be enough. Mel had clearly doubted Mason's real name was John, but at that point, Artec wouldn't know what was the truth and what was fiction.

Keira slunk back toward the access hatch. She pried it up in increments, biting her tongue with each subtle creak. As a sliver of the room below came into view, Keira tilted her head to see the lookout who had been left behind.

He stood in the open doorway, arms crossed. He was facing outside. *Good.*

Keira kept her eyes fixed on him as she dropped the slip of paper through the gap. It spiraled down, twirling through the air, and landed in the middle of the seat. Keira carefully lowered the hatch back into place, then slunk away from it.

"What's happening?" Zoe's voice was low and husky with dust.

Keira couldn't spare the breath to explain, so she pressed a finger to her lips, begging for silence. Zoe gave a stony-faced nod.

Doors continued to slam as the rooms on either side of them were searched. Keira waited, counting seconds in her mind. The footsteps were growing more agitated. The commander barked out a string of instructions—*search the convenience store, look in the trees*—but his increasing frustration was palpable. Like she'd suspected, it only took a moment for three of the men to return to Keira's room.

"Search it again," the commander said, and his voice suggested there would be no leniency for failure. "Look in every crack. She can't have just vanished."

Come on. Come on.

Keira inclined her ear toward the hatch as footsteps spread out through the room again. Then, just like she'd hoped: "There's a note."

"Give it to me." The commander was silent for a second as he read it. "Was this here before?"

Keira closed her eyes. She was certain they would hear her racing heart in the silence.

"I—I didn't see—"

"Damn it." A fist slammed into the wall. It would leave a hole, Keira suspected. "The receptionist lied to us. She already left. You two—watch the motel. She might still come back. The rest of you, follow me."

There was a crackle. A communications unit being turned on, Keira thought. The commander's voice continued to echo through the ceiling cavity, even as he left the room. "All available personnel, meet at the turnoff just before the overpass. Stay discreet. Await further orders."

The room's door closed a final time. Keira dropped her head and let it rest on the rough wood beam. Clumps of dust clung to her skin and itched her, but she held still, listening. It didn't sound like anyone had stayed inside the room.

But the motel was still being watched. They would need another way out.

Keira waited until the screech of tires told her the vans were leaving, then shuffled to sit up on the support beam. The nest containing her old belongings was just behind her. She picked through the items, ultimately deciding to leave the matches and charcoal where they were but pocketing the cash and newspaper clippings.

Then Keira raised Mason's light. It was small and dim and only managed to light about ten feet of the ceiling's cavity. There were no walls that she could see. It should be theoretically possible to crawl the entire length of the building.

She kept her voice to a whisper as she turned back to her friends. "We're going to head for the opposite end of the motel."

"Not that I'm complaining or anything," Zoe said, "but I just want to remind everyone that I was freshly showered just ten minutes ago."

"Yeah." Keira couldn't repress an apologetic smile. Zoe's damp hair was full of cobwebs and dust. "Sorry."

"Also my pizza is now making friends with the ground, which honestly feels like a crime."

"It had anchovies mixed with pineapple," Mason said, shuffling around as they prepared to crawl along the narrow beams. "I'd say it met a justified end."

CHAPTER 32

THE PASSAGE ALONG THE motel's length was agonizing. Keira couldn't be certain exactly where the suited men were stationed, and some of the rooms beneath them were still occupied by irate visitors, so they couldn't afford to make any kind of noise.

The rough wood beams worked splinters into her palms and snagged threads loose from her clothes. The dust was smothering. Outside would be bitingly cold, she knew, but the roof seemed to cling to warmth, making her feel uncomfortably hot and turning her mouth and throat dry.

Keira led the way as she used Mason's flashlight to illuminate their path. The roof wasn't high and she had to crawl, pausing frequently to navigate around vertical beams that blocked her path. Cobwebs clung to her. As she stopped to flick a spider aside, she raised her flashlight to check their progress. The motel's end was in sight.

Her muscles burned from crawling in cramped conditions for so long and her knees would likely have some bruises. But they were on the other side of the reception area, and Keira thought that might be far enough.

She found a roof access panel in among the pink insulation and dropped onto her stomach to pry it up. She moved slowly, afraid there might be someone in the room below, but the bed was neatly made and there was no sign of luggage in the space.

"This is it," she whispered as Mason and Zoe crept up behind her. "Follow behind me. Stay quiet. We'll probably need to run. We might even be forced to split up. If that happens, find the drainage ditch again, okay? We'll meet up inside."

"Got it," Mason said.

Zoe muttered, "I swear I never would have suggested this trip if I'd known it would involve so much running."

Keira opened the hatch completely. She slipped through the gap. With no chair below, there was more of a drop, and she lowered herself from the support beams until her cut arm couldn't take it anymore, then let go.

Even though she landed carefully, she still made a soft thud on impact. Keira grit her teeth as she slipped over to the chair and carried it back to the ceiling access.

Zoe came through next, and Mason took a second to close the hatch behind them, so their escape route wouldn't be detected. Keira returned the chair to the room's corner, then crossed to the window and twitched back one corner of the curtains.

Flecks of rain coated the glass. She could see half of the parking lot, with reception jutting out of the row of rooms to their left. Its barred window allowed a glimpse inside. Mel sat hunched at her desk. Her lamp's light painted her in unnatural shadows. She was facing away, toward Keira's original room.

"Quietly," Keira reminded the others. "Keep to the shadows."

The door was designed to open from the inside without a key. Keira nudged it open and edged her way through the narrow gap she'd created. Half her attention stayed on Mel's silhouette. The other half of her focus was used to scan for the two guards that would be stationed somewhere nearby. As she stepped out of the room, she saw them. They were at least sixty feet away, at the edge of the floodlight's circle. One of them slowly turned to scan the highway, the convenience store, and the trees surrounding the motel's rear. The other had his attention fixed on Room 108, like Mel.

Keira waited, breath held, until the first guard was turned far enough away that she thought they wouldn't attract attention, then began moving.

Zoe and Mason followed close behind. They moved at a quick lope: not quite running, but as fast as they could go without making noise. Cold rain coated her face and arms within seconds, but Keira was grateful for its muffling and shielding effects.

They aimed for the lanky trees surrounding the motel. Keira didn't stop once they were inside but led her friends off at an angle to put as much room between them and the motel as she could.

Even through her ragged breathing, the tapping rain, and the rustle from the branches she pushed through, Keira strained to listen for foreign sounds. Cars rattled along the highway and someone laughed as they exited a takeout place. No one yelled. There were no rapid footsteps except for her friends'.

Still, she didn't take chances but led them on a weaving path through backroads. Her subconscious remembered the area, even if she didn't, and kept her away from dead ends. She didn't dare stop until even the highway's noise faded into the distance.

They stumbled to a halt and leaned their backs against an office's brick wall. Zoe, gasping, muttered repeated curses under her breath. Mason ran his fingers through his damp, dusty hair to get it away from his face.

"I think we're okay." Keira couldn't fight the smile that grew over her face. The relief was euphoric. "We should be fine."

"Yes, but at what cost?" Zoe, grimacing, pressed a hand to the stitch in her side.

Mason asked, "Should I try Adage again?"

"Not yet." Keira's eyes turned toward a dark, familiar wall in the distance. She'd felt her subconscious drawing her back toward the cemetery during their escape, and she hadn't tried to stop it. "I think we're going to get your car back, Mason."

"Sorry, what?" Zoe's eyes were squinted as she tried to catch her breath. "I thought we unanimously agreed that was a terrible idea."

"I'm pretty sure we can do this." Keira rubbed the dust from her hands onto her jeans. "It would take Adage at least an hour to reach us, even if he answered his phone right now. And every minute we spend waiting out here gives those people a chance to find us. We won't be safe going through the gates, but if we can climb over the cemetery's wall again…"

"Won't we be, like, shot on sight?" Zoe asked.

Mason made a faint, uncomfortable noise in the back of his throat.

"The *on sight* part is the bit that counts. I don't think we'll be seen. The note I dropped in the hotel room said I'd be at the overpass."

"Sorry," Mason said. "Which overpass?"

"No idea. But I assumed there had to be *some* kind of overpass nearby. And apparently, I was right. They've gone there in the hopes that they can trap me. *All* of them."

"Oh," Zoe said, her eyebrows rising.

"*All available units,*" Mason murmured.

"There might be some left behind," Keira said. "Someone to guard the cemetery's gates. Those two at the motel. But it will be a fraction of what was here before. We have a very narrow window to get your car back, and it's right now."

Mason took a quick, tight breath, then said, "Okay. I'll trust you."

"Good." Keira silently prayed that his faith wouldn't be misplaced. "Look for crates, boxes, anything sturdy enough to climb on."

As they wove through the backstreets at the edge of the suburb, they snagged up two empty milk crates from behind a dumpster and a small pallet from the back of a store. Their path was winding but led them inexorably toward their destination.

The cemetery was positioned right at the edge of town, with

empty fields, parks, and wooded areas surrounding it on most sides. They had to cross a major road to reach the wall. Keira's senses were on high alert as she watched for the shimmer of white vans in the distance. The distraction seemed to be holding, at least. Whatever overpass the suited men had found their way toward was keeping them occupied.

The rain was growing heavier. Keira's hair clung to the back of her neck and her clothes felt heavy. She wove around the cemetery until they reached the section of the wall that faced the park. That would put them as close to the parking lot as they were likely to get without being in sight of the front entrance. The three of them huddled in the shadows cast there, between the manicured shrubs and the brick wall, and stacked their milk crates and pallet into a makeshift ramp that likely wouldn't last under any sort of strenuous testing. That was okay, though; they only needed it once.

"Mason, if you give me your keys, I'll bring the car around to pick the both of you up," Keira whispered.

His expression, which had been tense with nerves, tightened. "I thought we agreed we wouldn't go into the cemetery alone."

"We agreed *you* wouldn't," Keira countered. "I can be quick and quiet. I'll be out in two minutes."

"Whatever danger this place might have for me, it's magnified a hundred times for you," Mason retorted. He took an unsteady breath, then continued in a softer voice. "I know I'm nowhere near as competent as you are in a crisis, but at least give me a *chance* to help if something goes wrong."

"I, also, have a craving for death," Zoe added.

Keira glanced between them, frowning. They matched her expression.

Then she remembered the spike of terror she'd felt at the idea of Mason entering the cemetery by himself. Of being caught while Keira was powerless to help him.

He felt the same way about her. If it came down to it, they might not be able to save each other if things went truly wrong. But they at least wanted to *try*.

Keira reached for both of her friends and pulled them into a damp hug. It was strangely warm and soggy and comforting all at once. "Okay. Okay. But you have to promise me to be careful."

"We will," Mason said.

"Follow my instructions."

"To the letter," Zoe promised.

"Okay. Let's do this."

Mason stood guard at the ramp's base while Keira scrambled up it first. She hesitated as her head came level with the top of the bricks and she stretched to peer over.

The cemetery was still open in the evening, though there were very few visitors. Lights, spaced at regular intervals between the manicured trees, illuminated the fields in a soft glow. It would have felt comforting if Keira didn't know what was hidden beneath the surface.

She didn't try to activate her second sight but skipped her gaze across the umbrella-bearing stragglers still in the cemetery. None of them wore uniforms. None seemed in any way watchful. She thought she'd been right in her hope and that anyone who might have been standing guard inside the cemetery would have raced to the meeting point to search for her.

Keira lifted herself up and over the bricks. She dropped as lightly as she could but still felt the reverberations run through her legs as she landed. One of the closer visitors lifted his head at the sound, but Keira was swallowed by shadows at the edge of the garden and he turned back to his path without seeing her.

The cemetery's emotions felt like a physical pressure on her skin. Keira swallowed, bracing against them. The sensations were growing easier to shield against as she spent more time in the graveyard, though they would never be impossible to ignore.

Two more thuds came at Keira's back, signaling that her friends had arrived. Zoe and Mason stayed close behind her as they crept out of the garden and joined the main path.

To their right were the parking lot and entrance gates. Keira thought she could even see their car, half-hidden behind the immaculate shrubs. It didn't seem like it had been touched, which was a good sign. The men in suits might have assumed she'd arrived on foot.

Keira led them past the rows of identical gravestones at a quick walk. She kept her head down but her eyes moving. She couldn't hear any sounds of alarm. An older couple sent them a curious glance as they passed, and Keira realized they were still caked in dust and traces of dried blood. It was too late to do anything about that now. They were halfway to the car.

It was impossible to ignore how toxic the ground was. Keira

had felt it on her first visit without truly realizing what it signified. The emotions bubbled up around her then, though, and it was almost like she could hear the screams of the chained figures.

She hadn't planned on opening her second sight once they were inside the cemetery, but, at that moment she couldn't stop herself. She cast a final furtive glance around them, then pulled on the muscle behind her eyes and felt the veil lift.

CHAPTER 33

FIGURES SHIMMERED INTO LIFE around her. The shades, locked onto the earth by chains that vanished into their burial sites, twisted as they screamed. One to her left was so close that she could have reached out a hand and run her fingers through the smokelike form.

Keira's mouth was dry. Her heart ached until it felt like it was going to burst. The first time she'd seen these spirits, she'd only felt fear and repulsion. Now, she was filled with grief. The gaping mouths no longer looked as though they were trying to bite her but like they were crying out for help. The twitching fingers, locked at their sides by their bindings, seemed to be begging for release. They writhed, but not with malice, only with misery.

A hot tear formed a track through the dust on her cheek, and Keira was glad the rain would disguise it. She wondered which one of the figures belonged to the older woman who had tried to warn her about what was happening at the hospital. The shades were as identical as their gravestones; all individuality had been stripped from them as they were shaped into unnatural forms that only barely resembled humans.

I'm going to help. I promise. I'll find a way to help.

Somehow.

They were nearly at the parking lot. Mason pulled the car keys out of his pocket. He looked impossibly stressed; his pulse leaped in his throat and perspiration dotted his pale face. He was keeping it well contained, though; his strides were steady and his jaw set.

Zoe, more comfortable with tense situations, had managed an easy lilt to her steps, even though Keira could feel the undercurrent of tension masked by it.

Keira nudged her arm. "Put some mud over the license plates. Just in case. I'll meet you there in a second."

"Keira—" Mason cut himself off, but his eyes still pleaded with her.

"In a second," she promised.

As her friends continued toward the car, Keira turned back to the graveyard.

What do I need to do to set you free?

A shade stood ahead of her, its jaw twitching. The spectral chains pulled across its body as it strained against them.

Keira's chest was too tight to breathe properly. She set her feet in the soft grass covering the grave and pulled down the mental walls she'd built to shield herself.

Talk to me. Tell me what I have to do.

The emotions hit her hard and from every direction. Her skin prickled as though pure electricity coursed over it. The air in her lungs seemed to turn to ice, and she choked on it.

The figure ahead thrashed. She thought, at the very edge of her hearing, she could detect the chains clinking as they shuddered against one another.

Please. Show me.

She reached out. The gaping jaws ahead of her stretched wider, wider than any living human could have survived, until the black pit inside seemed to contain an infinity.

Keira's fingertips touched the chains. Her skin burned on contact, ice and fire at once, racing up her arm. She jolted back, shuddering.

The pain didn't immediately fade. Her hand looked normal, but it ached as though she'd plunged it into liquid ice. That couldn't be happening to any of the visiting guests. Pleasant Grove had so many visitors that there would have been complaints if the shades could hurt anyone who stumbled onto a grave or reached an arm out too far. No—this was exclusive to Keira. She'd made herself vulnerable by opening herself to the spirit.

She looked back up at the shade. It quivered. It seemed to be straining backward, against the little give its bindings allowed it.

It doesn't want to hurt me.

Fog coalesced around them. The night was cold, but not cold enough to justify the icy chill that suddenly rolled through the cemetery. Keira strained to see through the swaying mass of dead to glimpse the other visitors. None of them seemed to notice that mist was suddenly swirling around their legs. Keira exhaled and felt the condensation turn to ice particles on her lips.

It's the shades. They're turning the cemetery cold. Why? Fear…or maybe hope? Or are they trying to warn me, to drive me out?

She couldn't afford to linger much longer. She'd already risked too much just delaying that long. Still, she couldn't tear her eyes from the shade ahead of her.

There had to be an answer. An explanation for what had been done to them. A way to break the chains.

The ache in her arm was fading, but it still sparked with pins and needles. Her whole body did, in fact. The air was alive with electricity. She didn't think she could afford to touch the chains—or the shade's body—too many more times. Not without causing genuine damage.

What am I supposed to do?

Maybe she hadn't known, even in her past life. If she had, she would have at least cleared some of them. The cemetery—the parts she could see, at least—was fully occupied.

Keira's tongue was heavy. Her fingers were growing numb as the chill engulfed her. She tried to stay focused, but it was growing harder to think as the electrical pressure grew denser all around.

It has to come back to the chains. Those aren't natural. They're the only things holding the dead here.

She dropped to her knees. The lush grass felt sharp under her hands as she crept toward the point in the center of the grave where the chains vanished into the earth. They looped around the shade's body, tangling and overlapping, before weaving together just before entering the soil. There was no visible disturbance to the grass where the spectral bindings passed through, no burning, no bare patches. But as Keira reached her hand toward them, she felt sparks of energy fizzing off the metal.

How deep do they go? Is there an anchor holding them in place? Something that I can dig up, maybe?

She pressed her hands into the ground just ahead of where the chains dipped into the earth. The prickly grass surrounded her palms. She dug her fingers down until their tips touched earth, then focused.

There was energy under the ground, she was certain. The same kind that radiated off the shade. It didn't just go straight down, though.

Keira's fingers shook as she dragged them through the grass, tracing the path the energy took. It traveled directly down at first, for perhaps half a foot, but then turned toward her. Even through inches of soil, she could feel it: a clear line of electricity, running toward the walkway behind Keira. Like a ribbon through the earth.

She crawled as she followed it. Faintly, she was aware of the few lingering visitors sending her uncertain glances. If any of them went to the guards at the gates, she would be as good as done. But she felt as though she was close to something. *Very* close. If she just followed it a bit farther…

The electricity changed just before reaching the path. It speared off to either side, running parallel to the edges of the graves, and became a hundred times stronger. As Keira pushed her fingertips into the soft, icy soil, she felt her breath being sucked out of her by the sheer force of it.

The spectral figures surrounding her redoubled their efforts to twist free from their bindings. Jaws stretched impossibly wide. The distant, not-quite-there clink of chains grew overwhelming. She'd found something significant. And they knew it.

What? What's under here?

Keira pressed her fingers deeper into the earth and gasped. She lifted her head, glancing from grave to grave. The cemetery's neat layout—unassuming if uncanny—suddenly took on new significance. The graves were placed in tight lines and segmented into manageable sections.

For efficiency's sake.

The graveyard's layout struck her as uncannily like a circuit board. Because that wasn't far from the truth. Each grave had a line of chains running from it and connecting to a main line. Those main lines traveled farther. Where, she wasn't sure.

Keira's mouth was dry. Her head throbbed. Her heart ached in her chest.

The spectral energy wasn't a side effect of the shades' presence—it was the entire reason they were here. It was being gathered. Concentrated. Carried somewhere. Unknown to every visitor who stepped inside its walls, cabling ran under the beautifully maintained lawn, and it connected every single burial site.

A wild desperation hit Keira unlike anything she'd felt before.

She began clawing into the damp dirt. Clods of grass spun away from her as she dug deeper and deeper, following the hiss of electric current into the soil. It wasn't deep. Only another few inches down. Her breathing was ragged as it caught in her throat.

Somewhere behind her, a woman began muttering. Mason's voice cut in, tight with panic. "It's fine! She's my friend. I'll take care of her." He was running distraction. That was good. She only needed a minute more.

The very dirt seemed alive with the energy infused in it. It stuck to Keira's hands and burned when it got under her nails. She tried to swallow and tasted only tacky froth. Deeper and deeper, her hole exposed a pit of heavy, loamy earth, shockingly dark against the jewel green of the grass. Worms writhed in the soil she dragged away. They felt the energy too.

Chains rattled on all sides as the shades grew into a frenzy. The mist swallowed her until she couldn't see more than a few feet in any direction, and it was possible to imagine she was cast away on an island, perfectly isolated. She didn't even dare to blink as her freezing hands tore into earth.

And then she found it.

A cable ran through the soil, exactly where she'd pictured it. It was nearly as wide around as her wrist. A large knot formed where the spectral chains had been lashed to the cable. That sight would be repeated every few feet, she knew: one for each grave. Funneling their energy into one source.

She touched a fingertip to the cable and flinched. It burned her on touch, just like the chains on the shade had.

This was it, though. This was why the shades had been restrained. Why the cemetery's owners wanted her dead. What her life had led to.

The cable looked heavy. She bent down to see it better through the pooling fog. It would be strong, yes, but she thought she might be stronger.

Breaking the cable could very well kill her.

But she still wanted to try.

CHAPTER 34

KEIRA REACHED BOTH HANDS into the hole she'd carved. Her skin seemed to want to creep off her flesh as she drew nearer to the cable. Icelike fog burned her throat with each tight, agonizing breath.

Please, let this work.

Her nerve endings seemed to catch on fire as she touched the cord. The sensation raced up her arms, like a sudden, intense grip had formed over her skin and squeezed tighter with every second. Keira's teeth clenched and the hairs across her head all stood on end. Her vision turned gray.

Please...

She pulled on the cable with all of her strength.

It began to peel up out of the earth. Clumps of dirt seemed to vibrate around it as Keira's fingers dug into the black casing. She twisted the cable, hoping the pressure might be enough to break it.

The chains rang like a symphony around her, and for the first time, the screams broke through the veil between the living and the dead. A thousand voices joined in wordless, howling cries.

Her face was wet with rain and tears. Her nerve endings screamed. She twisted the cable, pulling, tearing, and some of the casing broke.

Hissing, fizzing lines of electricity arced out of the tear in the cable. They hit her skin, and although they vanished on contact, she felt them *inside* her. Running along her bones. Through her muscles. Passing into her lungs and out of her mouth with each gasping breath. They were living things. Like eels squirming in the damp gaps between her bones and flesh.

Keira clenched her teeth harder and tasted blood. The tear in the cable widened. The electricity, which had only come out in sparks until then, flooded into her.

Her vision shot to white, then black. At first, she didn't know what had happened. Her hands were empty. She was on her back, she realized, facing the bleak sky and the heavy, dripping rain.

And lightning was trapped inside her body.

It knocked me out. That makes sense, I guess. The lightning bit, not so much.

She didn't know how long she'd lain there. It couldn't have been long, though. Only a few seconds. Mason was calling her name as he tried to rouse her.

"Don't touch me." She wasn't sure how Mason heard her—the words had come out as a voiceless gasp—but he pulled back regardless, his hands still outstretched in case she changed her mind.

"I'm sorry," he whispered. "But we really, *really* have to go. Right now."

Through the fog, she heard another voice. Someone yelling. They'd been found.

She refused to take Mason's hand but rolled onto her knees and then onto her feet. The electricity still rocked through her, jittering along every limb as it looked for a way out, and she didn't want to let it hurt either of her companions.

"Quick," Zoe hissed. "He's coming."

Keira could barely see. Between the rain, the dark, and the sparks that moved over her vision, the world had transformed into an alien place. But she could see her friends, one on each side of her like guides, and followed them blindly.

The shades twisted and howled. She wasn't sure if she could still hear their voices or if her ears were full of the echoes of their screams. But she could hear something else: Footsteps behind her. A voice, shouting for her to stop. Her subconscious emerged from the stupor and screamed in the back of her mind: *Run. Run. Run!*

Her strides lengthened. She barely had any air left in her lungs. Her head pounded. She staggered, first on wet grass and then on wet asphalt, and then, abruptly, they were at the car.

Mason dragged the back door open for her and Keira threw herself inside. Their bags scattered over the floor as she shoved them out of the way. Two more doors slammed as Mason and Zoe leaped into the front seats.

"Stay low," Zoe whispered. "Stay hidden."

Keira slid down into the footwell. The car rumbled as Mason

pulled out of the parking lot. She felt every bump and jolt as he took the corner too fast.

"Keep down," Zoe whispered, her voice squeaky with tension. "Keep down…keep down…"

Then Keira felt tingles race across her spine. She gasped as the overwhelming pressure of the cemetery faded.

That was the gates. We're through. We're out.

Confirming her suspicion, Zoe turned to look behind them, breathing heavily as she ran a hand over her face. "Okay, that was close."

"Mm" was all Mason could manage. His knuckles were white as he turned the car onto the main road. He was still driving too fast.

Keira rose up so she could look through the rear window. The gates were fading into the darkness and rain behind them. She could see two men in rainsuits huddled together at the gates, their arms jerking as they argued furiously. They kept glancing toward the road but made no move to leave the cemetery's entrance.

"I put mud over the license plates, like you told me to," Zoe said. Her owlish eyes glimmered in the car's dull lights. "I don't think that guy who spotted us actually recognized you, Keira. I think he was, like, an intern or something. He was trying to stop you from digging holes in the lawn."

Mason took a sharp breath. "Vans ahead. Dip down, Keira."

She slid back into the footwell. The space was cramped and musty, but she pressed her head against the back of the driver's seat, trying to be as small as possible.

From her position, she could see a sliver of Zoe's face. She almost looked calm except for the shimmer of sweat and the dogged, wide-eye stare fixed dead ahead. "Gun it," she whispered.

"Absolutely not." Mason's own voice was hoarse and barely audible, as though he was afraid the people in the vans would hear him. "We're going to be the most nondescript, law-abiding car possible and hope the vans pass us by without even looking at us."

Keira pressed her eyes closed. She could hear the engines like the rumble of thunder on the horizon. They were going fast. Racing closer. Right on top of them—

Mason's car rocked as the vans sped past in the opposite direction. Keira counted three of them. She waited for signs indicating they were slowing or turning, but the motors faded until she couldn't even hear their echoes.

Mason released a shuddering breath he must have been holding. "It's okay," he said. "We're past them."

"I still say we should have gunned it," Zoe muttered.

Keira gingerly climbed back into her seat. Every movement jarred her. She felt like she was on the verge of falling apart, like a poorly constructed clay sculpture.

"You all right?" Zoe asked, twisting around in her seat.

"I think so." Keira examined her hands. They were caked with loamy earth, numb. She tried flexing the fingers and felt pins and needles prickle through them.

Electricity in my bones. In my blood. In my sinew.

Mason glanced at her through the rearview mirror. "Are you sure? You don't look good. What happened?"

"I figured it out." She swallowed thickly. "Zoe, remember how your contact—the guy who's scared of airplanes—thought Artec's logo had something to do with renewable energy? Well, he was right."

"Wait, seriously?" Zoe looked incredulous. "How does that even... *Oh.*"

"They're harvesting power from the dead," Keira said, answering Zoe's horrified glance. "Ghosts draw energy from the ether. Normally they use it themselves—to materialize, to make the air colder—but Artec has found a way to harness it and drain it from them as quickly as they absorb it. That's why the cemetery is full of shades. They're more efficient at gathering energy than a regular spirit is."

"Damn," Zoe said. "So they're being paid by grieving families to inter their loved ones, then they're turning around and using those same loved ones as unwilling labor to produce power that they...what? Sell?"

"I'm assuming so."

"It turns out the real enemy is capitalism after all," Zoe muttered. "That is so disgustingly typical."

"So there's no supervillain, world-ending scheme behind this." Mason looked exhausted. "Just greed. Renewable energy is already a valuable industry and will only be worth more as time passes. And Artec's cemetery must have very few expenses compared to solar panels or hydro. Just the cost of the land and the burials, which is already being paid for by the families."

"And it's scalable," Keira added. "Assuming one cemetery is

profitable, ten will be even more so. The only limit on their rate of expansion is how quickly the local population dies."

For a second, none of them said anything. Keira watched the trees flash past her window as the ache in her chest grew worse and worse.

"There's nothing we can do legally, is there?" Zoe asked. "I mean, there are rules against tampering with corpses. If we could somehow prove Pleasant Grove was trapping ghosts against their will, we could stop it. But…"

"*How* can you prove something like that?" Keira finished for her. "The chains around the spirits are spectral. The cables are real, at least; I could touch them and break them, which meant they were made of real rubber and wires. But as far as any regulatory body would be concerned, it's not illegal to run wire around your cemetery, even if it is unusual. We're back to that same problem of needing to prove ghosts exist before anything legal could be done."

"So…what are we going to do?" Zoe asked.

"Right now?" Mason worked his jaw. "I'm getting us back to Blighty. I'll hide the car in a back shed, just in case. Then we're going to actually eat a real meal. And shower. And change into clean clothes. And maybe sleep for a few hours. We'll figure the rest out after."

Keira flexed her hands again.

Touching the cabling in the cemetery had felt like being struck by lightning. She wouldn't have been shocked to discover she'd been caked in soot like some cartoon character post-electrocution.

Instead, the face that stared back at her in the rearview mirror was pale and had dust and cobwebs tangled in its wet hair. Otherwise, she looked no different than she had before.

Underneath, though…

Under the skin. In the nerves and tendons and bones.

Her flesh was alive with lightning. It coalesced in her chest, in the space around her lungs, and pulsed into her limbs with every beat of her heart.

It had come very close to killing her, she was aware. A few more seconds would have been enough. She was lucky she'd collapsed backward and not on top of the cabling.

She was overcharged. Filled to her limit with spectral energy until it threatened to unravel her very DNA. She was fairly sure she could push it out of herself if she tried, press her hands into the earth or let it fill her lungs and then exhale, and gradually release the excess.

Instead, she held on to it, even as it set every bone in her body jangling.

Keira dabbed her tongue over her cracked lips. "I'm all for heading back to Blighty, but we're not going straight home. Take me to Dane Crispin's house."

CHAPTER 35

IT TOOK SLIGHTLY OVER an hour to reach Blighty. Keira sat rigidly straight for the entire drive, her hands clenching and relaxing in her lap. The energy was growing hotter with every second she held it. What had started as lightning in her bones began to coalesce into something more like an inferno infusing every fiber of her body. She felt as though she could have melted the car if she'd released even just a little of it.

Mason kept sending her uncertain glances in the mirror, but Keira stayed quiet and still. The energy didn't want to be contained. It kept looping through her limbs before coursing back into her chest, looking for a way out.

It was wild and raw. Powerful. Terrifying.

And it was valuable, she knew. Incredibly so.

The clock on the car's dashboard said it was approaching midnight when the scenery outside the window changed to something familiar. They passed the sign marking the driveway to the church and Keira's own home. The road looped them through a tunnel of tall, bare-branched trees before letting them into the town's center. Mason sent her another quick, searching glance as he neared the roundabout.

"You're sure?" he asked.

"Yes." She didn't try to hide a wolfish smile. "I've got some work to do."

He nodded once, then turned down the road that led to Dane Crispin's house.

The mansion's high fences rose through the fog that permeated Blighty's roads. Some kind of skittish bird took off from the vines, its wings creating a black silhouette against the starry sky. The energy was fighting harder to escape, and Keira clenched her teeth as she struggled to keep it contained—a breath in, a breath out. Then the car drew to a stop and the engine turned off as Mason parked by the gates.

Keira shoved her way out of the car before the others had even undone their seat belts. They were tired. Probably sore and covered in bruises too. Not to mention still wearing damp clothes.

All of the same could be said for Keira, but she barely felt it under the electric roar traveling through her tendons and bones. She shoved on the gate and tiny sparks escaped her fingers as they pressed against the metal. She swallowed and refocused.

Hold it. Just a little more.

There were lights on in the foyer of Dane's house. She was glad he was nocturnal by nature.

Zoe and Mason jogged to catch up with her long strides as she pressed through the overgrown plants to reach the mansion. The doors were closed and the windows too grimy to make out anything beyond, but she thought she heard a whisper of voices coming from inside.

"Hey, Dane!" Keira yelled as she slammed her shoulder into the door, shoving it open. "You better not be busy because this place is overdue for some cleaning."

Two pale faces turned to stare at her. Dane Crispin and Harry Kennard sat on opposite sides of a small round table. Six candles, all different sizes and shapes, were arranged in a circle between them. Several dozen more candles had been scattered around the foyer—poised precariously on side tables, beneath the portraits lining the walls, and in clusters on the floor. The whole room was cast in a sickly, uneasy glow of flickering lights.

"Hello." Harry looked entirely nonplussed. He tilted his head a fraction, shifting his black fringe away from his eyes. "We're conducting a séance. Would you like to join us?"

From the grim exhaustion on Dane's face and his defeated posture, Keira suspected the séance had been entirely Harry's idea and that Dane had simply not been willing to turn him away.

"Sure," Keira said, and cracked her knuckles. Sparks of sharp blue light fizzled around her hands. "But I'll be doing my own kind of séance tonight. Hold on."

Opening her second sight no longer felt like pulling on a muscle. It had always been an effort before. Now, overcharged as she was, it felt more like releasing her hold on a veil. The mansion's secret denizens flooded into her vision, clearer and crisper than she'd ever seen them before.

Six of them clustered around Dane, their jaws stretched wide as their needlelike teeth burrowed into his throat and shoulders. Another two hung around Harry, prodding and exploring his skin with long fingers.

She bared her teeth as she charged toward the spirits around Dane. They paid her no attention…until her hands plunged into their chests. She found the bundles of threads inside the nearest two and wrapped her hands around them.

What had hurt her the first time she tried touching the threads was now barely a tickle. The parasitic spirits lifted their heads as they felt her grasp tighten around them. Two sets of nervous eyes turned toward her. One struggled to pull away. The other stretched its jaws wide in a voiceless howl. Keira didn't let either of them go as she squeezed tighter.

"Good riddance," she told them, then sent a hissing, crackling burst of electricity into them.

The forms contorted like putty sculptures being crushed. Heads heaved backward as their chests became concave. Their agony only lasted for a second before their entire forms disintegrated into mist. It pooled around Keira's arms before fading into the ether.

The other spirits gathered around Dane stared at her with blank, stricken eyes. They turned as they attempted to escape her reach.

"No, you don't," Keira said, lunging forward to seize a third spirit. She dispatched it with the same ease as the first two, then turned to examine the room, breathing quickly.

The spirits had tried to fade out of sight. She could still sense them, though, like a distant shimmer against the room's shadows. Keira narrowed in on one and willed it to stay still as she circled around the discarded furniture to reach it.

The spirit flickered back into sight as soon as Keira touched it. She recognized the woman who had antagonized her so aggressively on her first night there. Her thin lips and pale eyes flickered in and out of sight as she tried to fade again, but Keira pinned her in place as she reached into her chest to take hold of the threads that kept her whole.

She squeezed, forcing pure spectral energy into the threads and crushing them in one motion. The woman contorted as her hands reached toward Keira, attempting to gouge holes across her face. She barely lasted a second before her form vanished into a swirl of fading mist.

"Hello, Dane," Mason said, calm and polite. "Hi, Harry. How's your night going?"

"It's getting more interesting," Harry said, matter-of-fact.

"Um" was all Dane managed. He'd keeled forward in his chair, one hand pressed to his chest, his eyes wide.

He must be able to feel the connection to the spirits being broken, Keira realized.

She turned to examine the foyer. The spirits had all fled the space. That wouldn't save them, though. She could still sense their presences like an invisible pull leading her deeper into the house.

"Stay here," she told Dane. "I'll be done soon."

Zoe yawned as she pulled two new chairs up to the table. Mason, hands on his hips as he examined the scene, said, "I'm going to get us something to drink. Dane, did you want tea or coffee?"

"Coffee." He blinked furiously. "Please."

Keira grinned as she followed long hallways through the crumbling building. She felt as though she were flying as she took corners in stride and leaped around obstacles. Dark wallpaper and looming portraits passed in a blur. The spirits tried to scatter when they sensed her coming but never made it far. Again and again she plunged her hand into their chests, eradicating them in a heartbeat, sometimes without even slowing her stride.

Some tried to hide. Some raised their arms in an effort to shield themselves. She would have been tempted to feel pity for them if she didn't know that they had been spending the last decades of their existence leeching from their descendant.

Others tried to fight back and sunk their needlelike teeth into her arms. It ached like pure ice was being poured into her veins, but they never managed to hold on for long before Keira swiped them away into mist.

She cleared one wing of the house, then turned back to retrace her path. Energy still flowed through her, as hot and fiery as an inferno in her chest. She passed through the foyer in search of more spirits and saw her four friends seated around the séance table, lit only by candlelight. Mason was pouring drinks from a delicate china teapot. Zoe lifted her own cup in a *cheers* as Keira passed by, heading for the massive, carpeted staircase that would carry her into the upper floors.

It was like a sixth sense crawled through her skin, leading her inexorably to each cowering specter. Two of them had tried to hide in Dane's bedroom, which was strewn with discarded clothes and loose blankets. Another hid in a secret compartment behind a bookcase. It took Keira a couple of minutes of tugging on the thick novels to find the one that opened the door. Still more attempted to squeeze between walls and under floors, but she was able to pull them to herself like tugging on a gauzy strip of fabric blowing in the wind.

Her seemingly endless energy was starting to wane as she finished in the upper levels and bounded back down to the foyer. Dane and Mason were engaged in quiet conversation. Zoe and Harry had pulled their chairs a little distance away and were embroiled in a slightly more heated discussion of their own. Keira heard the words *Mothman* and *enormous bug zapper* float out of the argument, and decided not to ask anything further.

"Hey," Zoe called as she spotted Keira on the stairs. "Nearly done?"

"Just a few left." She was breathless and dotted with perspiration but still smiled. The sheer speed at which she'd covered that half of the house had left her euphoric.

"Take a look at this," Zoe said. She pointed up to the walls of portraits. "Their eyes fade out each time you get one."

"Huh." Keira tilted her head. "That's neat. Creepy but neat."

Above her, the portraits were changing subtly. The eyes, which had seemed to stare down at the house's occupants with an unsettling level of perception, were growing cloudy. The irises and pupils bled out until the eyes were a milky, blind white.

Their skin seemed to be changing too. It was growing papery and sunken, closer to how the shriveled, bony spirits themselves appeared. It was possible, she supposed, to be so attached to a family and a legacy that your identity became entwined with the mementos left from your life.

Keira recognized many of the altered portraits as belonging to spirits she'd already eradicated. Only a handful were left.

She turned to the last section of the house she had to cover. Her heightened sensitivity to the ghosts told her there were only a half dozen of the spirits left, and they were all huddled in the darkest section of the mansion. Keira rolled her shoulders as she headed toward the final passageway.

"That part of the house is collapsing—" Dane called.

"Cool," Keira responded before pushing through a cracked doorway.

Most parts of Crispin Manor had been neglected, but it was clear no human had been in this wing in quite some time. Fractured beams hung down from the ceiling, causing Keira to clamber and crawl to get around them. Doors hung off their hinges. Wallpaper was shredded from the walls and seams split along the carpet. Keira pressed a sleeve to her face as the smell of rot and mold began to hit her.

She pulled on her second sight once more. As the energy faded, her ease of using it bled away as well. She flexed, testing herself, and was pretty sure she had just enough of a charge left to deal with the remaining spirits.

The first was lurking in a hole that had been punched through the wall. It lunged at her, almost catching her off guard, and she had to duck to avoid taking the spiky teeth to her face. As it arced over her, she thrust her hand up and gripped its life-force.

You're done.

Tendrils of mist floated behind her as she strode forward again. Two were somewhere to her right. It took her a while to locate the doorway into a long-forgotten nursery.

Two bassinets had been abandoned there. If Keira had to guess, they had last been used during Dane's infancy. Thin, fluttering curtains were draped above them, moving in the cold wind coming through a broken window, and they gave the impression of being rocked as two of the parasitic specters leaned over the baskets, cooing into the rotting blankets and pillows.

"Hey," Keira said, coming up behind them. "Looking after some fake babies, huh? Hoping it'll soften my heart enough to make me hesitate so that you can ambush me?"

Almost on cue, the two twisted, bony women turned on her. Bulging eyes stretched papery skin as their grasping fingers reached for Keira.

They must have thought they could shock her into pulling away. Instead, Keira leaned forward, meeting them halfway, and unraveled their cores just as their howling faces grazed her own. She felt the chill of spectral energy, followed only by the soft dampness of thinning fog on her skin.

As she'd suspected, the bassinets were empty. All that remained was a cloth animal toy, partially tucked under the desiccated blankets.

Three ghosts left.

She could see them in her mind's eye. They were close. Even though her breathing was becoming labored and her limbs were growing heavy, she broke into a jog as she returned to the hunt.

CHAPTER 36

HER FOOTSTEPS ECHOED THROUGH the hallway. The sound reverberated off every cracking wall and exposed beam of wood as Keira chased one of the final three spirits. An older man fled from her. His face might have been full once, but death had distorted him until flaps of loose cheek skin hung in clumps beneath a thick beard.

He darted through a door. Keira tried the handle and found it was locked.

Clever. Maybe not clever enough, though.

She stepped back and angled her shoulder at the door. That part of the house had suffered massive water damage. The wood was bulging and rotting. She hit the door harder than she even needed to and released a thin laugh as the remains of the fractured wood barricade collapsed onto the floor.

The older man flickered weakly as he tried to fade out of her sight, but Keira fixed her gaze on him and compelled him to hold still. It only took a few short steps to cross the distance between them.

Done.

Mist swirled around her hand as she withdrew it from where the ghost's essence had resided. She took a breath to center herself as she prepared to restart the hunt, only to feel something sharp and piercing dig into her back.

Oh, clever.

One of the remaining spirits had stalked her while she was chasing the older man. She reached behind herself but her fingers only grazed icy air.

Sharp puncturing pains ran from the back of her neck and down her spine. The spirit was going to try to feed on her, she realized. It had guessed—correctly—that she would be unable to dispel it if it could drain enough of her remaining energy. And she only had seconds before the balance tipped in a direction she couldn't afford.

Keira grit her teeth and squeezed her eyes closed. She forced some of the remaining energy toward the spirit. It sent a shock wave through her skin. The needlepoint teeth tore away from her as the ghost was knocked free.

She turned in one deft movement and plunged her hand into its chest. The motions had become so familiar that she could have done it blind: grip the threads; squeeze; send in a surge of energy.

The ghost's form bulged and then collapsed, evaporating into condensation that would soon fade into the air.

That last push of power had taken more from her than she'd expected, and Keira staggered. She closed her eyes, breathing quickly as she reassessed.

She was almost out of the charge she'd gained from Pleasant Grove's cables. There was just enough for one more ghost, she thought.

There has to be.

There was only one left. And they were close.

Her leg muscles ached as she made them move again, carrying her back out of the office and into the decaying hallways. Her clothes were still damp. They'd been easy to ignore while the inferno roared, but now they made her feel heavy and chilled. She exhaled and her breath plumed in the thin moonlight that fought its way through the broken roof tiles.

One more. Just one.

It was growing harder to find the last spirit. She'd spent too much, too fast, and the last traces of energy were slipping out of her no matter how hard she tried to cling to them.

She couldn't falter now, though. Not when she was so close to freeing Dane. The infusion of stolen energy was the only thing making it possible to clear the manor, and she had precious little left.

Ahead, a grand staircase led up to a collapsing second floor. Spears of moonlight cut through the space at the top, and Keira had the uncomfortable, distinct impression that there was something up there watching her.

She was pretty sure the second floor wasn't in any way stable, but she couldn't afford to sit around and wait for better options to present themselves. Keira cracked the stiff joints in her neck, then set off toward the stairs at a jog.

The lowest steps groaned as she climbed them. The fourth step snapped entirely, and Keira had to clutch at the railing to keep herself from plunging through. She hung close to the banister, relying on the stronger wood at the stairs' edges, as she crept upward.

Two cold, gray eyes stared down at her. They were full of steel and malice. Keira met the hostile gaze as she neared the top of the stairs and saw what she was facing.

An enormous portrait hung opposite the landing, though its gilt frame was barely visible in the choking shadows. The man depicted inside looked enormous. A thick, luxurious coat had been tailored for his broad shoulders. A shimmering gray beard hung down past his broad jaw. And the eyes...

There was ice and iron in his gaze. It was the kind of look that belonged to a man who knew what he wanted and would go to any lengths to obtain it. Ethical or otherwise.

Keira's own eyes dropped to the inscription below the art. *Mortimer Crispin.*

She knew that name. He was the tycoon who had founded not just the Crispin estate and the mill, but the entire town of Blighty. Countless people had died in the mill under his oversight. But his ruthless tactics had made his family wealthy beyond imagination.

The portrait shifted subtly. Keira, on the edge of the landing, came close to slipping off the top step before she caught herself. Breathing hard, she clutched at the banister and squinted to see through the heavy shadows hung about the painting.

The image moved again, and Keira began to doubt her own eyes. The portrait seemed to come alive, twisting, and yet it didn't move at all.

"What..." She took a step closer.

The figure in the painting mirrored her movement.

An enormous ghost emerged from the artwork. The transparent skin stretched across his skull was sunken and mottled. The beard seemed to float as though suspended underwater. His broad shoulders led to arms that were inhumanly long. The fingers didn't end where they should, but extended into long, curved claws. It was impossible to tell where the flesh ended and the nails began.

His eyes had been steely gray in life. In death, they were empty pits of darkness. He opened his mouth to reveal the rows of viciously pointed teeth, longer than any others Keira had seen in the mansion.

"Mortimer," Keira whispered.

He'd become far more warped than any of the other parasitic specters. Probably, Keira realized, because he had started the family tradition and had been doing it for longer than any of the others. He was as old as the town itself.

Good thing I'm in the mood to kill some history.

Keira set her feet. Somehow, she doubted Mortimer would let her catch him as easily as some of his descendants had. But she had precious little time left to take advantage of the energy she'd stolen.

Although his skin had sunken and his bones had grown angular, he still felt far larger than any of the other spirits had. His head tilted back as he regarded her with disdain. Unlike the others, he wasn't afraid. He'd thought he was untouchable during life. And now, in death, he only believed that more.

Keira darted forward, trying to catch him by surprise, but he moved before she could reach him. The paint in the portrait shimmered as he raked his clawlike fingers through it, then he flickered along the hallway.

"Coward," Keira snarled, giving chase. She'd hoped the taunt would prompt some retaliation, but the thin, bloodless lips only spread wider into a wicked smile.

His form whipped in and out of sight as Keira fought to keep him in focus. It was a nearly impossible task: the roof in that part of the house barely existed, and angled columns of moonlight cut through the floor and walls in a way that made it challenging to see anything clearly.

Mortimer abruptly lurched in front of her.

He flickered away again. Not fast enough, though. Keira lunged to catch him. Her outstretched fingers passed through his massive barrel chest. She reached for the fizzing ball of delicate thread nestled inside…

…and realized there was no longer any floor underneath her feet.

The horrendously sharp smile ahead of her widened,

narrowing Mortimer's empty eyes into glittering slits. He'd led her to the second floor deliberately. He, more than anyone, knew how precarious it was.

The floor below Keira had crumbled away completely. In the hazy moonlight and in her eagerness to not let the final specter escape her, Keira had failed to see that the stretch of hall had crumbled away entirely. The space below her was nothing but a black pit.

A dozen thoughts flashed through Keira's mind. She was plunging toward the ground below and whatever hazards it held. Bricks. Exposed beams of wood. Shards of broken glass, perhaps. She didn't know, but she was fairly sure she would become intimately acquainted with them in about two heartbeats.

She could just barely touch the threads in Mortimer's chest. If she reeled her arm back she might still be able to snag the wall or possibly one of the rotting floorboards and slow her fall. It might be enough to save her life. But it would mean relinquishing Mortimer. Probably forever. He was not only clever but cunning; she doubted he would ever let her get this close to him again.

As she hung suspended in the air in that eternal instant, Keira decided she had already made enough bad decisions that day to justify one more. She twisted her body, exposing herself further to the hazards below but extending her arm the extra half inch it needed. She grasped the threads as tightly as she could. And she shot every last scrap of energy into them.

Mortimer's smile vanished. He'd been gambling on the belief

that Keira would be as self-serving as he had been during life. And he'd been wrong.

He lurched backward, trying to wrestle free from her hold, but she refused to let him go. They plunged into the inky blackness together. About halfway down, Mortimer's mouth stretched wide into a scream as his form melted into a clotting clump of mist.

Keira had just enough time left to smile, then closed her eyes and braced for impact.

CHAPTER 37

"OW." KEIRA LIMPED ALONG a hallway that seemed longer than she remembered. Tangy blood coated her tongue and she could feel swelling along her upper arm, hip, and rib cage.

She wasn't exactly sure what she'd landed on, only that it could have been worse, and it also *definitely* could have been better.

She was mostly sure she'd survived the fall, though.

Mostly sure.

A door ahead stood ajar, and faint conversation flowed through. Keira nudged it fully open, grimacing again as fresh bruises made themselves known, and saw the arrangement around the séance table had shifted again.

Mason and Dane had removed most of the candles and brought out a deck of cards. They chatted sleepily as they played.

Not far away, Zoe had somehow convinced Harry to sit on a cushion on the floor. She was perched on a chair behind him, painstakingly weaving his pitch-black hair into a dozen elaborate braids. He looked significantly more miserable than usual.

Keira hadn't kept track of the time, but more of it must have passed than she'd expected. Most of the remaining candles were down to stubs. It was probably closer to dawn than midnight, Keira realized.

"Hey," Mason called, a smile lighting up his face as he saw Keira before it immediately vanished again into concern. "You're hurt."

"Coffee," she said as she staggered toward the table.

"You hate coffee," Mason reminded her even as he moved to pour a cup.

"Don't care. Need coffee." She took the drink he offered her, swallowed a mouthful, then surfaced, gagging. "Oh, that's disgusting. Why did you let me ask for coffee?"

He'd already started pouring a spare cup of tea and deftly switched it for the mug in her hand. "There you go. Sit a moment."

She did, taking the chair Dane vacated for her and slumping forward over the table. All of the energy and fire was gone, and in its place were a hundred aches and scrapes. She thought she could sleep for a week.

"I'm going to get my kit," Mason said, heading toward the door. "Don't move."

She mumbled something that might have been assent. At that moment, not moving sounded like an amazing idea.

"You look like hell," Zoe said bluntly.

"If you were going to have that much fun, you should have invited us along," Harry added.

Keira gingerly sipped her tea. "It wasn't as entertaining as it looks."

"Did you…" Dane cleared his throat as he pulled up an extra chair. He looked almost frightened to ask. "Was there…much progress?"

"Oh, yeah." She lifted her head to give him a lopsided, swollen grin. "You're certified ghost free."

"Oh." He didn't seem able to look at her directly. His eyes were wet. A hesitant, terrified smile was trying to form. "I see."

It would probably take a while to hit him fully, Keira thought. He'd lived under his family's oppression for so long that it would be hard to believe that they were truly gone.

"Not to be a wet blanket or anything," Zoe said. She nodded toward the wall of portraits. "But is there any chance you missed one?"

It took Keira a moment of hunting to find the painting Zoe was referring to. Out of a wall of slack, gray faces and empty eyes, one of the portraits remained intact. An elderly woman, her gray hair pulled tightly back from her face, scowled down at the foyer.

Keira stared at the face, incredulous, then broke into rough laughter. "That's fine. The house is empty. I guess that's one of the few relatives you have, Dane, who didn't linger after death."

"My great-great-aunt Josephine," he said, gazing up at her likeness. "She married into the family. Apparently she was always a bit of a black sheep. She thought the Crispin empire was too full of itself. I…I am glad she didn't stay."

It was hard to imagine the severe, heavy-lidded woman above them was the rebellious one in the family. Her dress's neckline was high and the fabric and jewels visible were elaborate.

"I wish I'd been able to meet her," Dane added. "She passed long before I was born. But it would have been nice to know at least one person in my family who… Never mind."

One person in his family who didn't try to hurt him. Keira's throat ached. Dane was free from the parasites, but it would take a lot longer to truly heal from what had been done to him.

The front door creaked open again as Mason shoved his way in. He carried his medical kit under one arm and a bundle of spare clothes from their suitcases under the other. "Here," he said, draping one of his jackets over Keira's shoulder. "Let me take a look at you."

She endured Mason prodding around her bruised ribs and the sore point on her jaw. He seemed relieved when he finally sat back. "No broken bones, at least. I can bandage some of these cuts and give you painkillers. Everything else will just take rest."

"I am incredibly sorry," Dane murmured from his place across the table. "I did not expect the dead would be able to harm you like this."

She adjusted her numb fingers around the mug. "Not your fault. I'm the fool who ran into a crumbling hall."

He glanced aside, then took a deep, slow breath. "I can feel it, you know."

"Yeah?"

"The pressure is gone. The…the *drain*."

Keira smiled.

His eyes were damp as they turned back to her. "Thank you. So much. I…I promised I would pay you anything you wanted if you could free me."

"Don't worry about it," Keira said.

"No. You must let me give you *something*."

Harry looked up from his seat on the floor. "Skulls," he suggested. "She likes skulls."

"I'm perfectly fine with the one inside me, thanks," Keira said. "And honestly, you don't owe me anything. I've had enough trouble with dead things outside Blighty that I'm just relieved to know *one* problem is within my power to fix."

"Hm." Dane looked dubious. "Let's call it a favor owed, then. If you need help with those other problems—any kind of help at all—consider me your ally."

"Oh." Keira blinked down at her cup of tea. "Yeah. That… that would be good, actually. Thanks."

"But also if you have any spare skulls, I would take them as payment in lieu of her," Harry whispered.

Dane shrugged. "Sure. I'll see if I can find any in a cupboard somewhere."

It was approaching four when they finally left the Crispin estate. Mason kept his jacket draped around Keira's shoulders and had her lean against him as she stumbled her way toward their car. Zoe looked like a zombie as she squinted up at the night sky as though expecting to see the sunrise.

Harry, against all odds, tenderly held a yellowed skull in both hands. His mother would be horrified, Keira knew, but Harry radiated a quiet, satisfied joy, even though he stoically refused to smile.

Mason drove them home, dropping Harry off outside the florist and Zoe outside her own home before taking Keira up the church's driveway to reach her cottage behind the graveyard.

"You're sure you don't want company?" he asked as he opened the car door for her.

The cemetery was visible ahead. Keira pulled on her second sight just long enough to see the faint, transparent silhouettes move between the gravestones, then smiled. "I'm not alone."

"Ghosts don't count unless they have the dexterity and physicality to phone someone in an emergency," Mason said flatly.

Keira, chuckling, patted his arm. "Get some sleep. I'll catch up with you tomorrow."

"Okay. Take care until then."

Mason's headlights washed over Keira as she strode through the graveyard. She belatedly realized she'd forgotten to return his jacket to him. A small part of her was grateful. She pulled it tighter around herself as the fog rolled across her shoes with every step.

"Solomon?"

He flickered into view at her side. Keira, smiling, hiked the jacket higher around her neck to protect against the chill he radiated. "We did it. We got rid of the problem ghosts."

His one good eye creased as he smiled. It was the first time she'd seen that expression on him.

"Are you ready?" Keira asked. "Would you like to move over now?"

He only hesitated for a second, then he spread his arms to expose his chest and closed his eye.

"Thank you for everything," Keira said, reaching through him to touch the bright, delicate tangle of thread she found there. "Find your peace now."

She didn't squeeze the thread or force energy into it like she had with the parasitic spirits. Instead, she found the loose end and gently, softly tugged. It unraveled instantly. Solomon filled his chest with a final deep breath, and as he exhaled, he evaporated into nothing.

"Goodbye, friend," Keira whispered. She pulled the jacket around herself and stayed, staring at his gravestone, for a very long time.

The earliest tinges of light grazed the horizon by the time Keira closed the cottage door behind herself. She stripped out of the last layers of damp clothes, then crawled into bed.

She'd barely lain down when a small, purring shape leaped onto the mattress beside her. A wet tongue dabbed at her cheek and Keira grimaced against the affection. "Hey. Thought you were meant to be staying with Adage," she mumbled.

Daisy licked her once more before curling into a soft, warm ball at her side.

"Okay," Keira murmured, pulling the blanket over them both. "Sleep well, magic cat."

CHAPTER 38

"THERE." KEIRA THREW A clump of half-dead dandelions onto her growing pile of weeds. "That's looking better, huh?"

Amanda O'Reilly, dead 1914, gazed down at her gravestone. Just a few hours ago, it had been so badly overgrown that her name had barely been readable. Now, her marker was cleaned of moss and the weeds growing over her resting place had been pulled up. The stone still bore a deep crack and listed slightly, but at least it looked as though someone cared for it.

The spirit gave a small, shy nod. She didn't smile much, but she didn't seem to want to stop staring at her freshened gravestone.

Keira adjusted her gloves, then picked up the pile of weeds and carried it toward the compost heap she'd started developing by the forest's edge. She'd cleaned three stones that morning, focusing on the ones that carried spirits. *That only leaves…*

She squinted at the graveyard. *Scores more.* That was fine, though. She had time.

Mason had hidden his parents' car, just in case, and Zoe had kept her ear open for rumors of strangers in town, but Artec and the people behind the twisted cemetery hadn't seemed to have found their way to Blighty.

Keira knew her fate was tied to Artec now. She'd seen what was going on behind its cemetery's high brick walls. And she couldn't ignore it. She would have to find a way to free the shades. Somehow. And it would have to be soon.

Add it to the list of problems, she thought.

At least the shock of having to escape from Pleasant Grove and its suited employees had kept Mason from bringing up the Gavin situation again. The memory still weighed on her, though. And it would be doing the same to him.

And then there was Evan Radecki. Neither Mason nor Zoe had brought up the gentle medical student's fate, but Keira knew they all understood what had happened to him. Killed by Gavin for the crime of being too well-liked, then trapped by a faceless organization that cared more about profits than ethics.

And his was the only story Keira knew. There were hundreds of other souls stranded there, crying out for help. And she was the only one who could see them.

One step at a time. That was all she could do. One step, then another. That day, with ugly bruises still in their earliest stages of healing, she was focusing on the small plot of land around her cottage and the spirits that needed help there. Soon, she'd be meeting with Mason and Zoe at the café to begin the first of what she suspected would be many meetings to find a way to unravel Artec and Pleasant Grove.

Keira squinted against the light. The day was still young and Blighty's cemetery held very few living souls. One figure strode toward her, weaving between the aged grave markers. Keira smiled and stripped her gloves off before going to meet him halfway.

Dane's hair was still long and shaggy, but it was clear he'd trimmed it as well as shaved. The new clothes he wore fit him better than the old, patchy garments he'd lived in for the last decade. The plum color of his sweater made him look warmer and more inviting, and although the starkness about his face would take time to fade, two days had already made changes; his posture was straighter and he seemed lighter on his feet.

He carried a bouquet of tulips and marigolds at his side, and the bright wrapping told Keira it came from the florist's. He nervously tapped it against his leg as they neared one another.

"I received your text," he said, and held up his phone. A message was printed on the screen: *Meet me at the graveyard. Bring flowers.* He cleared his throat, unable to meet her eyes. "I don't want you to think I'm in any way ungrateful for your help, but I should let you know I'm not ready to be set up for any blind dates—"

Keira broke into laughter and gave his shoulder a gentle shove. "As if I'd set you up on a date at a graveyard. No. But there *is* someone I want you to meet."

She led the way through the stones to reach one tall, grand

monument. She'd spent the first part of that morning cleaning residue from more than a century of neglect off of its marker. The name underneath was now clear and crisp: *Josephine Crispin.*

The elegant Victorian-era woman gave Keira a sharp, derisive glance, then looked away again. She leaned on a cane that was embedded into the overgrown grass, and one long finger tapped on its elaborate surface.

"Oh," Dane said as he came up beside Keira and read the marker's name.

Keira said, "Jo and I have been acquainted for a while—can I call you Jo, by the way?"

She directed that last part to the spirit ahead of them. The older woman refused to even acknowledge the question.

"Right, so anyway, Jo and I have been friendly, but I never actually thought to pay attention to her name," Keira said. "I can't believe I didn't guess it earlier, to be honest. What other family would have such an elaborate gravestone?"

Dane glanced at Keira, then toward the marker. "Do you mean she's…here?"

"Your family hasn't been kind to you," Keira said. She breathed in deeply, then exhaled. "The other night, you said you would have liked to know Josephine. That maybe, out of the Crispin family, the two of you are most similar. I think you were right. And more than that, I think Josephine would like to know *you.*"

The Victorian woman refused to face them, but Keira noted that she was watching Dane out of the corner of her eye. Keira turned to the spirit and addressed her formally.

"Josephine, I'd like to introduce you to the last of the Crispin family, Dane. He's your great-great-nephew."

The prominent Adam's apple in Dane's throat jumped. His eyes flicked from the grave marker to the space Keira had spoken to. It must have looked like empty air to him.

She couldn't blame Dane for being cautious around spirits. He'd lost the first half of his life to them.

"Dane." She shuffled slightly closer to him. "Josephine has been kind to me. But I think she's lonely. I think…maybe…she's waited a very long time for someone from her family to visit her. I think she'd like to know that she's not forgotten."

"Oh." He blinked hard, uncertain of where to look, then glanced down at the flowers in his hand as though he was surprised to see them there.

Keira gave his arm a light squeeze before turning away. "It will have to be a one-sided conversation, but she's here if you want to talk."

"Thank you."

Keira strode toward the driveway that would lead her into town. Once she was far enough away that she thought she wouldn't be intruding, she glanced back.

Dane bent to place the flowers at the gravestone's foot. Morning light spread over his long hair and coat, painting him in soft, warm colors.

Josephine Crispin stood over him, her cane discarded. One hand pressed against her chest. The other reached out to carefully, tentatively caress Dane's face.

Keira smiled to herself as she thrust her hands into her pockets, then returned to the path to town. Mason and Zoe would be waiting for her when she arrived at the café. They had a busy day ahead of them. There was still a lot road to cover.

One step at a time.

ABOUT THE AUTHOR

Darcy Coates is the *USA Today* bestselling author of *Hunted*, *The Haunting of Ashburn House*, *Craven Manor*, and more than a dozen other horror and suspense titles.

She lives on the Central Coast of Australia with her family, cats, and a garden full of herbs and vegetables.

Darcy loves forests, especially old-growth forests where the trees dwarf anyone who steps between them. Wherever she lives, she tries to have a mountain range close by.

GALLOWS HILL

IT'S TIME TO COME HOME.

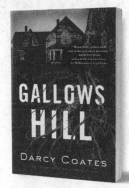

The Hull family has owned the Gallows Hill Winery for generations. Their wine wins awards. Their business prospers. Their family thrives: until Hugh and Maria Hull enter the dark halls of Gallows Hill one last time…and are found dead the next morning.

It's been more than a decade since Margot Hull last saw her childhood home. She was young enough when she was sent away that she barely remembers its dark passageways and secret corners. But now she's returned to bury her parents and reconnect with the winery that is her family's legacy—and the bloody truth of exactly what lies buried beneath the crumbling estate. Alone in the sprawling, dilapidated building, Margot is forced to come face to face with the horrors of the past—and realize that she may be the next victim of a house that never rests…

FROM BELOW

HUNDREDS OF FEET BENEATH THE OCEAN'S SURFACE, A GRAVEYARD AWAITS.

Years ago, the SS *Arcadia* vanished without a trace during a routine voyage. Now its wreck has finally been discovered more than three hundred miles from its intended course...a silent graveyard deep beneath the ocean's surface. Cove and her dive team have been granted permission to examine the wreck, film everything, and, if possible, uncover how and why the supposedly unsinkable ship vanished.

But the *Arcadia* has not yet had its fill of death, and something dark and hungry watches from below. With limited oxygen and the ship slowly closing in around them, Cove and her team will have to fight their way free of the unspeakable horror now desperate to claim them. Because once they're trapped beneath the ocean's waves, there's no going back.

For more info about Sourcebooks's books and authors, visit:
sourcebooks.com